SELMA LAGERLÖF (1858-1940) was born on a farm in Värmland, trained as a teacher and became, in her lifetime, Sweden's most widely translated author ever. Novels such as *Gösta Berlings saga* (1891; *Gösta Berling's Saga*) and *Jerusalem* (1901-02) helped regenerate Swedish literature, and the school reader, *Nils Holgersson's Wonderful Journey through Sweden* (1906-07), has achieved enduring international fame and popularity. Two very different trilogies, the Löwensköld trilogy (1925-28) and the Mårbacka trilogy (1922-32), the latter often taken to be autobiographical, give some idea of the range and power of Lagerlöf's writing. Several of her texts inspired innovative films, among them *Herr Arnes pengar* (*Sir Arne's Treasure*), directed by Mauritz Stiller (1919) and based on *Herr Arnes penningar* (1903; *Lord Arne's Silver*), and *Körkarlen* (*The Phantom Carriage*), directed by Victor Sjöström (1921) and based on Lagerlöf's *Körkarlen* (1912). She was awarded the Nobel Prize for Literature, as the first woman ever, in 1909, and elected to the Swedish Academy, again as the first woman, in 1914. Having been able to buy back the farm of Mårbacka, which her family had lost as the result of bankruptcy, Lagerlöf spent the last three decades of her life combining her writing with the responsibilities for running a sizeable estate. Her work has been translated into close to 50 languages.

SARAH DEATH has been a literary translator for over thirty years. Authors whose work she has translated include Victoria Benedictsson, Fredrika Bremer, Kerstin Ekman, Tove Jansson, Selma Lagerlöf, Astrid Lindgren, Sven Lindvist and Håkan Nesser. Three times the winner of the George Bernard Shaw Prize for Translation from Swedish, she was awarded the Royal Order of the Polar Star for services to Swedish language and literature in 2014.

Some other books from Norvik Press

Herman Bang: *Some Would Call This Living* (translated by Janet Garton, Charlotte Barslund and Paul Russell Garrett)

Victoria Benedictsson: *Money* (translated by Sarah Death)

Fredrika Bremer: *The Colonel's Family* (translated by Sarah Death)

Camilla Collett: *The District Governor's Daughters* (translated by Kirsten Seaver)

Vigdis Hjorth: *A House in Norway* (translated by Charlotte Barslund)

Selma Lagerlöf: *The Löwensköld Ring* (translated by Linda Schenck)
Selma Lagerlöf: *Charlotte Löwensköld* (translated by Linda Schenck)
Selma Lagerlöf: *Anna Svärd* (translated by Linda Schenck)
Selma Lagerlöf: *Lord Arne's Silver* (translated by Sarah Death)
Selma Lagerlöf: *Nils Holgersson's Wonderful Journey through Sweden* (translated by Peter Graves)
Selma Lagerlöf: *The Phantom Carriage* (translated by Peter Graves)
Selma Lagerlöf: *A Manor House Tale* (translated by Peter Graves)
Selma Lagerlöf: *Mårbacka* (translated by Sarah Death)
Selma Lagerlöf: *The Emperor of Portugallia* (translated by Peter Graves)

Amalie Skram: *Betrayed* (translated by Katherine Hanson and Judith Messick)
Amalie Skram: *Fru Inés* (translated by Katherine Hanson and Judith Messick)
Amalie Skram: *Lucie* (translated by Katherine Hanson and Judith Messick)

Kirsten Thorup: *The God of Chance* (translated by Janet Garton)

Dorrit Willumsen: *Bang: A Novel about the Danish Writer* (translated by Marina Allemano)

Memoirs of a Child
(Mårbacka II)

by

Selma Lagerlöf

Translated from the Swedish
and with an
Afterword by Sarah Death

Series Preface by Helena Forsås-Scott

Norvik Press
2022

Originally published by Albert Bonniers förlag as *Ett barns memoarer* in 1930.

This translation and afterword © Sarah Death 2022.
Series preface © Helena Forsås-Scott 2015.
The translator's moral right to be identified as the translator of the work has been asserted.

Norvik Press Series B: English Translations of Scandinavian Literature, no. 85.

A catalogue record for this book is available from the British Library.

ISBN: 978-1-909408-71-5

Norvik Press gratefully acknowledges the generous support of the Swedish Arts Council (Statens Kulturråd) and the Anglo-Swedish Literary Foundation towards the publication of this translation.

Norvik Press
Department of Scandinavian Studies
UCL
Gower Street
London WC1E 6BT
United Kingdom
Website: www.norvikpress.com
E-mail address: norvik.press@ucl.ac.uk

Managing editors: Elettra Carbone, Sarah Death, Janet Garton, C. Claire Thomson, Essi Viitanen.

Cover design and layout: Essi Viitanen
Cover image: *Narcissus maximus* Don. and *Narcissus bicolor* Linn. Image by Abraham Jacobus Wendel, from book *Flora: afbeeldingen en beschrijvingen van boomen, heesters, éénjarige planten, enz. voorkomende in de Nederlandsche tuinen* by H. Witte, illustr. by A.J. Wendel. Groningen: Wolters (1868).

Contents

Series Preface 7
Helena Forsås-Scott

Aline Laurell 15
Bible Interpretation 20
The Vow 38
Gårdsjö 47
Herrestad 51
Fear 54
The Game of Cards 59
The Marseillaise 64
Forty Below 73
Maja Råd 83
The Church Visit 88
The Kiss 95
The Sunne Ball 106
Elin Laurell 115
Pastor Unger 123
The Easter Witch 133
Anna Lagerlöf 141
Uncle Schenson 146
The Pond 155
Agrippa Prästberg 175
At the Jetty 186
The Well 192
At Fair Time 209
Earthquake 217

An asterisk in the text indicates an Endnote, see pages 223-231.

NOTES 223

Translator's Afterword 233
Sarah Death

Bibliography 251

Series Preface

In the first comprehensive biography of the Swedish author Selma Lagerlöf (1858-1940), Elin Wägner provided a snapshot of her at the age of 75 that gives some idea of the range of her achievements and duties. Sitting at her desk in the library at Mårbacka with its collection of classics from Homer to Ibsen, Lagerlöf is also able to view several shelves of translations of her books. Behind her she has not only her own works and studies of herself but also a number of wooden trays into which her mail is sorted. And the trays have labels: 'Baltic Countries, Belgium, Holland, Denmark, Norway, England, France, Italy, Finland, Germany, Sweden, Switzerland, the Slavic Countries, Austria-Hungary, Bonnier [her Swedish publisher], Langen [her German publisher], Swedish Academy, the Press, Relatives and Friends, Treasures, Mårbacka Oatmeal, Miscellaneous Duties'. Lagerlöf's statement, made to her biographer Elin Wägner a few years previously, that she had at least contributed to attracting tourists to her native province of Värmland, was clearly made tongue in cheek.

How could Selma Lagerlöf, a woman born into a middle-class family in provincial Sweden around the middle of the nineteenth century, produce such an œuvre (sixteen novels, seven volumes of short stories) and achieve such status and fame in her lifetime?

Growing up on Mårbacka, a farm in the province of Värmland, at a time when the Swedish economy was predominantly agricultural, Selma Lagerlöf and her sisters learnt about the tasks necessary to keep the self-sufficient household ticking over, but their opportunities of getting an education beyond that which could be provided by their governess were close to non-existent. Selma Lagerlöf succeeded in borrowing money to spend three years in Stockholm training to become a teacher, one of the few professions open to women at the time, and after qualifying in 1885 she spent ten years teaching at a junior high school for girls in Landskrona, in the south of Sweden. Mårbacka had to be sold at auction in 1888, and Lagerlöf only resigned from her teaching post four years after the publication of her first novel, establishing herself as a writer in a Sweden quite different from the one in which she had grown up. Industrialisation in Sweden was late but swift, and Lagerlöf's texts found new readers among the urban working class.

Lagerlöf remained a prolific author well into the 1930s, publishing chiefly novels and short stories as well as a textbook for school children, and she soon also gained recognition in the form of honours and prizes: an Honorary Doctorate at the University of Uppsala in 1907, the Nobel Prize for Literature, as the first woman, in 1909, and election to the Swedish Academy, again as the first woman, in 1914. Suffrage for women was only introduced in Sweden in 1919, and Lagerlöf became a considerable asset to the campaign. She was also able to repurchase Mårbacka, including the farm land, and from 1910 onwards she combined her work as a writer with responsibility for a sizeable estate with a considerable number of employees.

To quote Lagerlöf's most recent biographer, Vivi Edström, she 'knew how to tell a story without ruining it'; but her innovative literary language with its close affinity with spoken language required hard work and much experimentation. 'We authors', Lagerlöf wrote in a letter in 1908, 'regard a book as close to completion once we have found the style in which it allows itself to be written'.

Her first novel, *Gösta Berlings saga* (1891; *Gösta Berling's Saga*), was indeed a long time in the making as Lagerlöf experimented with genres and styles before settling for an exuberant and inventive form of prose fiction that is richly intertextual and frequently addresses the reader. Set in Värmland in the 1820s with the young and talented Gösta Berling as the hero, the narrative celebrates the parties, balls and romantic adventures throughout 'the year of the cavaliers' at the iron foundry of Ekeby. But it does so against the backdrop of the expulsion of the Major's Wife who has been benefactress of the cavaliers; and following her year-long pilgrimage and what has effectively been a year of misrule by the cavaliers, it is hard work and communal responsibility that emerge as the foundations of the future.

In *Drottningar i Kungahälla* (1899; *The Queens of Kungahälla*) Lagerlöf brought together a series of short stories and an epic poem set in Viking-age Kungälv, some distance north of Gothenburg, her aim being to explore some of the material covered by the medieval Icelandic author Snorri Sturluson in *Heimskringla*, but from the perspectives of the female characters. The terse narrative of *Herr Arnes penningar* (1903; *Lord Arne's Silver*), set in the sixteenth century in a context that reinforces boundary crossings and ambivalences, has a plot revolving around murder and robbery, ghosts, love and eventual punishment. The slightly earlier short novel *En herrgårdssägen* (1899; *A Manor House Tale*) similarly transcends boundaries as it explores music and dreams, madness and sanity, death and life in the context of the emerging relationship between a young woman and man.

A few lines in a newspaper inspired Lagerlöf to her biggest literary project since *Gösta Berlings Saga*, the two-volume novel *Jerusalem* (1901-02), which also helped pave the way for her Nobel Prize later in the decade. The plot launches straight into the topic of emigration, widespread in Sweden since the 1860s, by exploring a farming community in the province of Dalarna and the emigration of part of the community to Jerusalem. The style was inspired by the medieval Icelandic sagas, but although the focus on emigration also established a thematic link with the sagas, the inversions of saga patterns such as bloody confrontations and family feuds become more prominent as the plot foregrounds peaceful achievements and international understanding. Yet this is first and foremost a narrative in which traditional structures of stability are torn apart, in which family relationships and relations between lovers are tried and often found wanting, and in which the eventual reconciliation between old and new comes at a considerable price.

Lagerlöf had been commissioned to write a school reader in 1901, but it was several years before she hit on the idea of presenting the geography, economy, history and culture of the provinces of Sweden through the story of a young boy criss-crossing the country on the back of a goose. While working on *Nils Holgerssons underbara resa genom Sverige* (1906-07; *Nils Holgersson's Wonderful Journey*), Lagerlöf doubted that the text would find readers outside Sweden; paradoxically, however, *Nils Holgersson* was to become her greatest international success. Once perceived as an obstacle to the ambitions to award Lagerlöf the Nobel Prize for Literature, *Nils Holgersson* is nowadays read as a complex and innovative novel.

Körkarlen (1912; *The Phantom Carriage*) grew out of a request from The National Tuberculosis Society, and what was intended as a short story soon turned into a novel. The story of a victim of TB, whose death on New Year's Eve destines him to drive the death cart throughout the following year and who only gains the respite to atone for his failures and omissions thanks to the affection and love of others, became the basis in 1921 for one of the best-known Swedish films of the silent era, with Victor Sjöström as the director (Sjöström also played the central character) and with ground-breaking cinematography by J. Julius (Julius Jaenzon).

The First World War was a difficult time for Lagerlöf: while many of her readers, in Sweden and abroad, were expecting powerful statements against the war, she felt that the political events were draining her creative powers. *Kejsarn av Portugallien* (1914; *The Emperor of Portugallia*) is not just a novel about the miracle of a newborn child and a father's love of his daughter; it is also a text about a fantasy world emerging in response to extreme external pressures, and about the insights and support this seemingly mad world can generate. Jan, the central character, develops for himself an outsider position similar to that occupied by Sven Elversson in Lagerlöf's more emphatically pacifist novel *Bannlyst* (1918; *Banished*), a position that allows for both critical and innovative perspectives on society.

Quite different from Lagerlöf's wartime texts, the trilogy consisting of *Löwensköldska ringen* (1925; *The Löwensköld Ring*), *Charlotte Löwensköld* (1925) and *Anna Svärd* (1928) is at once lighthearted and serious, a narrative tour de force playing on ambivalences and multiple interpretations to an extent that has the potential to destabilise, in retrospect, any hard and fast readings of Lagerlöf's œuvre. As the trilogy calls into question the ghost of the old warrior General Löwensköld and then traces the demise of Karl-Artur Ekenstedt, a promising young minister in the State Lutheran Church, while giving prominence to a series of strong and independent female characters, the texts explore and celebrate the capacity and power of narrative.

Lagerlöf wrote another trilogy late in her career, and one that has commonly been regarded as autobiographical: *Mårbacka* (1922), *Ett barns memoarer* (1930; *Memories of My Childhood*), and *Dagbok för Selma Ottilia Lovisa Lagerlöf* (1932; *The Diary of Selma Lagerlöf*). All three are told in the first person; and with their tales about the Lagerlöfs, relatives, friends, local characters and the activities that structured life at Mårbacka in the 1860s and 70s, the first two volumes can certainly be read as evoking storytelling in the family circle by the fire in the evening. The third volume, *Diary*, was initially taken to be the authentic diary of a fourteen-year-old Selma Lagerlöf. Birgitta Holm's psychoanalytical study of Lagerlöf's work (1984) reads the Mårbacka trilogy in innovative terms and singles out *Diary* as providing the keys to Lagerlöf's œuvre. Ulla-Britta Lagerroth has interpreted the trilogy as a gradual unmasking of patriarchy; but with 'Selma Lagerlöf' at its centre, this work can also be read as a wide-ranging and playful exploration of gender, writing and fame.

With the publication over the past couple of decades of several volumes of letters by Lagerlöf, to her friend Sophie

Elkan (1994), to her mother (1998), to her friend and assistant Valborg Olander (2006), and to her friends Anna Oum and Elise Malmros (2009-10), our understanding of Lagerlöf has undoubtedly become more complex. While the focus of much of the early research on Lagerlöf's work was biographical, several Swedish studies centring on the texts were published in connection with the centenary of her birth in 1958. A new wave of Lagerlöf scholarship began to emerge in Sweden in the late 1990s, exploring areas such narrative, gender, genre, and aesthetics; and in the 1990s the translation, reception and impact of Lagerlöf's texts abroad became an increasingly important field, investigated by scholars in for example the US, the UK and Japan as well as in Sweden. Current research is expanding into the interrelations between media in Lagerlöf, performance studies, cultural transmissions, and archival studies. As yet there is no complete scholarly edition of Lagerlöf, but all her works and several background articles are available at litteraturbanken.se. Three works were completed by 2013: *Gösta Berling's saga*, *Osynliga länkar* and *Körkarlen*.

By the time Lagerlöf turned 80, in 1938, she was the most widely translated Swedish writer ever, and the total number of languages into which her work has been translated is now close to 50. However, most of the translations into English were made soon after the appearance of the original Swedish texts, and unlike the original texts, translations soon become dated. Moreover, as Peter Graves has concluded in a study of Lagerlöf in Britain, Lagerlöf 'was not well-served by her translators [into English]'. 'Lagerlöf in English', a series of new translations launched in 2011, aims to remedy this situation.

Helena Forsås-Scott
(1945-2015. First editor of the 'Lagerlöf in English' series.)

A list of further reading can be found at the end of the Translator's Afterword at the back of this volume.

Aline Laurell

And we are so pleased that we have such a kind-hearted governess here at Mårbacka.

Her name is Aline Laurell and her father lived in Karlstad and was the senior surveyor, and they were rich, to be sure, for as long as he lived. But when he died, Aline's mother was left poor, and Mrs Unger in Västra Ämtervik, who is Aline's aunt, arranged with Papa and Mama for Aline to come here and teach Anna and me to read French and play the piano.

And we are also pleased that she has brought with her a sister, who is called Emma and is only ten years old and is going to live here and be taught her lessons by Aline along with the rest of us. And you can tell that Emma was once rich, because she has so many pantalettes with dainty embroidery, which were passed down to her by Aline and her other sisters, and we have never worn anything like that here at Mårbacka. And on Sunday mornings, Emma struggles with tacking the pantalettes onto her bloomers and gets into a terrible bother, because some are too wide and some are too long and sometimes when she puts them on, one hangs right down to her foot and the other barely comes below her knee. We do not think pantalettes are at all pretty, especially when they hang crooked, but Emma probably thinks that as she has a whole drawer full of them, and they are so finely embroidered, she ought to wear them.

Selma Lagerlöf

And it is so funny, that just that autumn when Aline first came here, I was away in Stockholm and going to gymnastics* and living with Uncle Oriel Afzelius and Aunt Georgina and Elin and Allan at number seven, Klara Strandgata. I was gone all winter, so I did not see Aline until the spring of the next year. And I was very glad indeed when it was time for me to come home, but I was also anxious, because I knew that we now had a governess, and I thought all governesses were old and ugly and unkind.

And when I came home from Stockholm, I was wearing a panama hat with blue and white ribbon around the crown and a white feather with a clasp and a blue summer coat with shiny buttons and Aunt Georgina's dressmaker had made me a blue-and-white calico dress, so I was got up in all my finery when I came home. And I was so much better after attending gymnastics that you could barely see I had a limp. I had grown, so I was really tall, and I was not as pale or thin as when I went to Stockholm, but plump and rosy. I had my hair hanging down my back in a plait instead of pinned up round my ears, so that those at home barely recognised me. They said it was a completely new Selma who had come back from Stockholm.

When I first saw Aline, I was so surprised, because she was young and good-looking, and I liked her from the very first moment. But when Aline saw me, she thought I looked like a little Stockholm miss, and she was afraid I would be spoilt and full of airs and graces.

I had been away for so long. I had so much to tell everyone, and I could not stop talking. I talked about my visits to the Royal Opera House and the Dramatic Theatre* and the Smaller Theatre and being in Djurgården Park for the First of May, where I had seen Karl XV and Queen Lovisa and 'Lilla Sessan'*. And I talked about Louise Thyselius, who was the prettiest young girl in Stockholm and went to the same gymnastics classes as me, so I had been able to look at her every day, and about the house where Uncle Oriel lived, which was owned by a duke, who was a Frenchman named d'Otrante, and had a carriage and horses, a coachman and footman, and his

Memoirs of a Child

papa had been something dreadful in the French Revolution. And I showed everyone all the beautiful books that Uncle and Aunt had given me as Christmas presents, and I boasted about the big children's Christmas party at Mr Glosemeyer the wholesaler's, to which Elin and Allan and I had been invited and where we had been allowed to strip the Christmas tree and had each had a bag of sweets and chocolates to bring home. And I had been in the Leja shop* and seen so many toys, and I had seen chocolate cigars and a fountain with red, blue and green water, called *hulopinterokromatokrēne**.

And Aline Laurell sat there listening to all of this and saying precisely nothing but thinking what a precocious little girl she was, this Selma who had arrived home from Stockholm.

The worst part of all was that I said everything with a Stockholm accent. I was not aware of it myself, but Aline Laurell took it as proof of affectation and the way my head had been turned, for surely anyone born in Värmland would not be ashamed of speaking their own mother tongue.

I peppered my words with names like Drottninggatan and Berzelii Park and Slussen and Blasieholmen, I talked about the changing of the guard and the Royal Palace, I had been in the Catholic church, I had seen Saint George and the Last Judgement in Stockholm Cathedral*, I had been allowed to borrow all Walter Scott's novels from Uncle Oriel, and I had done my lessons with a kind lady teacher who said she thought I could certainly be a schoolmistress, too, when I grew up.

Aline Laurell sat there listening to all of this and thinking that this girl, so hoity-toity, was not someone she could ever make her friend.

And as there are only a few weeks left before the summer holidays, when Aline and Emma will go back to their mother in Karlstad, Papa says that there is no point in my starting to study with Aline, so I might as well be free and at leisure until the autumn. And I really do enjoy going into the kitchen and chatting to the housekeeper and looking at Gerda's dolls and playing with dogs and kittens and reading out loud to Mama from Nösselt's *General History for Women** and helping Aunt Lovisa to sow and plant in the garden, but when I have been

Selma Lagerlöf

back home for a few days, I do go into the nursery one morning in the middle of lessons, not to be made to read or write or do sums, of course, but just to see what they are doing.

Aline is testing Anna and Emma on the catechism. And Anna is just reciting that long part with the difficult language, 'On heathens who have not the law'*.

Once Anna has finished reciting, Aline starts talking to her and Emma about conscience. She explains all the difficult language so well that Anna and Emma completely understand its meaning, and so do I. I think Aline is so right when she says that we should always do what our conscience tells us to. Because that will save us from remorse.

When the lesson is over, the clock strikes eleven. Anna and Emma are allowed ten minutes' break to run out to play, but I stay there in the nursery.

I go up to Aline and my cheeks are burning as I ask, in such a quiet voice that she can hardly hear me, whether she can help me send twenty-four *skilling** to Laxå railway station to a lengthman's wife, who lives there.

'Ye-e-es, I expect I could do that,' says Aline, 'as long as you know her name.'

'No, I don't know it,' I say, 'but you see, I was coming home on the train and when it got to Laxå station, it ran over a lengthman. I didn't see him, but they said on the train that it cut him in half.'

'Ah, I see,' said Aline, 'and now you feel sorry for his wife?'

'She screamed so dreadfully,' I said. 'She came running along to the station. Aline, you just can't imagine the way she screamed. And they said she was poor and had lots of children.'

'I remember now that I read about it in the newspaper,' says Aline. 'But did they not make a collection?'

'Oh yes,' I say, 'they did. A conductor came into our carriage and asked if we wanted to help the lengthman's wife. And lots of people made donations, but I gave nothing.'

'You had no money, then?' says Aline.

'Oh, I did, two twelve-*skilling* pieces, but you see, I was planning to spend them on burnt almonds and nuts when I got to Karlstad, so I would have something to bring home with me for Anna and Gerda. And it all happened so fast, Aline. The conductor was in such a hurry, and he never looked in my direction. And I couldn't bring myself to hold out my money.'

'But now you want to send it anyway?'

'Yes, if you will help me to send it off, Aline. I didn't buy any burnt almonds in Karlstad so I still have the money. I felt ashamed of myself as I sat there on the train and it felt as though everyone else in the compartment was looking at me and wondering why I hadn't given anything, and I've felt ashamed every day since I've been home, too. I would dearly like to send that money to the lengthman's wife.'

Aline looks at me with her big grey eyes. 'Why haven't you spoken to your mother about this?' she says.

'I was planning not to tell a soul, Aline, but then I heard you talking about conscience.'

'I see,' said Aline. 'Well, I had better help you, then.'

And after that I go to fetch my two twelve-*skilling* coins and give them to her.

And since then we have been such good friends, Aline and I. I tell her all the things that I do not otherwise tell to anybody. I even tell her that once, when I was seven years old, I read such an entertaining book called *Oceola**, and I decided right there and then that once I grew up, I would do nothing but write novels.

Bible Interpretation

We think it such good fun to fetch the post on Sunday afternoons. It is only us big girls, Anna and Emma Laurell and I, who are allowed to go. We slip away before Gerda wakes up from her after-dinner nap, so she will not cry over not being allowed to come with us. You see, Gerda is only six years old and we think the route is too difficult for a little child like her, someone who cannot jump over a ditch or scramble over a fence without help.

Sometimes, Nursie Maja asks if she can come with us, because she thinks time goes so slowly if she has to spend all of Sunday sitting at home. Nursie Maja is Gerda's nurserymaid, and neither Papa nor Mama has instructed her to come with us and look after us. Seeing as Anna is twelve and Emma Laurell is eleven and I am ten, we do not think we need anyone to watch over us. Nursie Maja only comes along to amuse herself. She would rather go for the post with Anna and Emma Laurell and me than stand out in the yard at home talking to Lars Nylund and Magnus Engström. Nursie Maja says that those boys talk such a load of nonsense.

Nursie Maja is with us again today and the whole way, past the cowshed and down over the meadows and past Per in Berlin's* cottage, Nursie Maja tells us what it was like when she and Lars Nylund and the other young children in Högbergssäter used to mind the sheep in the woods at Åsskogen. And Lars Nylund once killed a viper, just as it was about to bite Maja's big toe. And once, Maja was sucked into

Stormossen bog right up to her chin, and would never have seen the light of day again, if Lars Nylund had not come and pulled her out.

I always like listening to Nursie Maja when she talks about things that happened when she was minding the sheep, but then Anna pipes up and says that you can tell Nursie Maja is in love with Lars Nylund. And Nursie Maya answers that there is no truth in it, because that is all over now. It was only a game when they were little. But I am not happy about Anna teasing Nursie Maja, because now she won't tell us any more stories.

It really is just as well that Gerda did not come with us, for just think how tiring it would have been for her, with her being only six. It is tiring for me, and I am ten. Not that I generally have any trouble walking a quarter of a Swedish mile*. My leg doesn't hurt at all since that winter I went to gymnastics in Stockholm. But, you see, the path from Per in Berlin's cottage to the inn in Högberg is as boggy as a marsh. When you lift up your foot, it makes a squelch. We did not know that the ice in the ground had melted to the west of home because it has only been thawing for a few days. Anna says we are bound to find that the postilion has been delayed by the poor state of the roads and we will get no post.

I do not understand how Anna can know everything. Just imagine, the very first thing we hear when we get to the inn is that the postilion has not yet been by to drop off the post bag for Mårbacka. Anna thinks we should go straight back, but Nursie Maja asks if we shouldn't wait for a while, because Lieutenant Lagerlöf is so dejected if we come home without any post.

I am glad, I must say, that Anna gives in, and we are allowed into the big room at the inn to rest for a while. The innkeeper's wife puts out some chairs for us, right down by the door, and we sit there in silence, because no one speaks to us. We look around the room instead. Butter, bread and cheese have been laid out on a big table over by the window, and another table is covered in cups and saucers. On the cast-iron stove there are several big coffee kettles, bubbling and hissing and sometimes boiling over. The innkeeper's eldest daughter is busy grinding coffee. Nursie Maja mutters that nothing smells as good as coffee, especially when a person is tired and wet and freezing cold, and we all think the same, but Anna hushes her because we do not want to give them the idea at the inn that we are expecting them to offer us anything.

Nor do they, and after a while Nursie Maja goes out to see whether the postilion carriage is coming into sight along the road. She stays outside for so long that we think we will never see her again, and we also start to worry because we can see a lot of people gathering in the inn yard. Some of them open the door as if to come in, but when they see us, they shake their heads and turn back. And we hear the eldest daughter, the one who is grinding coffee, whisper to her mother and ask if those little girls from Mårbacka are ever going to leave. And Anna whispers to Emma Laurell and me that she thinks there is going to be a party, so they want to be rid of us. And we do not want to be in the way, so we agree that as soon as Nursie Maja comes back, we will leave at once.

But Maja is still nowhere to be seen and I hear Anna whisper to Emma Laurell that she thinks Maja has arranged to meet Lars Nylund here at the inn and that is why she was so eager to come with us. But I cannot believe that Maja would be so cunning. I sit there staring out of the window the whole time to see if I can spy her.

And before my very eyes on the other side of the yard is the stable, with an old staircase built into one corner, and you can only see the bottom two steps. But standing on those steps there are two people. I cannot see who they are, because the only things visible are a pair of tall boots with a bit of trouser leg, and on the other side a pair of ankle boots and a section of striped kirtle. But they must have a great deal to say to each other, because they have been standing on those steps for a long time. The strangest thing is that I think I recognise that striped kirtle, although it would be very odd indeed for Nursie Maja to go and talk to a pair of trouser legs when she is meant to be on the lookout for a postilion's carriage coming along the road. I am about to ask Anna what she thinks about the striped kirtle when the innkeeper's wife comes towards us.

Memoirs of a Child

She does not speak to us but as she passes by she says, as if to herself, 'Well, it's going to be a real treat to listen to Paulus Andersson from Sandarne.'

As for us, we just sit still and are all ears. The innkeeper's wife is behind us now, getting logs from the log basket. 'I thank God that Paulus Andersson is coming to give a Bible interpretation in my house at four this afternoon,' she says to herself as she clatters about with the logs. 'All those who want to stay and listen are very welcome,' she goes on. 'All that the Father giveth me shall come to me, and him that cometh to me I will in no wise cast out, I say, like Jesus. But let those who fear man more than God be on their way.'

We turn our eyes to the big wall clock, all three of us, and there are no more than five minutes left until four o'clock. And Emma Laurell and I, we jump down from our chairs ready to go, but Anna does not move from hers, and she gestures to us to sit back down as well.

What on earth can Anna be thinking of? Does she mean us to stay and listen to a Bible interpretation? Doesn't Anna remember that colporteurs and itinerant pietist preachers are the worst thing Papa knows? Has she forgotten all those times Papa has said that if anyone from his household were to go to a prayer meeting, they would never be allowed through his door again?

There is no time for me to ask Anna what she has in mind, for in comes Nursie Maja. She is in a fearful hurry to tell us that there is to be a Bible interpretation in this room at four o'clock, so we must make ourselves scarce. Yet Anna does not want to.

'But Anna, you very well know that Lieutenant Lagerlöf won't want us to listen to a pietist preacher,' says Nursie Maja. But Anna replies that we cannot help it if they are holding a Bible meeting here, while we sit and wait for the post.

'But I'm so scared now that I think I shall run home on my own,' says Nursie Maja.

'I have wanted to go home all along,' whispers Anna, and you can hear how dreadfully cross she is with Maja. 'But you tricked us into staying here, Nursie Maja. Now you will have to take the consequences.'

And that is the end of the deliberations, for a couple of young hands come in and shift forward benches and chairs and when that is done, the crowd that has been waiting in the yard comes surging in, and the room is crammed full. But we do not leave. We just move our chairs right back against the wall and stay, for if Anna is not afraid, then it surely cannot be risky for the rest of us. And frankly we are all very curious to know what happens at a Bible interpretation.

Last of all, Paulus Andersson from Sandarne comes in, and he looks like any other peasant farmer and he seems to me to preach in quite the ordinary way. But I cannot properly follow what he says, because all I can think about is what is going to happen when we get home.

It will not help to tell Papa that we were waiting for the post. Anna must never imagine that it will. No, we will all be turned out of our good home, because we have been disobedient and inquisitive. It will be for us as it was for Adam and Eve.

What defence can Anna offer for us when we get home, and what will become of us then? We will have to go out on the road as beggars. Nursie Maja has her parents in Högbergssäter, and Emma Laurell has her mother in Karlstad, but Anna and I, we have nothing else but Mårbacka.

When I think that Papa always says itinerant preachers are a worse rabble than thieves and murderers and that the lot of them should be shut up in Marstrand fortress, we can expect nothing else but to be thrown out onto the road.

It is just as well for Gerda that she was not allowed to come with us today to fetch the post. She does not know how lucky she is.

Then Anna nudges me with her elbow, and I see that there is a man standing in the doorway, holding up a post bag. And we creep out and walk home, Anna and Emma Laurell and Nursie Maja and I, and we are so upset and angry and scared that not a single one of us says a word, the whole way home.

Memoirs of a Child

When we have gone past Per in Berlin's cottage and down over the meadows and up the slope to the cowshed we see that Lina, the big cook, is standing there waiting for us.

And she is always so nice. She is here because she wants nothing more than to warn us.

'Why are you all so late?' she says. 'You'd barely gone before the Lieutenant heard there was going to be a prayer meeting at the inn, and he's been complaining all evening about you children staying out, and been so afraid you'll be converted into pietists, just like that.'

We have no time to answer her as we hurry across the courtyard to the front steps, but just think, Nursie Maja does not dare to come with us through the main entrance, but slips away to the kitchen door.

But Anna is not a bit frightened, she just walks straight in. As she opens the front door, she tells us not to say anything about Nursie Maja and Lars Nylund. Because she does not want Nursie Maja to get into trouble. But she does not say a word about keeping quiet on the subject of the Bible interpretation

Anna walks straight through the hall and into the dining room and Emma Laurell and I, we follow her. Anna does not even take off her outdoor things, and neither do we. We think it best to do as she does.

In the dining room they have pulled down the blinds and lit the lamp, and Mama and Aline Laurell are sitting at the round table in front of the sofa, playing sympathy patience*. And Aunt Lovisa has Gerda beside her and is drawing a little flower for her, and Papa is sitting in the rocking chair, chatting as he usually does.

And although Anna knows that she has been to a Bible interpretation, which is against Papa's express wishes, she goes straight up to him and hands him the post bag. 'Here is the post, Papa,' she says.

But it looks as though Papa is going to ignore our arrival. Anna is left standing there with the post bag. He does not take it, but carries on talking to Mama and Aline Laurell.

And when Papa does that sort of thing, it is a sign of how angry he is.

Mama and Aline Laurell stop playing patience, and Aunt Lovisa stops drawing the little flower. And none of them says a word. Emma Laurell and I take each other's hand, because we are so scared that we think we will die, but as for Anna, she is calm and fearless.

'The road was so bad that the postilion was late,' says Anna. 'We had to sit at the inn and wait, until five o'clock.'

Papa just sits there rocking and does not hear what Anna has to say, but then Mama chimes in.

'Tell us, Anna, what did you do as you sat there waiting?'

'For the first hour we did nothing. Then a preacher came to give a Bible interpretation,' answers Anna. 'But as soon as the postilion arrived with the bag, we left.'

'But Anna,' says Mama, 'you know very well that Papa has told you all you are not to listen to pietist preachers.'

'Yes,' replies Anna. 'But you see, Mama, this was Paulus from Sandarne, and you know that he is the most dangerous of them all.'

'Yes, but my dear girl,' says Mama, 'why should his being dangerous have made you stay?'

'We had no idea that there was going to be a Bible interpretation until he was about to start,' explains Anna, 'and I thought that if we walked out at that moment, he might be angry with us and come here to Mårbacka and steal things.'

'Whatever is the girl saying?' mutters Papa, and stops rocking. 'She surely has not gone and lost her wits?'

And just then I see that Aline Laurell has turned bright red in the face and is puffing out her cheeks and bending over her cards so that no one will notice she is about to burst out laughing. But Aunt Lovisa is leaning back into the corner of the sofa and laughing so much that she has to press her hands into her sides.

'There you are, Gustav,' says Mama, and you can hear in her voice that she would very much like to join in the laughter. 'You see what happens when you exaggerate so wildly.' Then she turns back to Anna: 'Who told you that Paulus from Sandarne was a thief?'

'Well Papa said that he was a worse rogue than Lasse-Maja*,' said Anna, 'and should be locked up in a fortress.'

And by this time Emma Laurell and I are laughing too, because we have always understood that Papa only meant colporteurs and pietist preachers were as bad as convicts. We would never have thought that Anna, who was so sensible and twelve years old, would take him quite so literally.

Now that we are all laughing, it clearly starts to dawn on Anna that she has done something silly, and her top lip quivers, as if she is going to cry.

But then Papa gets to his feet and takes the post bag from her.

'Yes, that was well done, my Anna,' he says. 'You certainly are your father's daughter. Take no notice of all the others laughing, because we two are right, you see. Take Emma and Selma with you now, get those outdoor clothes off and change out of your wet boots. And then you can all ask your aunt for some syrup and almonds so you can make toffee, because I think you deserve a little reward for having waited so long for the post.'

The Vow

There is nothing we like more than having Papa come home.

He went away the day after the one when we found ourselves at the Bible interpretation, and he has not been at home since then. We think it is so tedious when Papa is away. There is nobody to talk as we have our dinner, and nobody to play with us in the evenings, after we have eaten. Nursie Maja says that he is travelling round collecting taxes, and according to her he has only been gone for a few weeks. But we do not trust Nursie Maja since she went to talk to Lars Nylund on the steps of the stable at the inn, and we think he has been away for many months.

Then one morning, Mama tells us he will be back in the evening, which makes us so happy.

All day long we open the front door whenever we get the chance, and run out onto the porch to listen and look. Mama tells us that we must stay indoors. We will catch cold from standing outside, but we do not care a single bit.

Aline Laurell complains that our minds are elsewhere when she tests us on our lessons. 'And if I did not know who is coming this evening,' she says, 'I would give you each a black mark.'

Gerda spends the whole day dressing her dolls. She dresses them and undresses them and then dresses them again. She is never satisfied with how beautiful she has made them.

Memoirs of a Child

Anna and I, we tell Emma Laurell that she can be sure Papa will bring toys for her as well as for us. She does not know our papa, if she can be in any doubt about that.

When four o'clock comes and lessons are over, Aline Laurell says we are excused any preparation for tomorrow, because she knows we will not be able to learn it. And we hurry out, Anna and Emma Laurell and Gerda and I, to meet Papa. First we go to the stable to fetch the big ram, which Johan broke in at Christmas, and we harness it to the sledge to mark this as a grand occasion. There is barely enough snow but we know Papa likes to see us on the sledge pulled by the stable ram.

And just imagine our good fortune – our 'stroke of luck' as Emma Laurell likes to put it! We have barely reached the top of the avenue when we hear the deep sound of sleigh bells. And then we see someone coming, and we recognise Brownie and the big sleigh and Magnus in Vienna and Papa himself in the big wolfskin coat. We only just have time to pull and push and chivvy the stable ram to the side of the road, because he is not yet trained well enough to move aside when he meets a horse, but digs in his back legs and sticks out his head and tries to drive the horse into the ditch.

But how strange it is that Papa does not stop to say hello to us! We are not far from home, it is true, but we were still expecting that Gerda and I, or at least Gerda, would be allowed up into the sleigh to ride to the front steps. But Papa just gives the tiniest of nods and drives straight past.

Now we regret bringing the stable ram with us, because we are in a hurry to get home, and the ram has not yet been trained to turn round when you pull on one rein, but the only way to turn him is for all four of us to stand on one side of him and push until he understands what he has to do.

And this all means we are too late to be there to receive Papa when he drives up to the front steps. But what a surprise that he does not wait outside for us! We simply cannot understand him.

We dash into the hall, but he is not there, either. He must have something special in store for us, we think, and wonder whether we should go into the bedroom. But at that very moment Mama opens the bedroom door and comes out to us. 'Walk quietly on the stairs please, children,' she says, 'and stay in the nursery, because Papa is ill. He has a fever and is going straight to bed.'

And Mama's voice trembles as she says this, and it frightens us terribly. And then, once we have crept upstairs and reached the nursery, Anna says she thinks Papa is going to die.

In the evening, when we get into bed, Mama comes in to listen as we say our prayers. We recite the Lord's Prayer and 'Lord bless us and keep us', and 'Now I lay me down to sleep' and 'Angels bless and angels keep'. Mama moves from bed to bed and we recite the same prayers, first Anna, then Emma Laurell and finally me. Emma Laurell also prays that God will keep her mama and her siblings and all good people. But the rest of us never say that prayer, because we did not learn it when we were little.

This evening Mama comes in to us as usual, even though Papa is sick, and sits down on Anna's bed. And Anna recites the Lord's Prayer and 'Lord bless us and keep us', and 'Now I lay me down to sleep' and 'Angels bless and angels keep' as she usually does, but she does not content herself with this and ends in the same way as Emma Laurell: 'God keep my papa and my mama and my brothers and sisters and all good people.'

Anna says this because she wants to pray to God for Papa, who is sick, and Mama understands this, because she bends down and kisses her.

Then Mama goes to Emma Laurell, and she recites the Lord's Prayer and 'Lord bless us and keep us', and 'Now I lay me down to sleep' and 'Angels bless and angels keep'. Then she prays for her mama and her siblings and all good people. And last of all she says, 'God keep dear Uncle Lagerlöf, so he doesn't die like my papa!'

When Emma Laurell has finished, Mama bends down and kisses her, just as she kissed Anna. Then Mama moves to my bed.

And I recite the Lord's Prayer and 'Lord bless us and keep us', and 'Now I lay me down to sleep' and 'Angels bless and angels keep,' but then I say nothing more. I really want to, but it is quite impossible for me to utter a word.

Mama sits still and waits for a moment, and then she says:

'Aren't you going to ask God not to take your papa from you?'

And I want to, I want it so terribly, and I know it looks bad for me to say nothing, but I cannot.

Mama sits and waits for a while and I know she is thinking about everything Papa has done for me, making the journey to Strömstad for my sake and letting me stay in Stockholm for a whole winter to go to gymnastics, but even so, I cannot get a single word out. And then Mama gets to her feet and leaves without kissing me.

And once Mama has gone, I lie there thinking that perhaps Papa will die, because I did not pray for him.

Perhaps God got so angry with me for not asking him to keep my Papa, that He will take him away from me.

And what shall I do to show God that I do not want Papa to die?

I have a teeny-tiny gold heart that was a present from Miss Spak, who was Aunt Wennervik's sister, and a little garnet cross. If I give them away, perhaps God will understand that I am doing it so Papa will be allowed to live. But I do not think Mama will let me give them away. I shall have to think of something else.

*

The doctor has been now, and after he left, Mama told us that Papa has pneumonia. Papa had damp sheets on his bed one night while he was away, and damp sheets are the most dangerous thing there is.

Aline Laurell took turns with Mama sitting up with Papa last night, and she is spending most of her time in the bedroom today, too. Mama does not know what she would do without Aline Laurell, because she is so sensible and calm. Aunt Lovisa is so dreadfully afraid of Papa dying that she is not much use.

Aline Laurell sets us lessons, but she does not come up to test us on them, and she gives us long sums to do, but she does not come up and check in the answer book whether we have got them right. And eventually we children find it too horrible sitting upstairs in the nursery, so far away from all the grown-ups. We tiptoe down the stairs, Anna, Emma Laurell and I, and we go in to Aunt Lovisa, in her bedroom off the kitchen. And there sits Aunt Lovisa at her sewing table, reading a big, fat book, and Gerda is on a little stool beside her, stitching away at a doll's dress.

We three, Anna and Emma Laurell and I, snuggle up on Aunt Lovisa's sofa and sit there without saying a word, and we find it very odd that Gerda can carry on playing with her dolls on a day like this. But then Gerda is only six years old and she does not understand that Papa is dying.

And it is as if we feel calmer, once we are in the room off the kitchen. Everybody always finds it so pleasant in Aunt Lovisa's room. They say that this is the place where they can recognise the old Mårbacka. Here is the wide bed where Grandfather and Grandmother slept and which Aunt has inherited from them. Here is their wall clock in its tall case, and here is Grandmother's beautiful chest of drawers, which the splendid carpenter of Askersby made out of apple wood and lilac from Mårbacka. The cover on Aunt Lovisa's sofa was woven by Grandmother herself, and its curious pattern was taught to her by Aunt Wennervik, who was married to Grandmother's brother. The chair where Aunt Lovisa sits is Grandfather's very own writing chair, and Aunt's mirror, which stands on the chest of drawers with a veil thrown over it, was also made in Askersby. But as for the tall wooden urns standing on either side of the mirror and filled with dried rose petals, she bought those at an auction at Välsäter, which was the home of her sister Anna, who was married to Uncle Wachenfeldt.

There is nothing here in the bedroom off the kitchen that Aunt would want to be rid of, except for the unsightly black framework over the steps down to the cellar, but whenever Papa talks of removing it, Aunt says it will be best to leave it, because it is old, and she would not know her way about the room if it were no longer there.

Above Aunt Lovisa's bed hangs a picture of a white church, surrounded by tall trees and a low churchyard wall with a wrought-iron gate. But the picture is not a painting; it is a paper cut, and the scissors were wielded by Aunt Anna Wachenfeldt. Aunt Lovisa always maintains that the picture is so cleverly cut and glued that it is really beautiful, but I think it has a slightly pitiful look.

Around the mirror hang four small pictures, painted by Aunt Lovisa herself when she was at boarding school in Åmål. The first is of a rose, the second a narcissus, the third a carnation and the fourth a dahlia, and I think they are very lovely. Aunt Lovisa still has both her paintbox and her brushes, but she never paints anything as lovely as those.

Aunt Lovisa owns another picture, too, which hangs above the sofa just behind us, and is of a fat boy and a fat girl who are out in a little round boat where there is scarcely room for them. The whole picture is done in cross-stitch on canvas, and Aline Laurell keeps saying that Aunt Lovisa ought to take it out of its frame and make it into a sofa cushion, but Aunt Lovisa does not want to change anything that is old, and so there it stays, hanging in its place.

Over by the window there are three big oleanders, covered in big pink flowers, and on the wall is the little bookcase, where there is only just room for the hymn book and New Testament and *A Life of Love* by Johan Mikael Lindblad* and the big book that Aunt Lovisa had to read when she was at boarding school in Åmål, where everything she needed to know about French and geography and Swedish history and general history and science and household hints was brought together between two covers.

Aunt Lovisa suddenly dabs at a tear in the corner of her eye, but she says nothing, merely carries on reading. Gerda gets up from her stool a few times and asks Aunt Lovisa whether the doll should have black or white trimming on her dress. 'Dear child, do as you wish!' says Aunt Lovisa, but a little later she relents and tells Gerda what she wants to know.

All the time I am wondering what I shall do to stop God taking my Papa away from me and I, too, would very much like to ask Aunt Lovisa's advice, but I am too timid.

It is not too long before the kitchen door opens and the housekeeper comes in with a coffee tray. 'Daresay you'd like a drop of coffee, Miss Lovisa,' she says. 'It would probably do you good, with things being so gloomy and all. Not that the Lieutenant's going to die, but all the same... Do you think, Miss Lovisa, that I can go in to the mistress with a cup as well?'

'You know what, Maja, I cannot face any coffee today,' said Aunt Lovisa. But then she perhaps decides that, seeing as the housekeeper has gone to the trouble of making the coffee, it would look unkind if she did not have any, so she pushes aside her book and pours herself a cup.

And the moment Aunt Lovisa takes her eyes off the book, I rush over to see what tome it is that she is reading. I know all the other books that are in the house, but I have never seen this one before. It is awfully large, and has stiff, brown leather covers that are scratched and faded, and a big brass clasp. The title is on the first page, but it is printed in such peculiar letters that it is almost too much for me to read them.

'Oh look, the regimental paymaster's Bible!' says the housekeeper. 'I haven't seen that for many a long day. I was wondering where it had got to.'

'It has been in the cupboard in my space in the attic ever since my mother died,' says Aunt Lovisa, 'but today I felt I ought to bring it down.'

'You did the right thing there, Miss Lovisa,' says the housekeeper. 'Paymaster Lagerlöf always used to say that that book was better than all the doctors and medicines in the whole world.'

'Yes, it was his comfort in all need,' confirms Aunt Lovisa. 'Do you remember my papa saying that he had read it all through fifty times?'

'Yes,' replies the housekeeper Maja, 'I certainly do. And just imagine how comforting it was, going to sleep out there in the kitchen of an evening, knowing that paymaster Lagerlöf was

Memoirs of a Child

lying here reading the Bible! It was as if no harm could ever come to you.'

Hearing my aunt and the housekeeper say that Grandfather read the whole Bible fifty times, I raise my head. 'Do you think, Maja, that God was pleased with Grandfather for reading the whole Bible so many times?' I ask.

'Of course he was, Selma, you must know that.'

And when I hear her reply, a remarkable feeling comes over me. It is not anything that I work out for myself. It is someone whispering to me what God wants me to do, to make Papa well again.

At first, I am struck with dread. Just think what a terribly long book it is! And to think that it is nothing but sermons and lectures! But that does not matter, as long as Papa is allowed to live. I put my hands together and make a vow to God that if he lets Papa get better, I shall read the whole Bible. I shall read it from cover to cover and not skip over a single word.

And no sooner have I made that vow than Mama appears at the kitchen door, and nods to us and looks quite different from yesterday.

'So kind of you to look after the children, Lovisa,' says Mama, completely overlooking the fact that we have abandoned our lessons. 'I wanted to tell you that Gustav has been better for a while now. He is not delirious any longer and he recognises us. It will take some time, of course, before he is well, but by the power of God, I think we will be able to keep him.'

*

I do not believe it was as hard for Grandfather to read the whole Bible fifty times as it is for me to read it through only once.

For you see, Grandfather could sit down to read whenever he wanted, and Grandmother brought him a light, so he could lie there and read in the evening.

And if I were to tell Mama or Aunt Lovisa that I have promised God that I will read the whole Bible to make Papa well, then perhaps I would get a light by my bed to read by, as well. But you see, it would never do for me to say anything. There was once a princess who had twelve brothers who were turned into wild swans,* and they could only become human again, once she had made each of them a shirt of stinging-nettle yarn. But she was not allowed to tell anyone why she was making those shirts. She almost got burnt to death because she stayed silent, yet still she did not say a word. And I shall not say a word, either.

The doctors at my gymnastics in Stockholm told me I had to lie down and rest for a while in the middle of the day, and I am supposed to carry on doing that at home, too, because it happens to be exactly what Papa has always insisted on for himself. And that gives me a chance to read the Bible. But I can never read for long, because Mama always comes and says that I must close the book and take a nap.

But it is certainly very fortunate – 'a stroke of luck', as Emma Laurell says – that Aunt Lovisa did not take Grandfather's Bible back up to her attic store and lock it away in her big cupboard. I think it must be God who made sure that she only put it in the round-fronted yellow corner cupboard that lives on the cover of the cellar steps. For that cupboard is never locked, and I can take out the Bible whenever I want to read it.

Aunt Lovisa just thinks it is a good thing that I am reading the Bible, because she always keeps a novel under the lid of her sewing basket, which she reads when no one is looking, and there were a couple of times when I borrowed one of those novels and forgot to put it back. But now, with me reading the Bible, she is left in peace with her novels.

Mama and Aline Laurell think the same. They do not like me reading any old thing, and once they found me with a novel called *The Woman in White**, and took it from me just when I was enjoying it most. But neither Mama nor Aline Laurell has anything against me reading the Bible, because the Bible is the word of God.

One other good thing is that it is light in the mornings. On Sundays, when I do not have to get up until eight, I can lie in

Memoirs of a Child

bed reading the Bible for several hours. But it really is awfully long. I feel as if I am getting nowhere.

Gerda normally sleeps downstairs in the bedroom, but on Sundays she comes up to the nursery before she is properly dressed, and she and I play together and have pillow fights. Gerda cannot understand why I now lie there reading and do not want to play, and she gets very upset. But there is no help for it. There are worse things than that to endure when you have to read the whole Bible and you are only ten years old.

I do wonder sometimes whether Grandfather read every single word in the Bible, like I am doing. I am reading all the genealogical tables and all the laws and everything about sacrifices and tabernacles and the high priest's garments. And I wonder whether Grandfather was able to decipher all the strange words well enough to understand everything he read.

You see, I have read in my Bible history about most of what is in the Bible. I already knew everything about Adam and Eve and the Flood and the Tower of Babel and Abraham and Joseph and David, but I am reading it all again, of course, word for word, because that is what I have undertaken to do.

*

It is a Sunday morning, and we are out walking along the road, Anna and Emma Laurell and Gerda and I. And we all find it very dreary that we are in the month of May, because that means there is nothing at all to do when we go out. It is so much better in winter, when we can put on our skates or toboggan down the hill or make the stable ram pull us on the sledge. Even April is better, because then we can dig canals in the slushy snow on the road and build dams to make waterfalls in the stream. But May, no! There is nothing to do but pick wood anemones. And picking wood anemones can be pleasant enough for a few days, but we are already tired of it. Now we just walk straight ahead, and we find it as dull as if we were grown-ups.

Anna and Emma Laurell walk on one side of the road, talking to each other in low voices. They must be saying something about boys and pretty dresses that they think Gerda and I are too little to understand. Gerda and I walk on the other side of the road, talking about when I was in Stockholm for my gymnastics. And among other things, I tell her about a really beautiful play that I saw at the Dramatic Theatre, called *My Rose in the Forest**.

Suddenly, Anna and Emma Laurell cross over to our side. They want to hear all about the play and they say what great fun it must have been. And Emma Laurell tells us that when her papa was alive and she lived in Karlstad, she and her siblings would dress up and act plays. Then Anna says that perhaps we could do that sometime. 'Perhaps we could do it today,' says Emma Laurell, 'seeing as Uncle Lagerlöf is well enough to be sitting up, out of bed, and we have prepared our lessons.'

We do not go a single step further along the road but turn on our heels and almost break into a run in our haste to get home and stage *My Rose in the Forest*. But we talk and deliberate as we go. Before we reach the avenue, we have allocated all the parts. Emma Laurell will be the young girl who is called My Rose in the Forest because she has such rosy cheeks. And Anna will play the young gentleman who loves her. Anna is pale and has dark hair, which fits well for a man. And the old man in the forest, who Emma Laurell lives with, that will be me, because I have long white hair, just like the old man had at the Dramatic Theatre. The hardest thing is to find someone to play the old man's housekeeper, because we think Gerda is too little for the part. In the end we agree that we will have to restore Nursie Maja to our favour, even though she loitered on the stable stairs at the inn talking to Lars Nylund, and let her be the housekeeper.

Gerda is upset when she realises she will not be allowed to join in the dressing up, and she starts to cry, because that comes so easily to her. And we are alarmed, because if Gerda wants to, she can cry all day long, and then the grown-ups think we have treated her badly, and then they may not let us put on our show. So we tell Gerda that she can be Emma

Laurell's little brother and sit on a stool and dress dolls. And she is content with that, thank goodness.

The first thing we hear when we get home, of course, is that it is time for the sermon reading, and that is quite a nuisance. But as soon as it is over, we tell Mama that we want to put on a show, and Mama lends us the key to her big attic storeroom, and we go in there and hunt out all manner of old clothes. And we try things on and dress up and have tremendous fun.

The theatre will be in the nursery, of course, and it will have to represent a big forest where there is a little cottage with a wall round it. We will not be able to get a forest in a cottage, but we think the wall is the most important part, because Anna will have to jump over it when she comes to woo Emma Laurell.

So that is why we first build a wall out of all the beds and sofas and chests of drawers and tables and chairs that are in the nursery, and cover them with blankets and quilts to make a sort of wall, because without those it cannot possibly be like it was in Stockholm. But it is very hard to make that wall stay up, it keeps trying to collapse. The performers who are not acting on stage have to hold up the wall.

The seats for the audience are out on the attic landing, and naturally we need no curtain, because as soon as we open the nursery door, the audience have the whole theatre in front of them. Inside the wall we have set out a table and a chair and the stool Gerda will sit on. And we hope that everyone will realise that the table and chair and stool represent the cottage where My Rose in the Forest lives with her grandfather. We act it all through once, with me teaching Anna and Emma Laurell and Nursie Maja what they have to say. And Emma Laurell finds it so hard to stop herself laughing that it really worries me. But Anna is excellent.

Just as we are starting our performance, Uncle Kalle Wallroth and Aunt Augusta bowl up from Gårdsjö in their carriage to find out how Papa is and to enquire whether he is well enough to come into Filipstad with them to Aunt Julia's wedding. This is very provoking, because now neither Mama nor Aunt Lovisa nor Aline Laurell can come to watch us, but have to keep company with Aunt and Uncle. But when Aunt and Uncle hear that we are about to perform a play from the Dramatic Theatre, they very much want to hear it, and this so enlivens Papa that he puts on a fur coat and goes up to the theatre with them.

It is a little vexing, of course, that we have to have Gerda sitting on a stool and dressing dolls, when she does not belong in the play. When we open the door and are about to begin the play, Papa asks her who she is meant to be, and Gerda answers exactly as if she were her usual self and not a brother of My Rose in the Forest. The other thing that is not good is Nursie Maja. She is so terribly affected. She has been allowed to borrow the real housekeeper's shawl, and she walks crookedly, with a stick which she keeps banging on the floor, and she pulls faces that make her look like a witch.

But Emma Laurell is lovely, and so is Anna. Anna is wearing Papa's uniform jacket from the time when he was earning his officer's stripes in Stockholm, and her hair is gathered up under a military cap, and we burnt a cork and used it to give her a sooty little moustache. And Emma has Mama's white wedding dress and her hair is down.

I have my long hair hanging loose, too, so I look like the old man at the Dramatic Theatre, and am wearing a little coat of rough homespun that Johan has grown out of, and the long trousers that I had for gymnastics in Stockholm, so I am pretty sure people will realise that I am an old grandfather.

And I am so relieved when I see that Anna can get over the wall without either of them falling down, because that is the most important thing.

One time when I am on stage, scolding Emma Laurell for letting Anna jump over the wall, I hear them laughing out on the landing. And when I look round, it is Gerda, holding her finger up to a doll and mimicking me. She is never going to be allowed to act in one of our shows again.

Emma Laurell looks very sweet, but she got a smut on her top lip when Anna kissed her, and after that we all found it hard not to burst out laughing.

When it is all over there is lots of applause, of course, and it lasts almost as long as it did for the actors in the play at the Dramatic Theatre.

Then we have so much to tidy away, not only in the nursery but also in Mama's attic storeroom, and it takes a good while for us to get it all done. When we come down, Mama tells us that Papa is tired, so he has retired to bed, but he wanted us to go in and see him. And we do, of course.

When we come in to Papa and stand there in a row by the bed, he says, 'I want to thank you, children! You know, I think this has done me more good than all Dr Piscator's pills*.'

And that is naturally the best thing we could possibly hear.

Then we go into the drawing room and to say hello to Uncle Kalle and Aunt Augusta, because we had not been able to earlier. And they are delighted, too, and tell us they have thoroughly enjoyed themselves.

We are starting to think that we are rather special, Anna and Emma Laurell and I, and Gerda too, even though she has done nothing but be a nuisance.

But when I come up to Uncle Kalle, he puts his hand on my head and turns my face up to his. 'Well, so this is the girl who is a theatre director,' he says in his kindly voice, and I am expecting him to say how clever it was of me to teach the others to act a play from the Dramatic Theatre. But instead, he goes on: 'Yet I heard tell that she was a little pietist, always dragging a big Bible around with her.'

I am so discomfited that I do not know what to do with myself. And I cannot explain the reason for my Bible reading.

Uncle must have noticed how upset I am, because he pats me on the cheek. 'We have not laughed so much for a long time, your aunt and I,' he says, 'and next time you all come to Gårdsjö, you will have to do your play there, as well.'

I realise that Uncle Kalle is trying to console me, but I am still upset. Just think if Papa were to find out that people say I am a pietist!

There is a great deal to endure when a person has set herself to read the whole Bible and is only ten years old.

Selma Lagerlöf

*

Aline Laurell has borrowed a novel from Mrs Unger in Västra Ämtervik, and it is apparently terribly entertaining. Aline lends it to Mama and Aunt Lovisa, and they are so eager to find out what happens that they can hardly bear to put the book down.

I have seen the book lying about in the bedroom and in the room off the kitchen, and I know that it is called *A Capricious Woman** and is by Emilie Flygare-Carlén, and I would very much like to read it too.

One Sunday afternoon, the book was left on the dining room table for several hours and I could have had a good long read of it, but I did not. Until I have finished the Bible, I do not want to start on any other book.

It is a good thing that summer is here.

Aline and Emma Laurell have gone home to Karlstad, and we never have to get up before eight, and we have no lessons, so I can read the Bible for several hours a day.

But the difficult thing about it being summer is that Daniel and Johan have come home from school.

They have found out, of course, that I am reading the Bible, and they cannot resist teasing me.

'Listen here, Selma,' they say, 'you're reading the Bible, so do you know where Jacob went when he was fourteen years old?'

'Or can you tell us the name of Zebedee's sons' father?'

'Or do you know what the twelve Apostles are doing in the Kingdom of Heaven?'

'Or what do you reckon to this? There was once an old woman who had read the whole Bible, and she said afterwards that she understood every word except for stone tablets, copper pots and stumbling blocks?'

But it does not matter one jot. A person has to endure worse things than that, when she is reading the whole Bible and is only ten years old.

Memoirs of a Child

Papa is up and dressed, but he lies on his sofa for several hours a day. He feels weak and feeble and cannot get rid of his cough. He says he is sure he will never be his old self again.

Papa and Mama and Anna have been in Filipstad at Aunt Julia's wedding, but that did not do him any good. Now Mama has come up with the idea that he should go to Strömstad for the bathing, because they have not felt as well before or since as they did that summer they were there and went bathing. I know that it is not necessary, because he is going to get well anyway, as long as I get to the end of the Bible, but I must not say that to a soul.

Perhaps it is God who has arranged for Papa to spend some time away, so I can get on with my reading.

While Papa is not himself, there is no one who wants to tell him anything to make him unhappy. So no one at home has told him that people think I was converted that time we heard Paulus Andersson from Sandarne speak at the inn, and that I am now a pietist.

But of course he could happen to find out about it anyway, and what would I reply if Papa were to ask me why I am reading the Bible? It would not be possible to lie, and it would not be possible to tell the truth.

At any rate, it is very good to have the long summer nights. When Mama has been up and we have said our prayers with her and Anna has gone to sleep, I slip out of bed and sit over by the window and read for all I am worth.

*

Now Papa is back home and we are all so happy, because he is well and himself again, his old self like he was before he went away to collect taxes and had to sleep on damp sheets.

And we have so many visitors, so many visitors. There are Uncle Schenson and Ernst and Klas and Alma, and there are Uncle Hammargren and Aunt Nana with Teodor and Otto and Hugo, and there are Uncle Oriel Afzelius and Aunt Georgina and Elin and Allan, and then Uncle Kristofer Wallroth, who is not married.

Aline and Emma Laurell have come, too, although not to start lessons, but just to be here for the seventeenth of August, when it will be Papa's fiftieth birthday.

It is such beautiful weather, and there are so many currants and gooseberries and cherries, and the Astrachans* are getting ripe. Everything is so very nice. There is only one tiresome thing, and it is that I have not found time to get to the end of the Bible. I am almost there, I have reached the Book of Revelations, but now there are so many guests that it is full everywhere, and there is not a single place in the whole house where I can sit in peace and quiet for a single hour, and finish reading the Bible.

But this afternoon Mama has come up with the idea that everyone will take a walk to Storsnipa to admire the lovely view. Off they have all gone, both big and small, and I am left on my own at home. I wanted to go with them, but Mama said it was too far for me. I had spent so much time running and playing these past few days, she said, that she was afraid I would start limping the way I used to before I went to Stockholm for gymnastics classes.

I am happy to stay at home, because I am thinking about the Bible, and as soon as the others have gone, I hurry into the room off the kitchen and take it out of the round-fronted cupboard. Then I go into the garden and sit down beside a gooseberry bush, and eat gooseberries as I read the Book of Revelations. And I am so happy. I am thinking about how soon it will be over, and then I will not need to keep any more secrets.

Just as I am busy with my reading, I see Uncle Kristofer walking in my direction, and when he catches sight of me sitting by the gooseberry bush with Grandfather's big Bible in my lap, he comes towards me. I was sure Uncle Kristofer had gone on the walk to Storsnipa like everyone else, and it catches me unawares when he comes up and asks what I am reading.

But I reply that I am reading the Bible, and when he wonders how far I have got, I tell him that I started from the very beginning and am now reading the Book of Revelations.

He says no more, but as he turns to go, he looks as if he would like to roar with laughter.

As soon as he has gone, I shut the Bible and take it inside, to the cupboard in the room off the kitchen. I understand, of course, that as soon as Papa and Uncle Schenson and Uncle Hammargren and Uncle Oriel get back from Storsnipa, Uncle Kristofer intends to tell them that he found me sitting by the gooseberry bush, reading the Book of Revelations.

And Uncle Kristofer is so droll when he tells a story that the others will be beside themselves with laughter.

I go into the kitchen and help Aunt Lovisa and the housekeeper to prepare the evening meal. I run down to the kitchen garden and pick parsley and dill, I run up to the storeroom to fetch pepper and onions. I run all manner of errands, just so I am not inside when the others come home and do not have to hear Uncle Kristofer tell them how funny it was to see me sitting there reading the Bible.

There is a lot to do when a house is so full of visitors. After the meal I help to wash the dishes. I stay out in the kitchen until it is time for me to go to bed.

When so many visitors come to stay, we children have to give up our beds in the nursery, because Aunt Nana and Aunt Georgina and Aline Laurell sleep there. Anna and Emma Laurell and Alma Schenson have to make do with the attic where we store the clothes, but my bed is the corner sofa in the main bedroom.

I lie down and fall asleep, but later that night I wake up and hear Papa and Mama talking about me.

'Did you hear what Kristofer said about Selma?' says Papa, not sounding at all angry, just a bit surprised.

'Yes,' says Mama. 'I do think Kristofer could have left the girl in peace.'

'Yes. I have been away this summer, of course, but you have noticed her reading the Bible, I expect?'

'She has been reading the Bible all summer, morning, noon and night,' declares Mama.

'But Louise, my dear,' says Papa, 'don't you think you should have forbidden it? It is no kind of reading for children, after all.'

'No,' says Mama. 'We talked it over and agreed, Aline Laurell and I, that it was better to leave her to it.'

'I suppose I shall have to speak to her myself then,' says Papa. 'I don't want her turning into a pietist.'

'Please don't, Gustav.'

'But I don't understand...,' says Papa.

'The matter of it is,' explains Mama, 'that I think she wants to read the whole Bible to make you get better.'

'But that can't be possible,' says Papa.

'Well, you know how upset she was when you were taken ill. It affected her more deeply than any of the others, and ever since then she has been reading the Bible.'

'But that can't be possible,' says Papa again, and clears his throat several times, as if he is finding it hard to get the words out. 'It can't be possible for the girl to be so simple-minded.'

Mama makes no reply, and Papa says nothing more, either. There is just silence.

It is so curious. The guests go on their way, and I know I can read the Bible as much as I like, now that Mama has come to my defence. But never again do I take it out of the corner cupboard and finish those few pages in the Book of Revelations. You see, once the secret was revealed, there was no longer any power in what I had vowed. There was no point in carrying on with my reading.

There was no use in any of it.

Gårdsjö

We think it is so enjoyable to go to Gårdsjö to visit Uncle Karl Wallroth and Aunt Augusta and Hilda and Emilia and Karl-August and Elin and Julia and Hugo.

We think Gårdsjö is so beautiful, because it is painted white and has two storeys and a slate roof. At home, our house at Mårbacka is painted red, and it has only one storey and a tiled roof. Nor do we have a big salon where we can play games and dance when there are parties, like they do at Gårdsjö. We only have a small drawing room.

At Gårdsjö they have a lake, and boats we can go rowing in when we come to visit. And we do so enjoy rowing out to pick water lilies. We also like rowing into the reeds to a round, open space where no one can see us and the reeds grow so high that everything is green, the water and the rowing boat and the oars and even us. We lie there in total silence, just waiting, and finally a mother duck comes swimming by with lots of ducklings following her in a row. We think they are so stately. We think it is a real shame that we do not have a lake to row on, back home at Mårbacka. We have nothing but a little duckpond.

At Gårdsjö they also have a river, and crossing the river there is a bridge, where you can stand and fish. As soon as we get to Gårdsjö, we each borrow a rod and go to the bridge to fish. And sometimes we get a bite and manage to pull out little roach and perch and ruff. We are always glad when we pull out a perch, for it is a good fish and worth frying, but the roach is so full of bones that no one wants to eat it. But it is nothing to be ashamed of, if you catch a roach. You just have to be thankful you have not caught a snot-fish, a ruff, which is so slimy all over that it is barely fit to feed to the cat. But we would certainly be as happy as anything to have a river like that at home to fish in. Our river is called the Ämtan, and it is a mere stream all summer, and it is so far away, and it is muddy, too. We have never tried to fish there.

The children at Gårdsjö have so many exciting things to look at that they hardly have time for them all, because Gårdsjö is a proper working estate with a hammer forge and a mill and brickworks and sawmill. We have nothing like that at Mårbacka. All we have is a tiny little smithy where Per in Berlin mends sledges and carriage wheels, and an old hand mill standing in the storehouse, which they use for grinding salt at slaughter time. When Papa built the cowshed, they took mud from the pond to make tiles, but they do not do that any more, and Lars in London and Magnus in Vienna generally saw wood outside the stables, but there is no excitement in watching that.

Down at the Gårdsjö estate, all the roads are black with cinders. We like the way they look, and we find them smoother and easier to walk on than roads made of ordinary grit.

When we get to the estate, we always go first of all to the edge of the millpond and stare down into it. It is in such an awfully dark place with tall trees on all sides, and the water in it is glossy and brown, and there was once a mill boy who threw himself in, because he could not have the miller's daughter. We think it is extraordinary to stand on the spot where another human being took their own life. No one has ever made the slightest attempt to drown themselves in the duckpond at Mårbacka, and we do not think it is deep enough for it to be worth trying.

We never bother to go into the mill itself, because there is so much flour dust in the air in there. We much prefer to go to the hammer forge.

The hammer forge is terribly big and black, and there is no other light in there but what comes through the semi-circular opening in front of the hearth. There are no windows in the forge, no wooden floor and no ceiling, so you can see right up to the roof tiles. Some of the tiles are broken and some have blown off, and that is very fortunate, because we would not be able to see where we were going otherwise, down in the darkness.

And we know from past experience that in the middle of the hammer forge there is a big, square pit, full of coal and water, and stumbling into that would be the worst accident that could befall us, especially when we are wearing our best clothes. We have to mind out and walk slowly and carefully when we are in the forge.

We could also accidentally tread on one of the bars of iron that is lying there on the ground looking like all the other bars of iron, but is newly forged and so hot that it can burn off the sole of your shoe.

We are so awestruck whenever we are in the old Gårdsjö forge. It is like being in a church, before the service has started. There they sit, old man Stjernberg and another blacksmith, on a little wooden bench right beside the forge itself, and they are dressed in nothing but long shirts and wooden clogs and goggles. But we have such fearful respect for old man Stjernberg, and for the other smith too; they look so grave and stern. We hardly dare speak, so as not to disturb them and be sent packing.

Sometimes it is Stjernberg, and sometimes it is the other smith, who stands up, goes to the forge and thrusts in an iron bar, bending and breaking something tough and gluey and heavy. And then sparks come flying out of the mouth of the furnace, and the smith has to make a hasty retreat. And sometimes coals roll down onto his feet, and he has to kick off his clogs.

In between times, the blacksmiths' boy comes in with his barrow and scoops wet coals out of that dangerous pit and shovels them into the mouth of the furnace. Nothing else happens for a long, long time, and we get pretty tired of standing waiting, but we never have the slightest inclination to leave.

Selma Lagerlöf

Finally the moment comes when both the smiths get to their feet and they each pick up an iron bar and start rooting around in the furnace. They bend and pull and break and the sweat pours off them, and before long something red comes rolling out, giving off sparks and light, and it is as soft as dough, yet still holds together. The smiths grip it with both sets of tongs and lift and drag it out of the furnace and across the floor and up onto the anvil.

With that, it seems the worst part is done, for now old man Stjernberg looks very satisfied. His fellow worker pulls on a rope, and then the big tilt hammer starts to descend. To see the hammer fall onto the melted red mass on the anvil and beat sparks from it is one of the finest and most awe-inspiring things I know. The hammer falls again and again, it roars and screeches, the water wheel outside keeps on turning in its wreath of foam and the sparks fly all over the smithy. It is so beautiful.

We enjoy going to the brickworks, too, because we get ocarinas there, and sometimes lumps of clay that we can flatten out into bowls and plates. And it is just as much fun to go to the sawmill, but that is further away, too far for me generally to go there with the others.

We children are not the least bit sad that Gårdsjö is painted white and has two storeys and a slate roof, or that it has a lake and reeds and rowing boats and a bridge and fishing rods and a millpond and a hammer forge and a brickworks and a sawmill and so much else that is not to be found at Mårbacka. No, we are not remotely sad, for as long as it is Uncle Kalle who lives there, we will be able to visit almost every Sunday, and it as if we have our share in everything that is there.

But when I grow up, I would very much like to live in a house that is painted white and has two storeys and a slate roof and a big salon with room for games and dancing when there are parties.

Herrestad

We think it is so enjoyable to go to Herrestad to visit Uncle Noreen and Aunt Emilie and Adolf and Hedvig and Arvid and Erika and Emilia. We at Mårbacka are not related to the Noreens, but they are cousins of our cousins at Gårdsjö, and that is almost the same thing.

We think it just as fine at Herrestad as it is at Gårdsjö, because that is also painted white and has two storeys and a slate roof and a salon where you can play games and dance when there is a party. But at Herrestad there is no working estate; it is just an ordinary property like Mårbacka.

We also think it excellent that Herrestad lies on the shores of Fryken, because Fryken is a big lake, so big that it is in the geography book and on the map. Fryken is eighty kilometres long, and back in the time when it could speak, it would say 'Measure my length, and you will know my depth.' So there is no doubting that Fryken is a proper lake.

At Herrestad there is a big park of spruce trees, where we enjoy walking. There are so many needles on the paths that they are all slippery. You slip on them like when you are walking on ice, and it is so funny. There are also big, bare rocky outcrops in the park, which are awfully good for sliding down on a little branch of spruce.

And in the park, Uncle Noreen has had a pavilion built, with proper glass windows and wallpapered walls, and we were there for the opening ceremony. And it had such a splendid floor of short blocks of wood at angles to each other, so we felt

Selma Lagerlöf

as if it was going up and down in waves, and we were really nervous about dancing on it. And Uncle Noreen had written verses that he read out at the ceremony, because he does not only give speeches but also writes verse and acts the part of Erik XIV*.

And it is so amusing, because Emilia Noreen, who is the youngest of all the children at Herrestad, can also act Erik XIV. She runs around and shakes her fuzzy hair, because she is supposed to be mad. 'The forest calls my name,' she says, 'the forest calls my name, but how does he know it?' And she makes her voice all deep, to scare us. But she is so small and sweet that it only makes us laugh.

It is most certainly Uncle Noreen himself who taught her to do her Erik XIV act, because he plays with his children and is kind to them, just like our papa.

There is a hole in the high rocks in the Herrestad park, and it has vertical walls and is called Bear Cavern, because a bear once tumbled into it and could not climb out again. We like to sit down under a big spruce that grows on the edge of the hole and pretend that the bear is still down in the depths. We hear it growling and climbing and its claws scraping the stone walls as it falls back down again.

Wild blackberries grow at Herrestad, and that is also remarkable, for blackberries do not grow anywhere else in the parish. It is my belief that the bear who fell into Bear Cavern was after some blackberries, because they are simply delicious.

I like Herrestad, because so many remarkable things have happened there.

An old woman once lived there, who never dared go out because she was afraid the magpies would eat her up. And a young woman once lived there, who was so unhappy that she would sit for long hours on the shore of the lake and think about killing herself. And there is a room there known as the Blue Cabinet, where a young girl once sat by the window and saw her fiancé drown in Lake Fryken. I sometimes stand at that window and I can always picture Fryken frozen over and a young man approaching across the ice on skates, and suddenly a huge crack gapes open in front of him. Then I turn away, because I do not want to see any more.

*

On one occasion there were some gentlemen – I think it was Uncle Schenson and Warberg the engineer and Pastor Unger, and Papa of course – sitting on the verandah at Mårbacka, and they were debating which was the best property in the parish, Gårdsjö or Herrestad. And one said it was Gårdsjö, and another said it was Herrestad.

Papa sat there quietly for a while, listening, but then he asked whether they had forgotten Mårbacka. When all was said and done, perhaps that was just as good as the other two.

The visitors fell silent and were slightly embarrassed, but then Uncle Schenson said: 'Of course it is true, brother Erik Gustav, that you have spent a good deal on Mårbacka and extended it, and that you run it excellently. But you must understand that it still cannot be compared...'

'Yes,' said Papa, 'I know, of course, that Gårdsjö is a working estate and Herrestad is the most beautiful spot in the whole of Fryksdalen, but can you tell me why it is that Gårdsjö and Herrestad are always changing owners? They have been bought and sold for as far back as I can remember. But Mårbacka has never been sold since the day the people first settled here. It has simply been passed down through the generations.'

'Indeed, there could be something in what you say, Erik Gustav,' said Uncle Schenson. 'There could well be. For if we think in terms of good cheer and a sense of well-being....'

Fear

We are having such a good time here.
Papa and Mama and Aunt Lovisa and Aline Laurell and Anna have gone to a party at the vicarage in Sunne, but Emma Laurell and Gerda and I were not allowed to go with them, because we are too young. And once we had finished learning our lessons for tomorrow, we came into the kitchen to sit with the housekeeper, and she has been telling us those tall tales of Kockelille, who was 'full to bursting of nuts' and the Old Man who ate up seven cartloads of porridge and seven cartloads of buttermilk. And we persuaded the kindly cook to sing the comical song of Olle Bock, who went to war with fifteen thousand men and would be back 'by Easter or Trinity Sunday'.

Then we baked apples in the tiled stove in the dining room, and later in the evening we had little pancakes with raspberry jam to make up for having to stay at home.

But as soon as we have had our supper, we go up to the nursery, because we do not feel happy downstairs when all the grown-ups are out. Gerda is going to sleep on the nursery sofa tonight because no one can expect her to sleep alone in the bedroom. So she and Nursie Maja come upstairs with us. The tall, red-haired scullery maid and the kind cook come too, not because they have any tasks to do in the nursery, but just to talk.

Nursie Maja adds wood to the stove and we settle down in front of the blaze to warm ourselves. The weather has been

Memoirs of a Child

terrible all evening, and we sit in silence for a while and listen to the rain as it lashes against the windows and the wind as it whistles round the corner of the house. The kind cook says she feels sorry for the family, who will have to travel home on a night like this. But Nursie Maja comfortingly reminds her that they are travelling in the big, covered carriage. We are all glad to hear it, because having the big, covered carriage will mean that they are able to shut themselves in so they will come to no harm from the wind or rain.

Then, of course, we ask the kind cook and the scullery maid to tell us ghost stories. But they reply that they dare not, because Mrs Lagerlöf has forbidden it.

But Nursie Maja gives us a wink to show that we need not worry, for she will find a way. First of all, she persuades Gerda to get undressed and lie down on her little bed on the nursery sofa. Gerda falls asleep as soon as her head touches the pillow, and Nursie Maja comes over to us.

And she says that we two, Emma Laurell and I, are so sensible that we are almost like grown-ups, so it will not matter a bit if someone tells us ghost stories. Gerda is so little that it is only natural for Mrs Lagerlöf to want her not to be frightened, but she is asleep now.

We sit there listening to one ghost story after another.

The tall red-headed scullery maid says that at the place where she was in service last year, the master died. He was far from the best of men, and people had plenty to say about him. Well, she does not know how it all fitted together, but the day he died, a big black dog with gaping, blood-red jaws came running up to the house. It stood on the front steps and barked and howled for a good hour to be let in, but no one dared open the door. It was in the middle of the day, and the farm hands were in the kitchen for their dinner, but they just sat round the table and left the food untouched.

She remembered that there was a big dish of potatoes on the table, and one of the hands took a potato, but then he just sat there with it in his hand and could not bring himself to peel it. The scullery maid sat there in the kitchen with the others, and she would never forget how awful it was with

Selma Lagerlöf

everybody sitting there in total silence, listening spellbound to the dog barking on the steps.

Finally, the mistress came out to the kitchen. She was pale and so fearful that she had to hold onto the doorpost so as not to fall. She just wanted to ask, she said, whether there was anyone in the whole house who would dare to drive away that dog from the front steps.

At that, the eldest hand got to his feet. He pushed his chair back so fiercely that it crashed against the wall and then went to the stove, grabbed the fire tongs, picked up a flaming billet of wood with them and bore it out to the hall. The front door was bolted and barred, but the farmhand unlocked it and opened the door a crack. Then he hurled the burning brand straight into the mouth of the shrieking Creature, at which the dog let out an even more piercing howl. It could be heard far and wide, and sounded for all the world like a human voice shouting and cursing uncontrollably. But he did then turn tail and ran off up the avenue in a cloud of sparks and smoke, so it was very plain what manner of being he was.

And I do not even know that I have such a tight grip on Nursie Maja's hand until she leans down and asks me if I am scared.

There have certainly been cold shivers running up and down my spine the whole time the scullery maid has been talking, but it is frightfully exciting all the same. I instantly take my hand out of Nursie Maja's and shake my head.

Yet it is true that I wish they would keep to tales of elves and trolls, because those do not frighten me. But please, none about the Evil One! You see I have always had the idea that he is hiding in the attic outside the nursery in the dark corner where all the worn-out spinning wheels and weaving looms are piled up. I am always in a hurry to get past the part of the attic where I imagine him to be, because he could just happen to step forward out of the darkness and I would see him. But as soon as I have my hand on the key of the nursery, I feel safe, because he will never come in there. As long as he does not venture in now, what with the tall, red-haired scullery maid having said so much about him! Who knows? Perhaps he will suddenly knock at the door and open it and come in.

Now it is the kind cook's turn to tell a story. She begins by admitting that this is not an adventure she had herself, but she knows it to be true, all the same, because her uncle saw and heard it all.

Our cook's uncle was felling timber, way out in the forest, and as his workmate he had a man who must have had some kind of contract with old Nick. They had just sawed through a spruce and were waiting for it to fall, when they saw that it was not leaning the way they had expected. It looked as though it was going to fall right on them, and there was no time to get out of its way.

But then our cook's uncle heard his mate shout out to the big spruce: 'Rise up in the name of The Fiend!' At that, the uncle saw the tree stop in mid-fall, rise again and sink to the other side.

And it is stupid and mortifying, but I am so frightened. The whole time the kind cook has been telling the story, I have heard the patter of steps out in the attic, and just as the spruce falls, I shout to her to be quiet.

And all at once there is a terrible gust of wind and a loud crash, and I am convinced that the door will open and that the one I dare not name will show himself to us.

I jump up and start crying and I say again that I want to hear no more.

'Oh Selma, surely you could hear that it was just a tile blowing off the roof,' says Nursie Maja, 'but of course we'll stop now if you're scared.'

I realise at once that Nursie Maja is right and that it was nothing but a roof tile. I feel so ashamed of myself that I could die.

Emma Laurell says I am behaving like a child of six. She thinks the kind cook could very well carry on, but Nursie Maja says she can't be held responsible for that, so they will have to stop now.

Later that night I lie awake and am annoyed with myself for having been frightened, for I know very well that the Evil One is not actually lurking in the heap of old spinning wheels. It is just my imagination.

It is shameful to be afraid of nothing and burst into tears because a tile falls off the roof. That will never happen again.

I think about Frithiof and Sven Duva and Sandels*. I definitely fall very short of them.

But the next day there is a little girl standing ready in the kitchen when it is time to prepare dinner, and if the housekeeper wants anything fetched down from the storeroom, she instantly offers to run and get it. She goes up the attic stairs and across the landing and into the storeroom with calm and steady steps, and she carries on doing that, day after day.

The housekeeper praises her for obligingly running so many errands, but the little girl is only doing it to harden herself. And she soon reaches the stage of being able to pass the heap of spinning wheels in the corner without averting her eyes and without feeling her heart pound as she comes back down to the kitchen afterwards.

The Game of Cards

At Christmas, when Daniel and Johan and Uncle Wachenfeldt are here in Mårbacka, they play cards in the evenings with Aunt Lovisa. They play a game called Preference, although they call it whist, and it is great fun. I have learnt it by watching when the others were playing. But it is generally only grown-ups who can play whist. Neither Anna nor Emma Laurell knows how. They only know Knaves and Flurst and Comet and Snip Snap Snorum and Black Peter and Elevens and Beggar My Neighbour and Kille and Napoleon.

This evening, Papa has gone away, and taken Johan with him. And Daniel and Uncle Wachenfeldt are sitting there wondering how they are going to get a game, because they have no fourth player. They ask Mama whether she would perhaps like to, and Mama can do anything, but she does not like playing cards, so she says no. Then Aunt Lovisa says that it would be all right to take Selma as their fourth player. 'It can't be possible for the girl to know how to play whist, surely?' says Uncle Wachenfeldt. 'I mean to say, she's only twelve.'

'Why not try her and see, Wachenfeldt,' says Aunt Lovisa. 'She is not bad, you know. She has joined us a few times, when Aline and Mrs Lindegren at Halla and I felt like a game.'

So I am allowed to make up the numbers, and now here I am, playing and having a terribly good time, especially as I have Daniel as my partner, sitting opposite. Because Daniel plays so well and is always content, whether he wins or loses. He is so jolly, too. He always says something to make the rest of us laugh, like 'Diamonds out! said the jewel thief,' or 'Spades, all gone digging,' or something like that. Aunt Lovisa fingers her cards for a long time, but as soon as she has played a card, she regrets it and wants to take it back. Uncle Wachenfelt certainly knows how to do things, for he was a great player in his time, but he has a cataract in one eye and cannot see very well out of the other one, either, so he sometimes accidentally plays the wrong card. But Daniel does not mind in the slightest that the others play badly. He never loses patience with them.

To start with, everything goes quite well for me, but later in the evening I get such bad cards that I just keep on losing. And of course we are not playing for anything, but it is provoking all the same, for Daniel and Uncle Wachenfeldt might easily think my bad luck is because I am twelve years old and do not understand the game.

But just imagine, shortly before it is time for the evening meal and for us to stop playing, I get good cards! I have the ace, king, queen, jack and ten of spades and five lower cards, and that is ten tricks I am bound to win, if I can only get in. I also have the ace of diamonds and the queen and a lower card in hearts, but not a single club.

Because I have sat there watching all evening, I want to take the lead and show what I am made of. I say 'Preference' on my own initiative, for I will surely be able to win ten tricks with cards like those.

Opposite me I have Daniel and he is my partner. To my right I have Aunt Lovisa and to my left Uncle Wachenfeldt. The two of them are in league against Daniel and me.

And because I am the one who has said 'Preference', Aunt Lovisa is the one to go first, and she fiddles with her cards for ages. But finally, she plays a club, a suit in which I do not have a single card. Then it turns out that Uncle Wachenfeldt has some good clubs, too, and he and Aunt Lovisa win five tricks with their clubs, while I am forced to throw away my splendid spades. It makes me so impatient and anxious and I have to hide my hand, the one holding the cards, under the table so that no one will see how it is shaking.

And when they finally run out of spades, Uncle Wachenfeldt lays a heart, and Aunt Lovisa adds the ace, and I throw down my low heart card. As Aunt Lovisa is gathering up the cards, she laughs and says, 'This is going well for us, Wachenfeldt.' But Daniel, who is normally so patient, cannot help asking what I based my 'Preference' call on.

Then my aunt plays a jack of hearts, and I lay my queen, and Uncle Wachenfeldt does not beat my queen but puts down a low heart, so it looks as though I will win the trick.

I see it before me, the moment in which I am saved. Now I will be able to play my spades and my ace of diamonds and can win my seven tricks.

But before Daniel lays his card, he turns to Uncle Wachenfeldt.

'But why don't you outdo Selma's queen, Uncle,' he says. 'You have the king there, after all.'

Uncle Wachenfeldt brings his cards up to his eyes and studies them with his big, rounded cataract glasses.

'Well well, so I do, though I overlooked it,' he says. 'But the card I played must stand.'

'Oh, no need for that,' says Daniel. 'You certainly have the right to exchange your card, because you could not see.'

I understand, of course, that Daniel is doing the right thing by offering Uncle the chance to take back his card. But I so much want to win, and I simply cannot agree with Daniel.

'Didn't you hear Uncle say that the card he played must stand?' I ask.

But Daniel pays no heed. 'Let's see that king, Uncle,' he says, and passes back the low card that Uncle has already laid.

With that Uncle Wachenfeldt throws down his king, Daniel lays a low heart, and the play is back with our opponents. Now they will get seven tricks, and there is no way for me to win.

Aunt Lovisa reaches out to gather up the four hearts from the table, but I have reached the end of my patience. I throw all the cards I still have in my hand onto the table in one go.

'I don't want to play any longer,' I shout, and get to my feet, 'because you are not playing fair.'

Selma Lagerlöf

And I am so angry. I am so angry that the blood is boiling in my body. I think that Uncle Wachenfeldt is a rogue and a cheat, and it feels so good to throw the cards on the table and tell him as much. And Daniel is not a bit better than he is. They are not the sort any decent person can play cards with.

But it is far from usual at Mårbacka for anyone to throw their cards on the table and cry that the others are playing unfairly, so it creates a great commotion. Mama has been sitting at another table with Anna and Gerda, devising a logogriph, and she gets up at once and comes towards me. And I rush over to her: 'Mama, they are not playing fair,' I cry, and throw my arms around her and am in floods of tears.

Mama says nothing, either to defend me or to scold me. She just takes a firm grip on my wrist and leads me out of the dining room. We go through the front hall, up the attic stairs and into the nursery. I keep on crying the whole way and shouting the same thing: 'They are not playing fair, Mama, they are not playing fair.' But Mama does not say a word.

Once we reach the nursery, Mama lights the lamp and starts to prepare my bed. 'Get undressed now, so you can go to bed!' she says.

I do not do as she says, however, but sit down on a chair and sob and say as before, 'Uncle Wachenfeldt wasn't playing fair.'

As I repeat it, something strange happens. It is as if my eyes are reversed. Instead of looking out at the nursery, as they were before, they are looking inward. They are looking right into me.

And what they see is a big, empty, gloomy cave with wet, dripping walls and ground that is like a swamp. Nothing but slime and mud. And that cave is inside me.

But as I look down into it, I can see something starting to move, deep down in the filthy mire. There is something trying to work its way out. I see a huge, horrible head with gaping jaws and spikes on its forehead, rising up out of the depths, and behind that I glimpse a dark, scaly body with a big, jagged crest along its back, and stubby front legs. It is like the dragon that St George does battle with in Stockholm Cathedral*, but much bigger and more terrifying.

Memoirs of a Child

I have never seen anything as dreadful as that monster, and it scares me to death that it is dwelling inside me. I realise that until now it has been sunk in the mud and has not been able to move, but now that I have let rage get the upper hand, it feels bold enough to emerge.

I can see it, working its way up. It rises and rises, and more and more of its long, scaly body comes into view. It must be so glad that it has broken free and is no longer trapped in the mud.

I must make haste before the wild beast can expose its whole, long body, because by now then I may be able to force it back into its prison.

I jump off the chair and start to undress. I am no longer crying, but am as quiet as can be and terribly afraid of what I have seen.

I climb into my bed as soon as Mama has got it ready and as she tucks me in, I take her hand and kiss it.

Then Mama sits down on the edge of the bed. She can see that I am no longer angry, and perhaps she also knows that I am afraid of myself, for Mama knows everything.

'Tomorrow you will ask Uncle Wachenfeldt's forgiveness,' says Mama.

'Yes,' I answer at once.

Mama says nothing. I lie there and think about the great monster that I have living inside me, and I tell myself that I will never lose my temper again. It will have to stay down there in the mud for as long as I live. It will never break free again.

I do not know what Mama is thinking. She should be chastising me, but she is not. She knows everything, so she probably knows there is no need.

A little while later she asks me if I want any supper, but I say no, I can eat nothing.

'Say your prayers then, and I shall sit here until you fall asleep,' says Mama.

The Marseillaise

If only Uncle Kristofer had not seen me sitting beside the gooseberry bushes and reading the Book of Revelations, and if he had not told Papa, and if Papa had not questioned Mama, then I am sure he would have got properly better. But when he found out about it all, before I had finished, it could not be helped that the illness remained with him.

When it is summer, Papa is fairly well, but as soon as it turns cold in the autumn, his bad cough returns and will not leave him, even though he has tallow rubbed into the soles of his feet each night and sleeps with the sock that he has worn on his left foot wrapped round his neck.

Mama is forever asking him to send for the doctor from Sunne, but Papa says that he really does not want to call Dr Piscator here, because he is one of those perpetual students, says Papa. The man spent all his life in Uppsala, and grew accustomed to sitting up late at nights, talking and drinking toddy. It is impossible to get rid of him before two o'clock in the morning at the earliest, and Papa finds that trying.

Instead, Papa tries to cure himself. He stops going for walks along the roadway, which he would normally do every day, because if he meets anyone, he is obliged to stop and talk to them, and he thinks he will catch cold while he is standing still. Mama thinks there is no need for him to pause and talk, he could simply say good day and carry on past, but Papa says that is impossible for him.

Memoirs of a Child

Papa is determined to eat porridge made with water every evening. He no longer accepts invitations to go out in the evening, because he cannot have his porridge at other people's houses. Mama can barely persuade him to come with her to the vicarage in Sunne to visit Professor Fryxell*. He did not even want to go to Gårdsjö until Aunt Augusta came up with the solution of asking their maid Stina to cook porridge for him. He is not happy when we have guests at home, either, because Aunt Lovisa feels awkward about him eating porridge in company, so she pretends to forget it. But Papa will not give in. He will never get better, he says, if he does not have his porridge, so Aunt has no choice but to serve him a dish of porridge, however many guests we have and however grand they may be.

Papa has also hit upon the notion of taking a nip before breakfast and two before dinner. He says that schnapps is the best of all medicaments and that if only he can continue taking this medicine for long enough, he will be restored to perfect health. Papa is utterly convinced of it. Papa had never tasted schnapps until he was seventeen, but then he got a high fever and the shivers and Grandmother cured him by giving him schnapps. Mama and Aunt Lovisa both say that to judge by everything they have seen, drinking schnapps only brings folk to rack and ruin, but Papa will not concede this and insists he is feeling better with every passing day.

But we children, we can see that Papa is poorly, for he never runs to play tag with us in the evenings any more.

Papa has spent one whole winter curing himself and is now well into the second. But his cough is so bad that it gives him no peace, day or night.

Mama wants to send for Dr Piscator right away, but Papa resists for as long as possible, for war has now been declared between France and Germany, and since that happened it has been even more risky to fetch him.

You see, the doctor supports the Germans, and no one else does. He thinks them so clever that he can never stop talking about them. We have heard that when he was at the Nilssons in Visteberg, he and Mr Nilsson got into such a dispute about

65

Selma Lagerlöf

France and Germany that they sat there arguing all night, and Mrs Nilsson had to give the doctor breakfast before he left. So it is very true what Papa says, that it is a hazardous undertaking to send for Dr Piscator.

But Mama gets her way, even so, and one afternoon the carriage is sent to fetch the doctor. It is not even four when he arrives and we are quite sure that once he has examined Papa and written the prescription and had coffee, he will go on his way.

But he sits there talking and talking and when five o'clock comes, Papa asks for hot water and sugar and brandy to be brought to the bedroom, so the doctor can have his toddy. He thinks that is what it will take to make the doctor leave.

It has not been an overly cold day, but towards evening it suddenly turns extremely cold. By half past five, the thermometer is showing minus twenty. We sit in a circle round the table in front of the sofa in the dining room and work on our knitting and embroidery and sewing as usual, but we feel the cold come creeping across the floor, turning our feet to blocks of ice. We say what a shame it is for the stable hand, who will have to drive the doctor home to Sunne on such a cold night.

When six o'clock comes, Aunt Lovisa starts to ask whether the doctor will stay for the evening, but Mama and Aline Laurell reassure her that they cannot believe he will. Why would he stay? As a doctor, he should presumably have the sense to realise that Papa needs to get to bed in good time.

Just as they are discussing this, the housekeeper comes in to say that there is a grand sight in the sky, and she thinks the mistress and everyone should go outside and look. We throw on our shawls and coats and all go running out.

Outside, we see that the sky is all red, as if it were in flames. Aline Laurell says at once that it is the aurora borealis, although it is rare for it to be such a vivid red. And we stand there gazing at it, for we have never seen anything like it. All along the top it is hanging down like rows of red organ pipes, and suddenly there are hazy clouds of blue and green as well. We think we can hear a sizzling sound as they swirl in.

Someone says it could be reflections from the Siege of Paris*, which is currently in progress. Aline replies that this is a sheer impossibility, but that it could still be a sign that there is sorrow and anger up in Heaven, because the Germans are so wicked that they want to bombard a city such as Paris.

We think that it is all too horribly awful. The cold means we cannot stay outside for long, but when we go in, we feel as if we have had bombs and grenades hurled down on us. We think we can really appreciate how they must be feeling in the big, encircled city.

By the time we come in it is half-past six and Aunt Lovisa starts asking again whether the doctor will be here for the evening meal. She has a sausage soaking in water, she says, but she is afraid it is still too salty, and she has to have something for the smörgåsbord. Mama replies again that she can only imagine the doctor will soon be on his way. There will be medicaments to be sent out for Papa from the pharmacist's in Sunne, and that will be impossible if the doctor does not leave until bedtime.

When the time reaches seven o'clock, Papa comes to us in the drawing room with the good news that the doctor wishes to leave. He asks us to get the message to the stable hand to harness up the horse. Anna runs straight to the kitchen with the message, and we are all so pleased that the doctor is leaving, so Papa can have some peace.

Before Papa goes, Mama takes the opportunity of asking him something.

'My dear, what is it that the two of you are talking about?' says Mama.

'We are talking of nothing but Bismarck,' says Papa, 'and what a remarkable man he is.'

We feel very sorry for Papa, who is obliged to sit there listening to praise for Bismarck, for we know that everything befalling France is his fault. We are so caught up in event, you see, now that we have been outside and seen Paris under bombardment.

The stable hand loses no time in bringing the horse round. We hear the deep sleighbells as he arrives at the foot of the front steps, and we think the gentlemen sitting in the bedroom must have heard them, too. But they are still talking away in there.

'You go in, Selma,' says Mama, 'and tell them the horse is here.'

I go, of course, and when I open the door, I see Papa and the doctor seated at the desk with the toddy tray between them. The doctor is so animated that he slaps his hand down on the desk and cries: 'It was that damned Spanish hag, you must see that.'

When he catches sight of me, he breaks off to hear what I want, and when I tell him the horse is waiting, he simply waves his hand. 'That's good, my girl,' he says, and turns back to Papa as before.

I return to the dining room, where I obviously tell them what the doctor said. And Aline Laurell is very cross and says that it is a shameful way to speak of a poor, deposed and exiled empress*.

We sit and wait in the dining room again and check the thermometer, which now shows minus twenty-five, and we are so worried about the stable hand and the horse. Mama sends out a fur for the man and a hide rug to put over the horse. That is all she can do, she says.

At half past seven we hear the stable hand come into the hall and direct his heavy footsteps to the bedroom. We cannot hear what he says but we realise, of course, that he wants to know whether he is to carry on waiting. It does not take him long, at any rate, and he comes back into the hall and opens the door to the dining room.

'What should I do, mistress?' he says. 'I'm afeared the mare'll freeze herself to death.'

'What did the gentlemen say in there?' asks Mama.

'What did they say?' repeats the stable hand. 'The Lieutenant never got a word in. I was no sooner in there than the doctor poured me a big nip of brandy, and then he gave me two *riksdaler** and sent me out.'

'I see,' said Mama. 'Well in that case I think it best, Jansson, for you to unharness the horse and take her back to the stable.'

Just after the stable hand has closed the hall door behind him, Papa comes in through the door from the drawing room and says he is convinced the doctor will not leave until he has had a meal.

'We can give him a meal by all means,' says Mama, 'as long as he does not sit there all night afterwards.'

'Well, who can say,' replies Papa, 'but we cannot turn him out in any case.'

Then he goes back to his room and Aunt mutters something about things going the same way for us as they did for the Nilssons at Visteberg, so we will have to give him breakfast too. And Mama says that it will be too much for Papa. 'I shall have him back in bed tomorrow, if that happens,' she says.

When Mama says that, we are all very distressed, and we are so cross with Dr Piscator for outstaying his welcome. To us it feels just as awful as that evening when Papa came home suffering from pneumonia.

But just as we are all sitting there feeling at our most dispirited, Aline Laurell starts to laugh out loud. 'I think I know a way to make the doctor go home,' she declares, 'if you will allow me to try it, Louise.'

'Of course I will, as long as you do not do anything to make him angry with us,' says Mama.

'Oh no, I shall certainly do no harm,' says Aline.

With that, she tosses aside her needlework and gets to her feet. And Mama and Aunt Lovisa and Anna and Emma and Gerda, they are all ashen-faced with cold and worry. But Aline has red roses in her cheeks and a sparkle in her eyes.

In the old days we had nothing to play on except a clavichord but when Grandfather died a few years ago we inherited his piano, which now stands in the drawing room. At this point, Aline goes into the drawing room and we hear her open the piano. Then she lights candles and we can hear the rustle of paper, and we realise she is hunting through the pile of sheet music. And all at once, she starts playing a march.

We sit in silence, transfixed, for we are so curious that we can neither knit nor sew.

'What is she playing?' says Aunt Lovisa. 'I think I have heard it before.'

'I think so, too,' says Mama. 'You know what? I am sure it is the Marseillaise.'

'Yes, I do believe you are right,' says Aunt Lovisa. 'It is a very fine march, and I am glad to hear it again.'

'They were forever playing it in Filipstad in my young days,' says Mama, 'and I remember how much Papa always enjoyed hearing it.'

Mama and Aunt Lovisa look quite exhilarated, but Anna and Emma and Gerda and I, we have no idea what is going on.

'The Marseillaise,' says Anna. 'What kind of piece is that?'

'It is a French march,' says Mama. 'It was the one that they played and sang in France during the French Revolution. Can you hear how lovely it is?'

'I have never heard Aline play so well,' says Aunt Lovisa, 'but I do wonder what Dr Piscator will make of this piece.'

It starts to come back to me that I have read about the Marseillaise, either in Nösselt's *General History for Women* or somewhere else.

'I remember that the French liked it so much that they became twice as brave whenever they heard it,' I say.

Then we sit there and listen with rapt attention to Aline playing the Marseillaise. She plays it over and over again and goes at it non-stop without tiring, playing with great vigour and force.

I do not know how it happens, but it sounds so remarkable, that march. It is as if you can no longer sit still and just knit or sew. It makes you want to leap up and shout and sing. It makes you want to do something great and extraordinary.

Never before have I heard Aline Laurell play like that. And none of us knew that there was so much sound in Grandfather's old piano. I think I can hear the drums, I think I can hear the shooting and fighting, I think the ground is shaking. I think I have never heard anything so beautiful.

The bedroom where Papa is sitting with Dr Piscator is right next to the drawing room so they, too, must be able to hear

Aline playing the Marseillaise. And I cannot help wondering whether they think it beautiful as well.

When Aline sat down to start playing the Marseillaise it was just about eight o'clock, and now it is a quarter past, but she carries on, just as energetically and tirelessly.

There is something that Aline wants to tell us, her listeners. I can hear it, but I cannot put my finger on what it is. Perhaps it is that we should not despise the French, for they are a great and admirable people in spite of everything. Or perhaps it is that we should not grieve that they have been defeated, for they will rise again? Something along those lines, I think it must be.

But a little while later, Papa appears at the drawing-room door.

'You can stop playing now, Aline,' he says, 'for the doctor has gone.'

Then Papa tells us how peculiar it was when Dr Piscator heard the Marseillaise. At first he took no notice of it, but kept on talking as he had before, and when the music did not stop, he cursed a little and said that it was disturbing him.

But soon he fell completely silent and just sat there listening. Then he started stamping his foot in time to it and singing under his breath, and Papa rather thought there were tears in his eyes.

All at once he had leapt to his feet and made for the door, where his fur was hanging, threw it on in great haste and rammed his cap down over his ears. 'Farewell then, Erik Gustav!' he cried. 'I must go home right away.'

He opened the door and went out into the hall, but father hurried after him.

'My dear fellow, surely you will wait for the horse to be brought round?' Papa said. 'Come back in for a moment, while I send word to the hands' quarters!'

But the doctor wanted only to get the front door open as fast as he could.

'Do you not think I can find my own way to the hands' quarters?' he asked. 'I can stay no longer. If I sit here and listen to the Marseillaise, I will be as infatuated with the French as all the rest of you.'

Forty Below

It is Saturday today, and when we were at dinner Mama told us that since it was the end of our lessons – we always have Saturday afternoons off – and it was such lovely weather and the road was in such good condition, she thought Aunt Lovisa and Aline Laurell could venture out in the sleigh and get some fresh air. It so happened that Aunt Augusta at Gårdsjö had promised Mama a few samples of cotton fabric and it would be useful if they could fetch them for her. They would not need to stay so long at Gårdsjö, said Mama, that Aunt Augusta felt she had to invite them to supper. They could come back home once they had had coffee.

Aunt and Aline made themselves ready, and at half past three they set off. Then Papa sent a message to Anna and me, asking us to come down to the office to collate fire insurance policies. It is Papa who is in charge of all the fire insurance in Östra Ämtervik, and there are supposed to be three insurance policies for each house and farm, and all three are supposed to be exactly the same, there must be no mistakes in them.

We sit at the big desk in the office and we each have one of the big fire insurance policies opened out in front of us. And we think it is so solemn and serious to be allowed to help Papa with the collation.

And Papa reads: 'New 1. Gd. condition 1. Old ½. Roof: Birch bark and turf.' It is the same in policy after policy, there is no variety at all, but we enjoy ourselves all the same. Papa says that Anna is Nyman the surveyor, and I am Erik at Korterud, because they are the two who normally do the collation with him. If I find a mistake, he says 'It is well that you are paying attention, Erik at Korterud,' and it sounds so funny that we cannot help throwing ourselves back in our chairs and roaring with laughter.

And as we are busy with all that, the office door opens and in comes a gentleman dressed in a long black fur coat and a sealskin cap, with a hand-knitted travelling scarf wound around him. He has so much rime frost in his beard and eyebrows that we do not recognise him at first, but we soon discover that it is engineer Frykberg from Gräsmark, who comes here each seventeenth of August to dance and see the theatrical performances.

Once engineer Frykberg has exchanged greetings with Papa and Anna and me, he says he has heard that Papa has had unusually fine oats this year. He wonders whether he could buy some, as seed oats, because all the oats at Gräsmark were blighted by frost last autumn.

Papa immediately puts away all the insurance policies and sends us children up to Mama with instructions to serve coffee to engineer Frykberg. We hurry over to the house with the message, and as Aunt Lovisa is not at home, we help the housekeeper to cut the sugar and arrange the biscuits.

We think we have laid a really nice table for coffee, but when engineer Frykberg comes into the dining room and sees it, he somehow looks disappointed.

'Don't all your women take coffee?' he says to Papa. 'There are only three cups set out here.'

'Oh yes,' says Papa, 'they have all mastered that art. But my sister and the governess have gone to Gårdsjö. You will have to make do with just us.'

It is curious that engineer Frykberg, who is a big, burly fellow with a long, full, black beard that is even a little streaked with grey, can be so put out by the fact that Aunt Lovisa and Aline Laurell have gone to Gårdsjö. First he blinks his eyes several times, very fast, then he takes out his big, red silk handkerchief and mops his brow and face, more than once. And as he passes his cup to Mama so she can pour him some coffee, we can hear the spoon chinking against the saucer.

All the time they are having coffee, Mama and engineer Frykberg talk about Aline Laurell. Mama says she will be very happy for as long as she has such an excellent teacher for her children, so organised, so unpretentious and pleasant to have in one's home. And so deft with her hands, too! It was really remarkable what beautiful things she could make out of more or less nothing.

Mama looks up for a few moments, but she is not at all startled to see engineer Frykberg looking so peculiar, and she simply smiles. 'They will not be staying at Gårdsjö all evening,' says Mama. 'I think we shall have them back here by six o'clock.' When Mama says this, engineer Frykberg seems to revive. He puts his handkerchief back in his pocket and his spoon no longer chinks against the saucer.

Mama invites engineer Frykberg to look at two corner cupboards made of leather-cloth* that we have in the dining room, presents from Aline to Papa last Christmas. 'Can you see, Mr Frykberg, how beautifully embroidered these corner cupboards are?' says Mama. 'And can you imagine, these roses and fuchsias and lily-of-the-valley are embroidered with nothing but fish scales? And for this lovely border she used the scales of spruce cones, painted with copal varnish*. I tell you, that girl has a fortune in her hands.'

Then Mama asks me to go and fetch Papa's pen rack to show engineer Frykberg. Aline cut thin strips of wood to make it from and glued them together, and Papa is so fond of it that he will simply have no other pen rack on his desk. 'And as you see, Mr Frykberg, this has not cost much money either,' says Mama.

Then she shows him the splendid bookshelf in the drawing room, which is made of three lengths of varnished wood, hanging on twists of brown wool. The wooden shelves are edged in black velvet, onto which Aline has sewn fish scales, white silk and bugles* to make flowers and leaves. 'This was her Christmas present to me last year,' says Mama. 'It is a lovely item, don't you think, Mr Frykberg?'

And yes, engineer Frykberg praises everything Mama shows him. But he is not as impressed as Mama had expected. Instead he says what a shame it is for a girl like Aline to have to embroider with fish scales and fir cones.

As soon as he has finished his coffee, he is seized by fresh anxiety. Time and again he fumbles in his waistcoat pocket for a big silver pocket watch, looks at it, reinserts it and takes it out again, as if he had instantly forgotten what time it showed.

Once Mama has got to the end of what she wants to say about Aline Laurell, Papa takes over and asks engineer Frykberg about the beautiful mountain they have up there in Gräsmark, which is called Gettjärnsklätten. He wonders if it is true that a Finnish boy looking after the cows up there last summer had found a gold nugget and exchanged it at Brockman's goldsmith's shop in Karlstad for three big silver goblets. Engineer Frykberg has not heard a word about the gold nugget, and I do not think Papa has, either. He just wanted to banter with engineer Frykberg because he knows how proud all the Gräsmark folk are of their mountain.

But if Papa thinks he can put engineer Frykberg in a more cheerful frame of mind, he is mistaken. Engineer Frykberg keeps looking at his silver pocket watch – he quite fails to notice that we have a big clock on the dining-room wall – and then he turns to Mama and asks if they are absolutely sure Miss Laurell will be home by six. No, not absolutely sure, replies Mama, for it could so happen that they are invited to stay at Gårdsjö for the evening meal.

Then engineer Frykberg stands up and paces round the dining table. 'Well then, perhaps I shall have to be on my way,' he says. 'As you know, Mrs Lagerlöf, I have a full thirty kilometres ahead of me to get home, and the light is already fading.'

He has his handkerchief out again, and speaks in such a pathetic tone. I think Mama feels sorry for him. 'Would it perhaps be appropriate for you to stay the night here, Mr Frykberg?' she says. 'We always keep a fire in the office, and there are beds there with warm bedclothes, so it is no trouble for us.'

At this suggestion of Mama's, engineer Frykberg is suddenly revitalised. He puts his handkerchief in his pocket and looks gratified.

Then Mama enquires about his mother. She asks whether she still lives with him and keeps house for him. 'Yes she does,' answers engineer Frykberg, 'but she is getting rather frail.' – 'It is probably time for you to find yourself a wife, Mr Frykberg,' says Mama, 'so the old lady does not have so much work to do.'

Engineer Frykberg makes no reply to this, but he goes red in the face and takes out his handkerchief. Papa and Mama look at each other and shake their heads a little. They simply do not know what to do with him.

'You know what, Frykberg,' Papa says next. 'The children always go out tobogganing at dusk. Go with them, and help them to steer! It may well be that Lovisa and Aline come along in the sleigh while you are all out with the toboggan.'

And just imagine, this puts engineer Frykberg in a merrier mood! Anna and Emma Laurell and Gerda and I take him out with us. Does he not want to put his fur coat on, we ask him, but he is unconcerned, because he has warm, homespun clothes, he says, and does not need any outdoor layers.

When he sees our toboggan, he declares it to be far too small. 'This won't give us a proper ride,' he says, and picks out a drag sled instead, the sort the stable hand uses to bring wood down from the forest. He pushes it up the avenue and then all the way to Resting Stone Hill. And we get off to a speedy start, I must say, when we take our places on the sled and set off down the hill. With engineer Frykberg at the helm, we are positively flying. There is no question of colliding with a hard rut of snow and overturning the sled, which is what generally happens when we steer. We have never experienced such a glorious toboggan run before.

We come down the hill many times over, and we think how kind it is of engineer Frykberg to push the heavy sled up to Resting Stone again and again, so that we can have fun. We talk to him about all sorts of things and he answers, and we make friends with him. We soon feel that we know engineer Frykberg as well as we do Daniel and Johan.

The really remarkable thing about being out this evening is that there is so much rime frost. It coats the spruces and birches so thickly that they hang down over the road. We feel as if we have a white roof over us and Emma Laurell says that it is just like in Karlstad cathedral, and when engineer Frykberg hears that, he asks if she has ever been in Karlstad. Then Emma tells him she was born there, and so it comes out that Emma is not our sister, but Aline's. And engineer Frykberg did not know that until this moment. Then Emma asks engineer Frykberg whether he is a surveyor, because she thinks she remembers seeing him at a party at her parents' home when her father was still alive and was the senior surveyor. And engineer Frykberg is so pleased that Emma is Aline's sister and that she remembers him.

Suddenly Anna says it is so dark now that we must go home, and we have to admit that she is right, although we would love to spend all night tobogganing down Resting Stone Hill. And engineer Frykberg lets me and Gerda ride on the sled all the way home, because he can see how tired we are. We all think that engineer Frykberg is the kindest old gentleman we have ever met, apart from Papa of course.

We are not so stupid that we do not realise engineer Frykberg has taken a liking to Aline Laurell and that this is the reason he has does not want to set off home until she gets back. But we do not think Aline wants engineer Frykberg, because he is quite ugly and quite old. We think it is a real shame he is not young and good-looking.

Just think, we have been out tobogganing for several hours! When we get back home, the table is already laid for the evening meal, and all we can do is sit straight down to eat.

Then after we get up from the table, Papa says that on Saturday evenings he generally has a game of Kille* with us children, and he wonders whether engineer Frykberg would give the children the pleasure of playing along too.

Memoirs of a Child

Yes, engineer Frykberg is instantly at our disposal, and we take out the counters and cards and we all sit down round the dining table, excepting Mama because she does not care for card playing.

And Papa and engineer Frykberg are so funny and try to outwit one another, as proper Kille players are supposed to do, and Anna and Emma Laurell and Gerda and I, we laugh at them and enjoy ourselves no end.

We are so busy laughing and talking that we do not hear the horse and sleigh arrive back from Gårdsjö. We are oblivious until the door from the hall opens and Aunt and Aline come in.

They are all white with rime frost, and they are wearing big, men's fur coats. They say it is so dreadfully cold outside, fully thirty-five below. Uncle Kalle lent them the furs, otherwise they would have frozen to death.

They also tell us how welcome they were made at Gårdsjö. Aunt and Uncle were so eager for them to stay for the evening meal that they could not say no.

When Aline came in, engineer Frykberg got up from the table where we were playing cards and withdrew to the stove corner, so she did not see him until she had taken off her furs.

'But who have we here? Engineer Frykberg!' she says, and holds out her hand in greeting.

And she is in no way impolite, yet at the same time she draws herself up and throws back her head. She is a little bit like Mrs Hwasser at the Dramatic Theatre, when she is playing the Queen and addressing a lackey*.

And Aline Laurell looks so beautiful, standing there. She has such a healthy look and the front of her hair is glittering with rime frost, and her big grey eyes are bright and flashing, the way they always are when she is in high spirits. And I think Aline Laurell seems so superior to the rest of us. She is a fine town girl, used to the company of the county governor and the bishop, whereas we are just simple country folk.

Above all she is superior to engineer Frykberg. It is as if I see him shrink as he looks at her, growing smaller and smaller.

He really does look awfully dishevelled with his big beard and homespun clothes. He shakes Aline's hand but he says nothing, and then Mama comes to his aid.

'Engineer Frykberg has come to buy some oats,' explains Mama. 'He has been so good with the children and been out tobogganing with them for hours. We have invited him to stay until tomorrow, because he has such a long journey home.'

We want to rush up to Aline and tell her what fun we have had, but we desist, because Aline is so stiff and dismissive. She is like a taut bowstring, making you fear an arrow through your vital organs if you come too close.

'Indeed, it would not be advisable for engineer Frykberg to make the journey home in this cold,' says Aline, once again as haughty as Mrs Hwasser, if not more so.

Aline must think that her papa is still alive and that she is standing in their fine apartment in Karlstad, receiving all the lowly surveyors from the country districts who have been invited to the senior surveyor's party.

Engineer Frykberg still says nothing, but he has taken out his red handkerchief to mop his brow, and now he is groping for his watch.

'Yes, you're right, Frykberg,' says Papa. 'It is nearly eleven. And now that we have our travellers home, we should probably think about getting to bed.'

When Nursie Maja comes into the nursery the next morning, she tells us it is forty degrees below.

'It'll be as well for you children to stay in bed,' she says. 'It's just plain impossible to get them downstairs rooms warm.'

But we do get up, of course. We have never experienced such piercing cold. We think it is as remarkable as if we had moved up to the North Pole.

When we come downstairs, all the windowpanes are covered in a thick coat of rime frost, and the daylight getting through leaves the rooms in no more than a half-light. And it is terribly cold.

The thermometer hanging outside one of the dining room windows is hard to see properly. But right in front of the bulb of mercury, strangely enough, there is a clear patch where we can see the mercury lying frozen and unable to rise up the stem at all.

And we cannot have any bread for breakfast, the housekeeper tells us, because all the loaves have frozen rock solid and if you try to cut them, they simply crumble.

Nor can we have any butter, because that has frozen, too. The pat of butter has big lumps of ice in it.

We would very much like to go out and see what minus forty degrees feels like, but we are not allowed to. We are not even allowed to put our bare hands on the lock of the front door. Because if you touch iron when it is forty degrees below, it burns you as if it were red hot, and pulls the skin off your hands.

But it is awe-inspiring to have experienced such intense cold, all the same. Neither Papa nor Mama, nor even the old housekeeper, has ever known minus forty degrees at Mårbacka before.

We are so distracted by everything to do with the cold that we quite forget engineer Frykberg, who was so nice to us the previous evening. But when it is time to sit down at the breakfast table, Anna asks whether we should wait for the engineer.

'No,' says Mama. 'Engineer Frykberg has left us. When he heard it was forty below, he got up at once and set off for home. He left word that he had to get back and make sure his sheep and pigs did not freeze to death. He did not even have time to say goodbye.'

'But isn't it dangerous to travel so far in such cold?' says Aline.

But Papa laughs. 'Dear dear, Aline,' he says, 'this is a fine time to turn warm-hearted. I do wonder whose fault it is that he left.'

'Oh, Uncle Lagerlöf,' said Aline, 'you really cannot claim I was anything other than polite to him.'

'I do declare that there was at least forty degrees of chill in that politeness,' says Papa.

And I think that Papa, and Mama too, were a little less than pleased with Aline. And Anna and Emma Laurell and I say, looking back, that it is certainly not possible for Aline to take a liking to such an old and ugly man, but that we feel sorry for him, even so.

And privately I wonder whether he was intending to let himself freeze to death when he set off in temperatures of minus forty degrees. I am waiting to hear that he did not get home alive. That would be going out in style, as Emma Laurell might say.

Maja Råd

And we do so like it when Maja Råd comes here to sew.
We get new dresses twice a year. Each spring we get a cotton dress and each autumn we get a wool dress. All our cotton dresses are home-woven and it is Mama who sees to the yarn and the dyeing and thinks out patterns and sets up the piece on the loom, because she is very good at that. When we were little Mama would make all our clothes herself, as well, but now that we are bigger Mama does not trust herself to do it, so Maja Råd comes here to help us.

Maja Råd always does her sewing in Aunt Lovisa's room off the kitchen, and Aunt likes that very much because it means she has company all day long and forgets to think about sad things. Mama also sits in the room off the kitchen when Maja Råd is here to help with the sewing, and Aline Laurell and Anna and Emma Laurell and Gerda and I sit there too. Gerda is so little that she only sews doll's clothes, but she does it so well that Maja Råd says Gerda is going to be a fine dressmaker. Anna is also good at sewing, but Emma Laurell and I, we are all fingers and thumbs and can never keep track of right and wrong sides, so we are only given tasks that are not too complicated, like stitching together the gores of a skirt or doing seam bindings.

But Emma and I still think it is fun having Maja Råd here, because we are excused our reading and arithmetic.

When Maja Råd is here, we set up a big folding table in the room off the kitchen, and that is where Maja Råd spreads out the lengths of fabric and does her cutting. Maja Råd never cuts crookedly or makes a mistake, and she always keeps track of the right and wrong sides. Because she is a proper dressmaker who did her apprenticeship with a tailor.

Maja Råd takes a German fashion journal called *Der Bazar*, which comes out once a month. We pore over it every day while Maja Råd is here and try to find the most attractive styles so we can have our cotton and wool dresses made up to those designs. Maja Råd thinks we should choose simpler styles to follow. She says you can never expect a dress to be as attractive when it has been made up as it looks in the drawings in her magazine.

Maja Råd cannot speak German, and nor can any of us, because Aline Laurell only speaks French and that is the only language she has taught us. We say that we cannot fathom how Maja Råd can make anything of her German fashion journal, and Maja Råd likes to hear us say that, as we are supposed to be such scholars and do nothing but read every day.

Maja Råd is always very spruce and has her hair combed sleekly back, but it is so thin that her white scalp shows through beneath the individual hairs. Her forehead has lots of little lines running close together and she has freckles all year round. We have freckles, too, which come in the spring and disappear in the autumn, but Maja Råd's do not do that. She also has a crinoline, although everyone else has stopped wearing them, and I wonder if there is something particular about Maja Råd that means she can never change. She can never discard things once she has them. She cannot give up either her freckles or her crinoline.

I often sit there looking at Maja Råd and wondering if she is made of wood. For she is so dry. If Maja Råd were to prick herself with the needle, I do not think she would bleed. I sometimes wish Maja Råd would prick herself, so I could see whether she really is made of wood.

We always ask Maja Råd whether she is going to buy a sewing machine, but she says she will never do that. Not ever, not for as long as she can still thread a needle.

Maja Råd does not have an ordinary thimble, but uses a sewing ring like tailors do. And it was a tailor who taught her to sew, after all. Maja Råd stitches so awfully fast that no one, neither Mama nor Aunt Lovisa nor Aline, can keep pace with her.

Maja Råd charges a *riksdaler* a day, and when she gets plenty of help with skirts and sleeves the way she does here, she can make a dress a day. So that means we can get our dresses made for one *riksdaler*, and we think that is a real bargain.

Maja Råd always sews the bodices herself, because that is the most important part. There has to be a back piece and two stay casings and two side pieces and two front pieces, and the front pieces have to have two darts, which are dreadfully complicated.

All the bodices have to fit smoothly to the body, with not a single wrinkle. And that is the hard part, but Maja Råd knows how to do it. And that is what she thinks Gerda will be able to learn, but when it comes to Emma Laurell and me, she plainly states that she does not think we will ever be able to learn to make a proper bodice.

Maja Råd gets up at six o'clock every morning and as soon as she is dressed, she sits down to her sewing. Then she sews all day long, until it is time for the evening meal. She never goes out for a walk. We try to persuade her to come out for a walk with us, but she immediately turns back and goes inside. She says she wants to do good work for her money and not go gadding around the high road. But we think she only says that because all she wants to do is sew.

Maja Råd also goes to do the sewing at Gårdsjö and for the Noreens and for the Nilssons in Visteberg and at Pastor Lindegren's. The children there get a new cotton dress each spring and a new wool dress in autumn, just as we do, so Maja Råd certainly has plenty to do.

The good thing about Maja Råd is that she never spreads gossip. You can say whatever you like about the other gentry of the parish in Maja Råd's hearing. It will never get back to them. The only thing she will reveal is that if she were to relay everything that the family of one house says about the family

Selma Lagerlöf

of another, then that would be the end of their friendship. So it is just as well that Maja Råd knows how to hold her tongue.

When Maja Råd is here, the housekeeper brings in coffee for the grown-ups at eleven o'clock. We children do not drink coffee, but we get a sandwich.

And while Maja Råd has her coffee, she likes to pass on the sort of news that does no harm. She tells us who is getting married and who is throwing a party and who is dead and who is leaving for America.

And when Maja Råd has been here so long that she runs out of topics of conversation, Gerda likes to bring out the book of a hundred riddles that she once had as a Christmas present, and make Maja Råd and the rest of us guess the answers.

'Maja Råd, do you know who it is who keeps on going but never reaches the door?' says Gerda.

And Maja Råd knows the answer as well as we all do, but she always says that she cannot answer, to make it fun for Gerda. She can never solve a single one of Gerda's riddles, even though she hears them twice a year, and there are always gales of laughter in the room off the kitchen at Maja Råd's foolishness.

Maja Råd told us that when she was young, she did not know how she was going to learn to make dresses. It was her sole wish in life. She did not want to go out into the countryside to look after the animals like her brothers and sisters, nor did she want to cook meals or scrub floors or churn butter or bake bread. She only wanted to sew.

Later, as she grew up, she did not care about going to dances or getting married, and she did not want children, either. She had only one desire, and that was to learn to sew properly, so she could become a dressmaker.

She asked her mother if she could go down to the Misses Myrin who lived next to the church and were skilled in all kinds of needlecraft. But when she went to them, they said it was impossible for a poor crofter's daughter to learn anything as difficult and delicate as making dresses.

So Maja Råd had to do the same as everyone else. She had to go and look after the animals and to shovel dung from the

Memoirs of a Child

dung pit and to cook meals, and to go up to the summer huts with the cows.

But just as Maja Råd had given up all hope of becoming a dressmaker, the most marvellous thing happened: her sister married a corporal, who was a tailor. And when the corporal heard that Maja Råd's greatest wish was to make dresses, he offered to teach her. He showed her how to take measurements and how to draw up patterns and cut out and how to try on and how to sew buttonholes and everything else she needed to know.

And when Maja Råd had finished her apprenticeship with her brother-in-law, she started making dresses for children and for young peasant girls who were not all that important, although Maja Råd tried to do her best anyway.

And things went well for her from the very start, and in the end she had such a good reputation that the housemaid at Mårbacka came and asked her to make a dress for her. She made that dress as well as she possibly could and by good fortune, Mrs Lagerlöf happened to see it. And she found herself sending for Maja Råd. And from Mårbacka Maja Råd went to Gårdsjö and from Gårdsjö to Herrestad and from Herrestad to Visteberg and Halla. And as a matter of fact, she had received enquiries from gentlemen's families in both Sunne and Ransäter who wanted her to go and sew for them.

And I do so like it when Maja Råd tells us how she learned to sew after yearning for it for such a long time, so she escaped from carrying water and scrubbing floors and shovelling dung. Now Maja Råd has no need to do anything other than what gives her the greatest pleasure.

I also like reading about Kristina Nilsson*, who once went round the fairs and markets playing the fiddle but has since been able to sing at the Grand Opera in Paris.

And I have just read about the students in New York who unhitched the horses from her carriage and pulled it to the hotel themselves, and I found it so touching that tears came to my eyes.

I always find it touching to hear about those who have known hard times, but have then enjoyed better luck.

The Church Visit

And we do so like the journey to church.

We have to get up such a steep slope before we reach the level ground in front of the church, but the stable hand cracks his whip at the horses so we arrive at a full trot. There is usually a collection of people sitting on the low wall that runs round the church, waiting for the service to start, and when they see the Mårbacka party approaching, they all get up and give a bow or bob, and we think that is a pretty courtesy. There are also a lot of people standing in front of the church or in the road itself, and they have to move aside at some speed as we drive up. And Mama shouts to the stable hand to go carefully, but Papa sits there with his hat in hand, greeting one and all and laughing, for he knows very well that Jansson will not run over anyone.

We stop outside the parish hall, where there is a little room set aside for those who want to tidy their hair or shake out their clothes after the journey, although it is only ever the gentry who trouble to go in there. And there we generally meet Aunt Augusta Wallroth with Hilda and Emilia and Mrs Nilsson from Visteberg with Emilie and Ingrid. And for as long as we are there in the room in the parish hall, we are so merry and chatter about all manner of things. But as soon as we come back out of the church, we go so quiet and solemn, because that is the custom in Östra Ämtervik.

Mama always brings a big bouquet of flowers with her to church, and after her visit to the parish rooms, she goes into the churchyard to lay it on Grandmother's grave and Anna and I go with her, of course. Mama clears away the dead leaves lying on the grass and tidies up the white briar rose that grows on the grave, and finally she says a prayer and lays the bunch of flowers.

I had a little sister who died, and who I never saw, and Papa and Mama loved her very much. She is buried next to Grandmother, and Mama always takes a couple of the prettiest flowers out of the bouquet and puts them at one corner of the grave, pushing their stalks into the grass.

I understand who they are intended for, of course, but I cannot help wondering whether Mama really does wish she had another little girl still living. It seems to me that she has so much to do, all that darning and mending and knitting and sewing for Anna and Gerda and me, that she should not have to cope with any more.

From the churchyard we walk straight to the church, and as soon as Mama sees some farmer's wife she knows, like Katrina in Västmyr or Mother Britta in Gata or Mother Katrina who is the daughter of Jon Larssa in Ås, or Mother Maja in Prästbol or Mother Kerstin Down There in Mårbacka, she stops to say hello and exchange a few words. Mama has been at their farms for funerals and weddings and knows how they are faring, so she is never short of something to say to each of them.

Then, when we get into the church, we take our seats in the front pew of the gallery, because that is where the gentry always sit. Our place is on the left side of the gallery. It simply will not do to sit on the right, because that is the men's side. If all the pews on the womenfolk's side were full but there was plenty of room on the other side of the aisle with the men, it would still not be appropriate to go and sit over there. We would rather stand all through the service.

When we get into the pew, we bend our heads and say a prayer, and then we sit and look around us. We look to see whether Melanoz the cantor is sitting at the organ and whether Mr Alfred Schullström, who keeps the shop in Älvsvik, is sitting beside him as usual, and whether the churchwardens have taken their seats on the little bench in the chancel and whether Mrs Lindegren at Halla is sitting in the vicarage pew just below the pulpit. We also take note of whether Jan Asker the verger is standing at the door of the vestry, watching to see when the churchgoers have arrived and the service can begin. We also look to see whether the hymn numbers have been put up on the black hymn boards and whether the organ-blower's shirt is sticking out behind the organ, so that we know he is in his place. And once we have looked around us and made sure everything is in order, we have nothing else to do for the entire service.

For see, it is very genteel to sit in the front row of the gallery, but the trouble with those seats is that you cannot hear anything of what the clergyman says, down in the church. Well, the first part of the service at the altar, you can hear all right, up to the confession of sins, but then it is as if everything is swallowed up by the walls and ceiling. You can hear that more words are being spoken, but you cannot distinguish between them. Or we children cannot, at any rate.

When the organ sounds, we can certainly hear it, but there is not much joy to be had from that either, for no one ever dares to sing in Östra Ämtervik church. We sit there with our hymnbooks in our hands and follow along, but none of us dares to sing a note. Once when I was little, I did not understand how things were meant to be, and I sang a whole verse as loudly as I could, because I like singing, and at home I sing all day long. But when the next verse was about to start, Anna leant down to me and asked me to stop. 'Can you not see how Emilie Nilsson is looking at you, because you are singing,' she said.

The only person who sings in church is Jan in Skrolycka, who is not really in his right mind.

And I sometimes wonder whether Melanoz the cantor loses his temper with the congregation for making him sit there and play hymn after hymn and making no attempt to sing, because sometimes, all of a sudden, he will do something with the organ to make it rumble and roar and howl so violently that we think the church roof is about to crash down on us.

Cantor Melanoz is such fun and so full of mischief that it would be just like him.

But not being able to hear the sermon, that is a real disappointment to me, because Pastor Lindegren lives at Halla, very close to Mårbacka, and we are good friends with him. He is always so kind to us children, and he is so splendid. He is always splendid, but never so much as when he stands in the pulpit to give his sermon. He speaks so eagerly and flicks the big handkerchief that he holds in his hand, and the longer he speaks, the more splendid he looks. And almost every time he preaches, he is so moved that he starts to weep. And then I wonder if he weeps because we are not improving and finding our way to God, however long his sermons are. But for those of us in the front pew of the gallery, at least, it is not that easy to follow his guidance, for we cannot hear a word he says.

The grown-ups are so used to being bored that they probably do not mind, but for us children it is very hard to make the time pass. Emilia Wallroth has told me that she counts the heads of the nails in the church roof, and Ingrid Nilsson says she looks down at the old farmers to count how often they offer each other moist snuff* to put under their top lip. Emilie Nilsson, she adds up the numbers on the hymn board, and when she has finished her addition, she subtracts and multiplies and divides. She says that as long as she keeps busy with that, she can have no sinful thoughts in her head. It would be worse if she were to sit there gazing at Hilda Wallroth's lovely hat and wishing she had one like it. But Anna says she sits there learning hymns off by heart, and we all think that is still to be preferred to multiplication and subtraction.

I do not do sums or watch people's snuff habits. I sit and think about what would happen if the church tower were struck by lightning and set the church on fire. Everyone would be scared and want to get away, and they would very nearly trample each other to death. But I would raise my voice from up in my seat at the front of the gallery, and urge them to calm down. And then I would make them all stand in a long line, just like it says in *Frithiof's Saga*: 'Now from the temple down unto the strand, of aiding hands is knitted swift a chain'*. And by my resourcefulness I would put out the fire and get my name in *Värmlandstidningen*, the local newspaper.

When the service is over, Mama and Anna and I go to visit the old Misses Myrin.

They live in the garret at the top of the schoolhouse, which is right beside the church, and Anna and I, we say that we would never dare to live so close to the churchyard. We would only venture out in the middle of the day, and never after dark, because then the ghosts in the churchyard could come and get us.

The Misses Myrin once lived at Herrestad, but that was long before our time. I know that they have fallen into real poverty now, but nobody ever mentions it, and talks to them just as if they still owned Herrestad today.

The stairs that lead up to the Misses Myrin's room are always newly scrubbed on Sunday and strewn with fresh fir twigs, because they anticipate that the gentry who have been in church will come up and see them. Mama always brings a bottle of cream or a pound of butter with her in her capacious bag when she goes up to the Misses Myrin, and she sets it down in their kitchen as she passes the kitchen door. And on the stairs, we almost always meet farmers' wives with something under their arms, to smuggle into the kitchen and leave there.

And the Misses Myrin live in a large and pleasant room, and are always dressed in their best and sit in their basket chairs waiting for visitors, blithely unaware of what has been left in their kitchen. They both wear big mantillas and black tulle caps, but Miss Marie Myrin is tall and white-haired and her fingers are twisted over each other by arthritis, and Miss Rora Myrin is small and dark and her hands are not afflicted by any infirmity, so you can easily tell one from the other.

And as soon as Mama comes in to the Misses Myrin, she starts admiring their curtains and their tablecloths and their antimacassars and their bedcovers. The Misses Myrin have made them all themselves, and they are all crocheted in lacy feather and fan stitch*. Miss Rora needs no second bidding to list all the orders they have had for tablecloths and curtains.

Memoirs of a Child

There are more of them than they can cope with. It is truly remarkable that all the residents of Östra Ämtervik have developed such a taste for feather and fan crochet, they say. And then Mama says she has to admit that the crochet work is the very reason for her own visit. She would so much like a big, round cloth for the table in front of the dining-room sofa. It is an alder-root table, says Mama, and its surface is so beautiful that she wants to keep it from getting scratched. It would be good to have a cloth to put over it. But perhaps the Misses Myrin have so many commissions that it would not be worth trying to buy a cloth from them.

Miss Marie looks a little doubtful, but Miss Rora is more decisive, and loses no time in opening a drawer, which is completely full of crochet work. Mama has only to choose; she can have as many tablecloths as she wants. And Mama is so pleased that she will not have to go home empty-handed. She buys not only a cloth for the round table, but also two antimacassars for the rocking chairs.

Once that is done, Mama thinks to take her leave, but then the Misses Myrin say she has made such a big purchase that they would like her to stay for coffee. Mama says that she could not possibly presume, but it does not help, and she is obliged to stay.

The Misses Myrin have a brother, who is rich and owns the Bada ironworks estate in Lysvik. And estate owner Myrin has three daughters who sometimes come to visit their old aunts, always bringing with them lots of pastries and biscuits so that their aunts have something nice to offer their Sunday guests. They are so generous, those nieces, that the Misses Myrin never have to do any baking from one year's end to the next.

And when the coffee tray comes in, Anna and I are so happy to see a big dish of pastries and biscuits in the middle of it, and they look awfully delicious. But Mama immediately starts talking about their kind nieces, and wonders when they last paid a visit. And the Misses Myrin tell Mama that they have not been to visit since a year ago last autumn.

And Mama restricts herself to a couple of rusks with her coffee and she urges us not to be greedy and pile our coffee saucers with pastries and biscuits. We must remember that the Misses Myrin themselves will probably want to eat some of those tasty treats that their nieces have given them.

And when Mama says that, we naturally only help ourselves to the very smallest items.

When we get back home, we are always pleased to have made our church visit, in spite of everything. Even though we were not allowed to sing the hymns and could not hear the sermon and dared only eat a few little biscuits at the Misses Myrin's, we still feel that Mama is right when she says it is good to spend a few hours in the house of the Lord.

The Kiss

And we think it so vexing that Aline Laurell wants to leave us this autumn.

Aline says she does not have knowledge enough to carry on teaching us any longer. She can only teach us French, and we ought to be having lessons in English and German, too. Nor is she as proficient at playing the piano as she ought to be. And it is very sweet of Aline to want to leave so that we can have a better education than she can give us, but we think it most vexing nonetheless.

Aline has a cousin named Elin Laurell, whom she likes a great deal. She knows both English and German, and is apparently an excellent pianist. Aline has arranged for Elin Laurell to come here and be our governess when she leaves. But we have heard that Elin is thirty years old, and as she is so old we are sure she will not want to play with us and dress up and join in all the fun like Aline does. And she is not pretty, either. I saw her once at a party at Pastor Unger's in Västra Ämtervik and I thought she looked very plain.

As for Aline, she is going to move to Västra Ämtervik and be governess to the little Unger children. They are nothing like as old as we are, so Aline thinks she will be able to give them lessons. And Mrs Unger in Västra Ämtervik is Aline's aunt on her mother's side, and Aline is terribly fond of her, so we wonder if Aline is leaving Mårbacka because she would rather be with her aunt.

Emma Laurell is not going to move to Västra Ämtervik with her, but will stay here at Mårbacka for a few months and do her lessons with Elin. Next year she will move back to her mother's in Karlstad and go to a girls' school. And we are pleased that at least Emma will be able to stay, for she is like a sister to us. We find it impossible to take in the fact that Emma Laurell was not born here at Mårbacka.

And I do not think Mama and Papa like the fact that Aline is leaving. They say nothing but Anna claims that neither of them believes Aline is leaving because she is not knowledgeable enough. They fancy that there is something behind it. And I think the same thing.

The idea of her moving came up so quickly. Last spring when Aline went home to Karlstad, there was no mention of her not continuing to give us lessons. And it was the same when she came back after the summer holidays in August.

Aline came back in time for Papa's birthday as she usually does, for there is nothing she enjoys more than celebrating the seventeenth of August at Mårbacka. And she was as merry as anything that day and in the days that followed, for as long as the visitors, the Afzeliuses and the Hammargrens and the Schensons and Mrs Hedberg and Uncle Kristofer, were still here. But as soon as they had departed, she began to talk of no longer being good enough to teach us and wanting to leave.

And we children think that Aline is not at all her usual self. Ever since she told us she was leaving, she has been so sensitive and quick-tempered. It is as though she is no longer friends with any of us. And whenever it is time for my piano lesson with her, I am full of foreboding. I have no talent at all for the piano, but Mama and Papa still think it would be good if I could get as far as knowing how to play a waltz or a quadrille when we have a party. They say it is something that will always be a source of pleasure to the player, no matter what their age. And Aline always used to have patience with me and my playing, but now the simplest mistake makes her cross.

And just imagine, when it is time for us to start our afternoon lessons, Aline does not arrive on time! That has never happened before in the four years she has been a governess at Mårbacka, so we are very concerned. We are supposed to have arithmetic, and we get our slates out of the desk drawer and sharpen our slate pencils while we are waiting. And Anna says that when she passed through the bedroom a little while ago, Aline was sitting there talking to Mama, so she cannot be far away.

Yet Aline does not come up to us until a quarter past two. And we can see at once that her whole face is flushed red, just as it looks when she has a headache. She opens the arithmetic book and tells us to do our sums, but she has no sooner done so than she throws herself full length on the nursery sofa and bursts into tears.

She does not say a word but sobs and weeps, making her whole body convulse. And we do not say a word either, but sit there with our sums on our slates in front of us. And we think it is wretched that we cannot comfort or help her, for we are all so terribly fond of her. But we think she would be angry if we tried to say anything to her.

We cannot do our sums, either. It is impossible for us to think of anything but her, lying there in tears. In the end, Anna gets to her feet, puts her slate in the drawer and gestures to Gerda and me to do the same. Then we all three tiptoe out of the nursery but we leave Emma Laurell there because Anna thinks that she, as her sister, should stay with her.

Then Anna takes me to the garden, and we sit down on a bench where no one can hear or see us, and then Anna starts to tell me about Aline.

For you see, Anna turned fifteen on the second of September, and she has always been awfully sensible, so mother asks her advice and tells her everything. And Mama has told Anna that she is very worried about Aline Laurell and cannot understand why she is leaving, and she has asked Anna if she knows what could be behind it.

But Anna knew nothing, and now she is saying that Aline likes me and talks to me a lot. She wonders if I can recall Aline saying anything in particular about Uncle Kristofer.

And I feel so proud, sitting there on the garden bench, that Anna is asking my advice on a serious matter, for that has certainly never happened before, but I cannot fathom what it is she wants to know. Why would Aline have had anything in particular to say about Uncle Kristofer?

Anna sighs, because I am so stupid and do not understand anything, and then she starts to explain it to me. She says that during the summer, when the visitors were here, Mama and Aunt Georgina Afzelius and Aunt Augusta from Gårdsjö were very keen for Uncle Kristofer to get engaged to Aline Laurell. For Uncle Kristofer has been a bachelor for long enough and he should seize the moment, while there is a girl as splendid as Aline on hand. And now he has also bought himself a little place outside Filipstad, called Hastaberget, so it would be a most appropriate time to find himself a wife. And Aline would be just the right one for him, because she is wise and kind and thrifty and careful and not deadly dull but ready to joke and banter, and fond of fancy dress and shows and socialising, just as Uncle is himself.

And I am so astonished to hear Anna tell me that. I cannot say a word, so Anna goes on with her explanations.

'And I am quite sure that Mama and Aunt Georgina have dropped a few hints to Uncle Kristofer about Aline,' she says, 'and he must have thought they were right, because he has been especially amiable and attentive to Aline this summer. And no doubt it was Uncle Kristofer's attentions that put Aline in such high spirits, right up until he left, because Uncle Kristofer is most definitely the kind who can make a girl fall in love with him, if he wants to.'

And because Anna is fifteen, she knows so much more about all that kind of thing than I do, being only twelve. It has never occurred to me before that anyone could fall in love with Uncle Kristofer, and I say as much to Anna.

'But think of how beautifully he paints,' said Anna, 'and how beautifully he plays and how nice he is and how much he has to tell about his time in Germany and Italy, and he is not at all old. He is only a few years older than Daniel.'

And when Anna says that, I remember having observed a few things that I did not really understand.

You see, it is usual that for as long as our guests stay with us after the seventeenth of August, we arrange some kind of entertainment each evening. Sometimes we move all the furniture out of the dining room, and Uncle Oriel teaches us to dance old country dances from Uppland, because Uncle Oriel grew up in Enköping. And sometimes Uncle Kristofer sings Erik Bøgh* songs and sometimes he and Mrs Hedda Hedberg put on their student caps and sing the 'Gluntarna' duets*, and sometimes we persuade Aunt Nana Hammargren to tell us ghost stories.

But now I am thinking of that evening when Uncle Kristofer sat there improvising. It all started when Uncle Oriel put on a women's hat with a wide brim and threw a mantilla round his shoulders and sang 'Emilie's Throbbing Heart'*. And it was terribly funny to see Uncle Oriel pretending to be a young girl and look shy and embarrassed, because Uncle Oriel must be sixty years old. But when Uncle Oriel finished singing, Uncle Kristofer stayed at the piano, for he had naturally been the accompanist, and played in a completely different way for a time. He had no sheet music open in front of him, so I asked Aunt Georgina what he was playing. And Aunt Georgina hushed me and said that Uncle was improvising.

I did not understand what she meant, but I realised it must be something special, for all the others were sitting there so quiet and solemn. Uncle Kristofer played for so long that the dining-room clock struck eleven, and I was so astonished that he had been able to learn that many notes off by heart.

While Uncle Kristofer was playing, I happened to look at Aline Laurell. She was sitting just as still as everyone else, but her face was full of life. It was as if she was listening to someone speak. Sometimes she smiled and sometimes she lowered her eyes, and sometimes she flushed as red as blood. And when I looked at Aline, I realised that she could understand everything Uncle Kristofer was playing, just as if he had spoken to her. For my part I could not make out any of its meaning, but she could.

And there was another time, too. It was the name day for the name Lovisa, the twenty-fifth of August. We always mark that day for Aunt Lovisa by dressing up and doing tableaux, because she enjoys that more than anything. This year we did 'The Visit of the Countess' by Mrs Lenngren*, presented in five tableaux, and it was a great success. And Aline played the dean, and padded herself out so that she looked all roly-poly and wore a big woolly wig on her head, and Uncle Kristofer played the countess in a floor-length silk dress and a big white silk shawl and a trim little hat with a white veil.

And Uncle Kristofer has been sporting a full beard ever since his time in Düsseldorf learning to paint pictures, and there was no concealing it under the veil. But the remarkable thing was that when Uncle turned his head and drew back his shoulders and spread out his fingers, we all thought of him as a proper countess, and completely forgot the beard.

And when it was all over and Aline and I were changing out of our costumes in the nursery – for I had played a part, too – I asked whether Aline had not thought as I did that Uncle Kristofer was very droll.

'Droll!' said Aline. 'You may very well say that. He is a born actor.'

She said it so fiercely that she really scared me and I did not dare ask any more questions.

But Aline went on: 'You all find him so droll, and you do not care about anything except the antics he devises to make you laugh. But, let me tell you, that is a real shame, because your uncle is a genius. He could become a great painter or a great composer or a great actor, whichever he chose. But nobody cares about that. You only want him to play the buffoon. Not one of you feels well enough disposed to him to uncover all the fine qualities he has inside.'

And after that I thought for a long time about how magnificent Aline was when she said that, but only now does it occur to me that it could mean she has feelings for Uncle Kristofer.

And now I tell Anna about it and about the piano playing, and Anna says she is pretty sure that these are signs that Aline is in love with Uncle Kristofer.

And Anna says that she thinks Uncle Kristofer proposed to Aline the day he was leaving, but she turned him down. 'Something must have got in the way at the last moment,' says Anna, 'but we cannot imagine what it could be, because she certainly does like him.' And Anna has noticed that a letter came from Filipstad today and she thinks that Mama was talking to Aline about Uncle Kristofer when Aline was late for our arithmetic lesson. Anna says she would not have wept like that unless she had feelings for Uncle Kristofer. Yet she still turned him down. We simply cannot understand her.

We sit there for a good while and consider the matter, but we are still none the wiser, and eventually we console ourselves with some fallen apples from under Papa's Astrachan tree.

I feel as if I have a big knot in my head. I cannot be rid of it until I have worked out what is making Aline behave so strangely.

In the evening, between six and seven, there is normally no one at all in the nursery, and I go up there and take out a lesson book and sit down as if to read, but in fact my thoughts are entirely on Aline.

A little while later, Nursie Maja comes in to get our beds ready, and she is clearly surprised to see me there, staring down into a book and saying nothing. 'What are you doing here this evening, Selma?' she says. 'Have you got to do your lessons over again?'

'No,' I say, 'I'm just sad because Aline is going to leave.'

And Nursie Maja had not heard that, although she generally knows everything. She agrees it is a shame that Miss Aline is leaving, 'because she was the kind you could really take to.'

Then Nursie Maja goes quiet for a while, but after that she says she does not understand why Mrs Lagerlöf has told Miss Aline to leave.

'Mama has not told her to leave,' I say. 'She is the one who has handed in her notice. Mama cannot make out why she is leaving.'

Nursie Maja falls silent again. She spreads out the sheets and tucks in Anna's bedcover and looks quite thoughtful, and then she says:

'I thought Miss Aline would be leaving soon, so I did, but I thought she'd be goin' somewhere else.'

'Where did you think she would be going, Nursie Maja?'

'Well Selma, I thought you were going to have her as your auntie.'

I give no answer to this, because I do not really like Nursie Maja knowing everything about us all.

Nursie Maja carries on tucking in covers for a while, and then says with a great sigh:

'Mebbe it's best this way. Who's to say it would've been any good for her.'

That makes me indignant on Uncle Kristofer's behalf. 'Why would Uncle Kristofer not be good enough for Aline?' I ask.

This agitates Nursie Maja and she leaves the bedmaking and comes over to me.

'Let me tell you what I saw on the seventeenth of August,' she says.

And then Nursie Maja says that on the seventeenth of August, one of the visiting ladies had the misfortune to tear her dress when she was out in the garden picking gooseberries. Nursie Maja does not want to tell me who it was, but will go so far as to say she was young and attractive and married. She was not from this parish, and this was her first year at the Mårbacka celebrations. The rest I would have to try to guess.

This beautiful lady, whose name Nursie Maja would not give, was in the garden in the company of Uncle Kristofer and Mrs Lindegren at Halla when the dress met with its accident, and she was understandably shaken and upset. Her entire sleeve was ripped and would have to be sewn back together, and she thought how embarrassing it would be to walk in such tatters through the whole crowd of guests to the big house in search of needle and thread. Then Uncle Kristofer suggested that she go into Papa's office, for she could make her way there unnoticed, and the place would be deserted at that time of the day. And Mrs Lindegren at Halla volunteered to go into the big

Memoirs of a Child

house for needle and thread and then to come down to the office and help her with the repairs.

The beautiful lady guest thanked Mrs Lindegren profusely for her offer and went off to the office with Uncle Kristofer. Mrs Lindegren went into the big house but it took her a good while to find any sewing things, for on a day like that, nothing was in its right place at Mårbacka. She finally found a sewing basket and hurried down to the office with it, because she felt she had kept them waiting for such a long time.

But it so happens that there is a little round window in the door of the office. It is just a little spy-hole so that the person inside can see who is there before opening the door. And when Mrs Lindegren at Halla arrived at the office door, she looked through the spy-hole. No doubt she wanted to check before she went in whether Uncle Kristofer and the beautiful guest were still inside waiting for her.

And what Mrs Lindegren at Halla saw then was Uncle Kristofer and the beautiful lady standing in the middle of the room, kissing.

And Mrs Lindegren at Halla simply did not know what to do. She did not want to go in while the two of them were kissing. But on the other hand, the beautiful lady visitor needed the sewing basket to get the sleeve of her dress mended. But then Mrs Lindegren caught sight of Nursie Maja, who was hurrying across the yard on some errand, and called her over. She asked Nursie Maja to take the sewing basket in to the lady visitor and help her to mend the sleeve of her dress, which had torn when she caught it on a gooseberry bush. 'But Maja, you must knock hard, three times, before you open the door,' she said.

So that was what Nursie Maja did. But before she knocked, she peeped through the little spy-hole in the office door, and then she realised why Mrs Lindegren at Halla did not want to go in with the sewing basket. But by the time Nursie Maja had knocked and opened the door as slowly as possible, Uncle Kristofer was over by the window, and the beautiful lady was by the tiled stove. He looked his usual self, but she was flushed and her hair was tousled.

Nursie Maja had not breathed a word of this to a single soul except me, for she had not dared to do so. But she could not say whether Mrs Lindegren at Halla had kept quiet about it as well.

As soon as Nursie Maja has finished, however, I cannot deny that I go running to Anna and tell her the whole story.

'And don't you remember,' I say, all happy and eager, 'that Pastor Lindegren and his wife were here the last evening before the visitors left, and we walked them home, because the moonlight was so lovely. And don't you remember that Aline was in conversation with Mrs Lindegren the whole way? And don't you think that Mrs Lindegren would have taken the opportunity of telling Aline about that kiss?'

And Anna agrees with me that this must be the case, because that evening marked the start of Aline's drastic change of mood.

'And don't you think it must be because Aline heard about it, that she refused Uncle Kristofer?' I say, still all eager and hopeful.

'I most certainly do,' says Anna, but she does not look the least bit happy.

'And don't you think that it is because Aline was so angry with Uncle Kristofer that she wants to leave?' I say.

'Oh yes,' says Anna, 'that is as clear as day.'

I look at Anna. I am so taken aback that she stays in her seat, not the least bit pleased, rather than dashing off to pass the news on to Mama.

'Aren't you going to tell Mama that you know what lies behind it all?' I say.

'No,' says Anna. 'With things as they are, I don't think it will be worth trying. Aline is so punctilious about that kind of thing. She will never marry him.'

'No, of course not,' I say. 'But can't Mama ask her if she will stay? There is no need for her to leave us, just because Uncle Kristofer kissed a lady visitor.'

Anna looks at me, and I can see that she thinks I am awfully stupid. 'Don't you see, it is the kiss itself that makes her want to leave?' says Anna. 'For as long as she stays here, she will be obliged to think about it every day. That is what she cannot endure.'

The Sunne Ball

We are so glad that we live in Östra Ämtervik and not in Sunne. There are many more people in Sunne, but they are not as jolly. They never arrange shows at parties, they have no brass sextet or singing quartet, and nothing like as many of them can make speeches and write verse as in Östra Ämtervik.

We belong with Sunne to the extent that we share a dean. But beyond that we have no dealings with the residents of Sunne. We never meet any of the Sunne gentry and their families but we have a distinct feeling that they think themselves far superior to us, because they live in a bigger place than we do.

Once a year we are invited to a party at the deanery in Sunne, but even then we do not encounter anybody who lives in Sunne. Because the area covered by the parish of Sunne is so large that the dean and his wife cannot invite all the gentlemen and their families at the same time. So they invite those who live in Östra Ämtervik and Västra Ämtervik and Gräsmark in one batch and those who live in Sunne in another.

But although we do not know the Sunne families, we have seen them all at the Åmbergshed fair, so we recognise the Petterssons from the Stöpafors estate and engineer Maule's family from Sundsberg and engineer Ingelius's family from Ulvsberg and squire Hellstedts' family from Skarped and the family of squire Jonsson, who live in the 'castle' in Sundsvik.

On the seventeenth of August, Mårbacka is teeming with young gentlemen who have come over from Sunne to dance and watch the entertainments. And we think that they must have spread word in Sunne that Hilda Wallroth at Gårdsjö and Anna Lagerlöf at Mårbacka have grown up to be the prettiest girls in all of Fryksdalen. Or at any rate, Papa receives a letter out of the blue one day from a couple of gentlemen in Sunne, asking whether we would like to come to a potluck ball.

The ball was to be held in the apartment above Nilsson's Stores, and there would be nothing to pay for the use of the premises. The gentlemen would provide the liquor and the ladies would bring coffee and tea and little cakes and biscuits and whatever was needed for the supper. It would all be very informal and would cost no more than a few *riksdaler* for candles and gratuities.

They have received the same letter at Gårdsjö, and Aunt Augusta comes over to talk to Mama and Aunt Lovisa about what to take, for they have no wish to be outdone by the residents of Sunne. Aunt Lovisa immediately starts preparations for large-scale baking of dainty pastries and biscuits and is in high spirits, for she remembers potluck balls like that in Sunne in her youth. Not for one moment does she intend to go to the ball, for she knows of course that she is too old to dance, but she says she is pleased that something so nice is happening.

It is the same with Gerda and me. We, too, think it great fun that there is going to be a ball, even though we are too young to go.

But that pleasure does not last, because the day before the ball as we are sitting round the dinner table, and naturally talking about the ball, Papa says he thinks Selma is big enough now to join the party.

I am sure Papa thinks I will be pleased to be allowed to go to a dance, but I am absolutely not. I have been to enough parties in Östra Ämtervik to know just how things would be for me at a ball in Sunne. I reply right away that I definitely do not want to go with them.

'Why don't you want to go to the ball?' says Papa, turning straight to Mama and asking: 'She has a dress, doesn't she?'

'Oh yes,' says Mama, 'she has her pale-grey harège dress, which will do very well.'

'And stockings and shoes, she has those too?'

'Not the shoes,' says Mama, 'but Anna has grown out of the grey cloth boots that she had for my sister Julia's wedding, so she can pass them on to Selma.'

'In that case, I see no reason why she should not come with us,' says Papa.

This makes me simply terrified. I am not really sure what I am terrified of, but I can think of no greater misfortune than having to attend that Sunne ball.

'But I'm too young to go to a ball,' I say. 'I'm only thirteen.'

'Emilia Wallroth is going,' says my aunt, 'and she is no older than you.'

So then I realise that they are all against me, Papa and Mama and Aunt Lovisa. I am entirely outnumbered, and I have no other recourse but to let the tears flow.

'My dear girl, there is no need to cry because we want you to go out and enjoy yourself,' says Papa.

'Yes, but I won't enjoy myself,' I sob. 'I am so lame that nobody will want to dance with me.'

I am not angry, for ever since I played cards with Uncle Wachenfeldt I have stopped myself getting angry. And Papa is not angry either. He just thinks I am being odd.

But for his part, he does not know how it feels when all the girls are asked to dance except you. Or when you only get asked to be part of the quadrille or by the sort of partner no other girl would want to dance with.

'Now that is enough nonsense from you,' says Papa, sounding really stern. 'I will not hear of my girls not going to the ball when they get the chance.'

'I do think she could wait until she was fifteen, at least,' says Aunt Lovisa, who is now trying to come to my aid, but it is too late. It would have been better if she had held her tongue about Emilia a few moments ago.

'Yes, of course she could,' says Papa, 'but who knows if there will be a ball in Sunne then? All these years there have been none at all.'

I know Papa does not like it when we cry. I would much more readily be excused from the ball if I could laugh and put on a cheerful face. But I cannot stop. The tears run down my cheeks all morning.

And they carry on all through my after-dinner rest and while we are at afternoon lessons and doing our preparation for tomorrow's and out tobogganing down the hill, and the whole time we are sitting round the table in front of the sofa in the dining room with our needlework.

Gerda is normally the best at long spells of crying, when she does not know her lessons, but I do not think she has ever cried without a break like that, from dinner right up until bedtime.

When mother comes up to say prayers with us, I hold back the tears just enough to say 'Our Father' and 'Lord bless us and keep us', but 'Now I lay me down to sleep' and 'Angels bless' are just too much for me.

'Is it really only the ball that you are crying about?' says Mama. 'Or is it something else?'

'Mama, can't you ask Papa to let me off going to the ball?' I say, holding her hand in a tight grip.

'Dear child, you know that Papa only wants you to have a nice time,' says Mama.

'Yes, but I won't get to dance,' I say. 'You know that, Mama. I won't get to dance.'

'Of course you will,' says Mama, and then she leaves us.

The first thought that comes into my head when I wake up in the morning is that this is the day of the ball, and I start to cry again. I cannot understand how a person can have so many tears in their eyes that they never come to end.

Anna and Gerda are talking about who will open the ball and who Anna will dance the first waltz with and whether the young Misses Maule will come in white dresses. Anna has put her hair in curl-papers and she is worried that the curls will not last to the end of the ball. But the more they talk of all this, the more I cry. If I could stop, I certainly would, but it is not within my power.

'You had better watch out, Selma, because your eyes will be all red this evening if you cry like that,' says Anna. And I really do make an effort not to cry any more, but it is no good.

Anna and Mama and Elin Laurell spend all morning at their toilette, sewing on ribbons and ironing starched skirts and trying on their shoes to make themselves as fine as they can. Aunt Lovisa says she finds it curious that one can go to a ball in a high-necked dress with long sleeves. That would not have done in her youth, but Mama says that Anna and I are still children, so we can certainly go in our ordinary party dresses.

In the middle of the morning, I go into the dining room, where Papa is sitting in the rocking chair as usual, reading *Värmlandstidningen*. I stand beside him with my foot on the rocker of the chair and put my hand on his shoulder. 'What is it now, then?' he says, turning towards me.

'Please could I be excused from the ball, Papa?' I say, as sweetly as I can, because a hope has crept over me that if I were to ask really humbly and politely, I might yet be able to persuade him. It is also my intention to remind Papa that I read the whole Bible for his sake. I think he ought to let me stay at home if he thinks of that fact.

'You know, Papa, that I will not get to dance,' I say by way of introduction. 'I limp so much that nobody will want to dance with me.'

But I get no further. I start to sob and not a word will come.

Papa says nothing but he stands up from the rocking chair, takes me by the hand and leads me out into the kitchen. There he asks the housekeeper to give me a really nice sandwich, a cheese one. And then he leaves the room.

I realise that I will be obliged to go to the ball and I feel very tempted to throw the sandwich on the floor, but I do not do it, because I never want to lose my temper again and give that monster living inside me a chance to break free.

I behave in a proper and decent fashion in every way, except for the fact that I am crying. I cry at dinner and I cry afterwards. I cry while we are getting dressed ready for the ball. I cry the whole time until we take our seats in the sleigh and are tucked firmly into the fur sleigh rugs.

And then the tears must finally have understood that they achieved nothing by falling. As we drive into Sunne, I sit in the sleigh with dry eyes.

I am wearing a dress of grey barège with a blue wool trim, and Anna's pale grey cloth boots, tied with red laces. At my throat I wear a pink rosette which is very beautiful and was a Christmas present from Uncle Kalle, who always gives us such lovely gifts at Christmas. Aunt Lovisa has combed my hair sleekly and evenly into a big bun at the back of my neck.

But actually, it makes no difference how I am dressed, because my face is streaked red and white and my eyes are red and swollen after all the crying. I am so ugly that I would not be asked to dance even if I had no limp at all.

In the apartment where the ball is being held there is a drawing room, and when we come into it, the Wallroth girls tell us that the young Misses Maule are still not ready, for they will be wearing gauzy white dresses, and to save the skirts from getting creased, two maids have had to bring them to Sunne on a carrying pole.

'That is easy enough for them, for they live no more than a quarter of a mile away,' says Anna. And we all think how awfully sophisticated it is.

But Anna and Hilda are so beautiful, I think to myself, that however fine the others make themselves, they cannot be as beautiful as those two are.

When the young Misses Maule come in, I have to admit that they look very elegant, and they are pretty, too, but not like Anna and Hilda, I cannot concur with that.

Emilia Wallroth is not at all beautiful, but everyone says that there is something attractive about her. Emilia always gets to dance. It does not matter that she is plain because she is so witty and engaging that she would be asked to dance every dance, even if she were lame.

The drawing room is packed with ladies and girls, and surely everyone must be here now, for the music strikes up.

Selma Lagerlöf

The brass sextet from Östra Ämtervik is playing, because in Sunne they have no musicians.

Squire Vilhelm Stenbäck at Björobyholm comes into the drawing room and says that as this is the first ball in Sunne for at least twenty years, he proposes that they open the evening with a processional polonaise, like they have on ceremonial occasions. And everyone agrees.

The old gentlemen come into the drawing room and find their partners among the old ladies: Mrs Maule and Mrs Hellstedt and Mrs Pettersson and Mrs Bergman and Mrs Wallroth and Mrs Lagerlöf, and they walk into the ballroom arm-in-arm. And the young gentlemen come in too and offer their arms to the girls and take them in to dance. And eventually there is no one left in the drawing room but me and Miss Eriksson of Skäggeberg. And Miss Eriksson must be at least fifty years old, and has thin yellow braids rolled into little coils around her ears, and long yellow teeth.

There is a stranger at the ball, a gentleman we have never seen before. He is in uniform, and they say he is an inspector at the railway station at Kil. He does not know anybody at all, and when he comes into the drawing room to ask somebody to dance, everyone is engaged but Miss Eriksson and me. I wonder which of us he will choose, but he turns abruptly and takes neither of us. There we sit, Miss Eriksson and I, and we do not speak to each other but I am glad she is there all the same, so I am not left entirely on my own.

The thought keeps flitting through my mind that it is a good thing not to be asked to dance, because now Papa will see it is true that nobody wants to dance with me. But that is a poor consolation. I have to endure this disagreeable time all the same.

I sit there thinking about Miss Eriksson of Skäggeberg. Who can it be who has forced her to come to the ball? For she surely cannot be there of her own free will.

When the processional polonaise is over and the dancers come back to the drawing room, they are so happy and exhilarated, young and old alike. Mama finds a seat on the sofa between Mrs Maule and Mrs Hellstedt, and they talk and

Memoirs of a Child

laugh as if they were old friends. Anna sits down beside Hilda Ingelius and they whisper together, and Hilda Wallroth comes in arm-in-arm with Julia Maule.

Then they have a waltz and a polka and a quadrille and a waltz and a polka and a quadrille, over and over again.

And Anna and Hilda and Emilia, they get to dance every single dance, of course.

They are so merry, and Hilda comes up to me and wants to say something kind to cheer me up. She suggests I could go with her into the ballroom and watch the dancing at least.

But this does not appeal to me at all. I do not know how to get out of it, but then Anna hurriedly comes to my rescue and says it is best not to talk to Selma because she might start crying again.

Mama and the other ladies do not dance any more dances after the processional polonaise, but they decide to go into the ballroom and watch the young people. So then the drawing room is entirely empty apart from me and Miss Eriksson. We two sit in our places all evening long.

And I try to think about all the people who are having a difficult time, the sick and the poor and the blind. What is there to grieve over, simply because one is not joining in the dances at a ball? Imagine being blind!

I wonder if this is a punishment for something I have done or said, or if it is to teach me humility.

I remember Miss Broström*, the lady Papa used to talk about, who the boys at the upper secondary school tricked into attending the ball at the end of the fair. I have always wondered what she thought about as she sat there on her own all evening and was never asked to dance.

She must surely have thought it remarkable that she was so disagreeable that nobody wanted to dance with her, or even speak to her. For that is exactly what I think myself.

The morning after, when we are having breakfast, Mama and Elin Laurell and Anna tell Papa and Aunt Lovisa about the ball, and how much they enjoyed themselves and how well done and successful it all was. I say nothing of course, because

I have nothing to say. And once Anna has listed everyone she danced with, Papa asks: 'And what about Selma?'

'Well, Selma did not get asked to dance,' says Mama. 'She was too young, I suppose.'

Then Papa is silent for a while, and after that he says:

'What do you think, Louise? Shall we not write to Stockholm and ask the Afzeliuses if Selma can spend another winter with them and go to gymnastics lessons? She got so much better last time she was there. I would like to see her in full health before I die.'

I sit wide-eyed. Perhaps Papa felt guilty last night for forcing me to go to the ball. Perhaps that was why he thought it over and came up with the idea of letting me go to Stockholm.

There really is no one as kind as my Papa.

Elin Laurell

And we are so pleased that Aline Laurell has come to Mårbacka to pay us a visit. We have not seen her since she moved to Västra Ämtervik last autumn.

Aline is just as she was, except that she has perhaps grown a little thinner. She is well and happy and when she stands on the front steps looking down at the side building and the office, it does not seem to worry her in the slightest.

Aline has come here all on her own and she is to stay for three whole days because Pastor Unger and Aunt Maria and Jonas and Anders and Johanna have made the journey into Karlstad for a wedding.

And when Aline arrived we were all, Papa and Mama and Elin Laurell and Anna and Gerda and I, out on the steps to receive her. And Aline took each of us in her arms and kissed us, except Papa of course.

It looked for all the world as though Anna and Gerda were as pleased to see Aline as I was, and Aline kissed them just as she did me. It is as well for them that Aline does not know they both like Elin better than they like her.

They say Elin is so pleasant and friendly to do lessons with. She is not as strict as Aline. She does not give us as much to learn for the next day, and she does not get as cross if we cannot answer all the questions.

But I do not care a bit if my preparation for the next day's lessons is shorter. I like Aline better, even so. No one can make me prefer Elin. I want to stick to Aline.

Yet I have to admit that it is not that easy not to like Elin, because it is true that she is pleasant, and she has so many interesting things to say. Sometimes she gets talking in the schoolroom and carries on for so long that there is hardly time for us to recite our lessons. And Anna and Gerda like that. And I sometimes enjoy it, too, but it does not seem right to me. Aline did not behave like that.

Sometimes when Elin is marking a written test we have done, she goes past a mistake without correcting it. But if I say that to Anna, she thinks that it does not matter. 'I am learning more with Elin than I did with Aline, anyway,' says Anna. 'Because Elin knows more than just what is in the books.'

And Anna is certainly right about that, but I do not want to like Elin. I do not want to be disloyal to Aline.

I think it is a good thing that Elin is plain. Her nose is too short, as if the tip of it has been sliced off. Her skin is greyish and she has a wart on one cheek. And she has a double chin like Field Marshal Klingspor in *The Tales of Ensign Stål**. But she has lovely fair hair, always nicely done. And it cannot be denied that she is tall and looks rather stately. And she has an attractive voice, and there is a certain something about her that I cannot understand. But the fact is that if Mama comes into a room, a little of Filipstad comes too – because Mama was born there – and a hint of coalfields and blast furnaces, and if Aline Laurell comes into a room, something of Karlstad and schools and fine parties comes too, but if Elin Laurell comes into a room, the whole world comes in with her. For Elin can talk about everything, and she feels equally at home in Greece and Egypt and Greenland and Australia. She knows what people are thinking about, everywhere that people are to be found. She is well versed in all things old but what is more, she knows all about everything new.

Elin is not appealing to men the way Aline was. We get no succession of single gentlemen making their way here as we did in Aline's time.

But I think old gentlemen like Papa and engineer Noreen like talking to Elin because she brings the whole world with her and is never afraid to state her opinion. She even dares to get into disputes with Papa about colporteurs and pietist preachers. But she does it so cheerily and makes such amusing remarks that he cannot be angry.

And she particularly enjoys teasing boys.

Elin Laurell stayed with us over Christmas, for she had only come from home in November and she did not want the expense of another journey so soon. And I think Daniel and Johan found her very good company. They stayed in with us much more than usual. She bantered with them on all manner of subjects, and provoked them most of all when she claimed that girls' brains could be just as good as boys' and they could learn the same things. And Daniel was kindlier, but Johan always tried to test her mettle. If she could not better him, she would leap up and try to ruffle his hair. He would slip out of reach and then there would be a chase, first round the dining table and then through the whole house.

But they would be good friends again in no time, and I do believe the boys have never had such an entertaining Christmas.

After dinner, Elin generally goes in to Aunt Lovisa's room to cheer her up with some serious debate. And they always argue about fate. For Aunt Lovisa says that no mortal being can prevent things turning out for her in exactly the way that was ordained from the start. If she is to marry, she will marry, and if she is not to marry, she cannot be married, however hard she tries. And then Elin Laurell asks whether life is preordained in all things great and small, or only in important matters like marriage and death. 'Yes, to be sure, every last detail is preordained,' says Aunt Lovisa. 'In that case I need not pray to God ever again,' says Elin, 'because if everything is decided and cannot be altered, then there is no point in praying for anything.' And that leaves Aunt Lovisa at a loss for an answer. 'Well you can see, Elin, that this is hard for me,' she says. 'I cannot work it out. I lack the brains for it, unlike you.'

But it raises her spirits that Elin comes in to debate with her, anyway.

So it is difficult not to like Elin, as I have set my mind to doing. But I am on my guard, as much as I can be. I am not impolite to her, of course, but I do not get drawn into any disputes with her, because it is clearly through disputing with her that people learn to like her.

I think to myself that if Elin were just as agreeable and witty as she is, but also young and beautiful like Aline, then she would be just the kind of person I would like to be when I grow up. So it is obviously quite hard for me not to be disloyal to Aline.

But now that Aline is here, I am glad that I have stayed loyal to her. I have never spoken to Elin of things that I never tell anyone else. I have never told her about *Oceola* or my reading of the whole Bible to make Papa well again.

Elin has always been kind to me, and at first it felt as if she was trying to make me talk to her about all sorts of things as I did to Aline, but she has stopped doing that now.

And when I was in such dreadful floods of tears over having to go to the Sunne ball, Elin did not lift a finger to help me.

The two of us, Elin and I, sometimes find ourselves sitting together in the nursery for a long time without exchanging a single word. Elin has undoubtedly noticed that I do not want to like her.

But now that Aline has been here for a couple of days, she seems to be giving me such strange looks. And she has asked me several times why I am so quiet, or whether I am feeling unwell.

And on the third day after dinner, Aline says she wants to go out for a walk, and she asks whether I would like to go with her. She does not ask any of the others, so I am the only one to accompany her. And I am very pleased about that. I imagine that we will enjoy ourselves as much as we used to, when the two of us were out together and Aline would say that it felt as if I was equal in age to her.

But Aline does not seem to be in the mood for talking. As we are walking up the avenue, she does not say a single word.

When we come out onto the road, she takes off my mitten and puts my hand into her muff between her two warm ones.

Memoirs of a Child

'Dear child, how cold you are,' she says.

Aline used to do that before, because I always have trouble keeping my hands warm. And I am so pleased that she has taken my hand into her muff once again.

'Well now,' says Aline, 'you must tell me how you are getting on with writing your novels.'

'But Aline, no! Surely you remember me saying that I didn't want to write novels until I grew up.'

'I want to tell you something,' Aline begins a little hesitantly, keeping a firm hold on my hand inside her muff. You mustn't be cross with me now . . . But I have been thinking, you see, that perhaps it was not really right of me to let you talk so much about your notion of writing novels.'

'Why not, Aline?'

'Well, you know . . . Perhaps it has given you fancies, and that might be partly my fault. But I did not think it impossible that you might have a little gift for writing. After all, your aunt Nana Hammargren is an awfully good storyteller, and your uncle Kristofer is a man of great talent, as far as I can judge. But then you are all related to Tegnér*, of course.'

'Us? Are we related to Tegnér?'

'Oh, didn't you know?' says Aline. 'Ah, your Papa, he is a strange one. There is no one he personally admires as much as Tegnér, but he is too unassuming even to let his own children know that he is related to him. Well anyway, your grandfather's mother was the sister of Tegnér's mother, so Tegnér and your grandfather were cousins. That was my very reason for believing you might have an aptitude for writing.'

Aline breaks off, as if she had expected me to reply, but I say nothing. I try to draw my hand out of her muff, but she holds it in place.

'You see,' says Aline, 'it is the most dangerous thing that can befall a person, for her to go imagining that she can become something great and remarkable for which she lacks the powers. When it then turns out that the ability is absent or is insufficient, such a person is generally left dissatisfied or a failure. It is best to root out such expectations right from the start, while one is still a child. It is not so hard then, but later it can become impossible.'

Aline speaks so gravely. It really does seem difficult for her to say what she is saying. I know full well that I have talked to her about wanting to write novels, but there was no deep intent behind my words on the subject. It was no more in earnest than what I used to say about wanting to become frightfully rich and build myself a grand house. It barely matters to me at all that Aline is saying I should not imagine I can attain any kind of greatness.

But I ask her anyway what has made her realise at just this point that I do not have the ability.

'When I moved away in the autumn,' says Aline, 'it was partly for your sake, so that you would have someone guiding your studies who was more knowledgeable and experienced than I. I thought Elin would be exactly the right person for you. But now Elin tells me . . . The thing is, you see . . . that Elin does not think there is anything exceptional about you. "There is nothing to indicate it," she says. She cannot find you to be any more gifted than the other children. You will probably be angry with me, but it is much better for you to hear this now. You can grow up to be a fine and splendid person all the same.'

And perhaps I am a little angry, but it is barely anything to speak of. For, as I say, all those notions about being an author were never anything I believed in myself. And especially now it has emerged that it is Elin who does not think I have the talent, I take it all very calmly. It is only because I have not been drawn into any disputes with her.

'Surely you are not crying?' says Aline, sounding so kindly and concerned.

'No, dear Aline,' I say. 'Of course not. It was good of you to let me know.'

After this exchange, Aline walks along in silence for a while, but then she starts to speak again. And this time she says that because she and I are equal in age, she wants to tell me that she is engaged.

Memoirs of a Child

And I am so amazed that I forget all about our previous subject of conversation.

She tells me that she is to marry a childhood friend whose name is Adolf Arnell. He has always been the love of her life. There have been times when he appeared not to care for her any longer, but that was only because he was not in a position to marry. Last autumn, when she was moving from Mårbacka, everything seemed to be virtually over between them, but now it was all fine again. And she could not be happier.

And I am so glad that she is happy and that Aline has shared her news with me. I am sure she has told Elin and Mama, but none of the others apart from me. Aline must know that I like her better than Anna and Gerda do. So when we return from our walk, Aline and I are just as much good friends as we were back in the days before she moved away.

When we have taken off our outdoor things, Aline goes into the bedroom to speak to Mama, but I go straight to the room off the kitchen, where Elin Laurell is sitting and debating fate with Aunt Lovisa as usual.

'You think everything simply happens by chance, Elin,' says Aunt. 'No,' says Elin, 'no, I do not think that. But do you know what I believe, Lovisa? Well, it is that if a person truly wants to be something, then they will do it.'

I am definitely not upset by what Aline was telling me, but I am very glad nonetheless to hear Elin say that. For perhaps I can become an authoress after all, if it only depends on will and not on talent. Because will is one thing I am quite certain that I have.

I feel so drawn to Elin when she claims that all you need is the will. I go to her side and listen eagerly to what she has to say. And without thinking what I am doing, I put my hand on her shoulder.

She turns her head slightly and smiles at me. And then I remember that I want to stay loyal to Aline and not to like Elin, or at any rate not to let her notice that I do. But then it comes back to me that Aline no longer cares whether a little girl at Mårbacka likes her. Aline has a fiancé and is to be married. Now I am entirely free. And I can like Elin as much as I want.

And now Elin and I are just as much good friends as Aline and I used to be, if not more so.

Pastor Unger

When we are sitting at the table over our evening meal, Aline tells us such a beautiful story about Pastor Unger. And it makes me happy to hear Papa and the others say that he showed himself to be a noble man, because I like Pastor Unger. If I had to choose from among all the gentlemen who come here to visit Papa, then I think I would say that he is the kindest and most jovial.

Pastor Unger comes here on the seventeenth of August, of course, and on other occasions when we are having a party, but the remarkable thing about him is that he does not come only then. He also comes on the kind of days when no one else would dare to venture too near.

We always say that we do not know how he works out which day in the midst of all our Christmas preparations everything will be most awkward and untidy. But as soon as two maids are on their knees scrubbing the bedroom floor and the bedroom furniture has all been moved out into the hall and two hired cleaning women are scrubbing the drawing-room floor and have moved all the drawing-room furniture and Mama is in the kitchen at one end of the baking table making saffron buns and the housekeeper is at the other end making the Christmas loaves of malted rye bread, and when Aunt Lovisa has moved everything out of the room off the kitchen so that she and Anna and Gerda and I can make the biscuits in there, when we are all wearing faded, outgrown cotton dresses and big baking aprons, and when Papa is sitting in the dining room practically walled up behind the drawing-room furniture on one side and the furniture from the room off the kitchen on the other, then we know that Pastor Unger cannot be far away.

When he then comes driving up to the house in his little cariole, we lament the fact that a visitor should come on a day like this, and we tell Papa he will have to go out and receive him, for the rest of us are wearing clothes that are not fit to be seen. But we do not lament anything like as much as we would have done had it been anyone other than Pastor Unger.

As soon as Papa comes out onto the steps, he calls to Pastor Unger that it will be best if he does not get out but goes on his way, because there is nothing in this house today but womenfolk baking and scrubbing. But Pastor Unger is not the least bit disconcerted and jumps out of his cariole and comes up the steps to Papa. 'Ah, so you are all in the middle of your Christmas cleaning, too,' he says. 'I might have known, for Maria has everything in such dreadful disarray at home that I was obliged to make myself scarce.'

Then he goes with Papa into the dining room. Papa sits in the rocking chair as usual, but Pastor Unger looks around for the worst chair he can find and pulls it up to the rocking chair. And he has barely sat down before he starts telling a funny story.

A little while later, Pastor Unger comes out to the kitchen and the room beside it. 'I heard that you dare not come in and say hello to me, Louise, nor you Lovisa,' he says, 'so there was nothing for it but for me to come to you'. And if they are up to their elbows in dough, then instead of shaking hands he gives them a couple of affectionate pats on the shoulder, sending clouds of flour into the air. And he says to the housekeeper that he can see that our Christmas is going to be a failure, for the malted rye loaves are as flat as the thinnest crispbread, and the housekeeper retorts that there must be something wrong with his eyes if he cannot see that they are as round as a dean's belly.

Then he passes on Maria's best wishes to Mama and Aunt Lovisa, and once he has taken a good look around him, he

Memoirs of a Child

declares that in this kitchen they are all dressed in their best, compared to how everyone looks at home. Then he asks to sample the ginger snaps, for they are his absolute favourite, and checks in the kneading trough to see that the dough is rising and goes over to the stove and lifts the lids of all the saucepans on the hob to see if there is anything passable to eat or if he will be forced to go elsewhere for his dinner. Last of all, he dips a whisk in a flour tub and flicks flour all over us children. We are not slow to retaliate. We take the wooden spoons we are using to mix the biscuit doughs and throw flour back at him. A wild battle ensues in the room off the kitchen. We laugh and shout, the baking sheets are knocked to the floor and the fine, shop-bought flour billows up into the air. Aunt calls out to us to at least use the home-ground flour, but Mama drives Pastor Unger out of the room.

'I can well understand that Maria was obliged to send you packing Alfred, today of all days,' says Mama. 'A madcap like you is the last person one wants around when Christmas preparations are in full swing.'

'Fine thing for a clergyman, I must say!' mutters the housekeeper, but so quietly that Pastor Unger cannot hear her.

When dinnertime comes, we have to try to make ourselves a little more presentable, and we all say that it is a real nuisance, but I do wonder whether Mama and Aunt are not actually glad of a little interruption to the work.

I know nobody whose words flow so readily as Pastor Unger's, and I like him for it, but Papa, who has now been listening to him for two hours, has doubtless grown weary, for he is never in the best of health in the wintertime. Papa does not say a word all through dinner and leaves Mama and Aunt to converse with Pastor Unger.

As soon as we have sat down at the table, Pastor Unger tells us that he will have to leave Västra Ämtervik. His stipend is so meagre that he simply cannot live on it. He has told us the same thing every Christmas for as far back as I can remember, so we children find it rather hard not to burst out laughing when he starts on his usual topic.

But Mama answers as earnestly as anything that it will be a great shame for us to lose such good neighbours, and asks which parish he will apply for.

Then Pastor Unger runs through all the parishes that are vacant and can be applied for in the present year, and does the same for those due to fall vacant in the coming year, and for those that he did not apply for the year before. Then, unbidden by Mama, he tells us all the advantages and disadvantages of the various places, and what the stipend and the accommodation are like. He knows where the land belonging to the property is deficient and where the forest has been cut down and where the stable floor has rotted and where the main house has a leaky roof. And he is so amusing that it is very funny to listen to him, whatever he is talking about. It is not just the fact that he is amusing, however, but that I also feel I am learning so much as I listen to him.

When he has spent some time talking of parishes and stipends and vicarages, he moves on to the clergymen who might want to apply for the same positions as him, and tells us what marks they got in their theological examinations and their pastoral examinations and how many years' service they have put in and how they preach and how they conduct themselves at meetings.

And I find it as enjoyable hearing about the vicars as I do about the vicarages. I never tire of listening to him.

I do not know what Mama thinks, but she lets him run on until the dessert comes in. But as the meal starts to draw to an end, Mama says:

'You know what, Alfred, I still do not believe you will move from Västra Ämtervik.'

'But I simply have to,' he says, throwing his hands wide. 'I have virtually no stipend. I have to tell you, Louise, that sometimes we do not have enough food for the day.'

'That may well be,' says Mama, 'but I think you are far too attached to Västra Ämtervik to leave it, Alfred. And just think how well liked you and Maria are over there! That much is plain from the new vicarage your parishioners have put

Memoirs of a Child

up for you. There are few even among the deans who have somewhere as nice as that to live.'

When Mama speaks so seriously and at such length, everyone falls silent and listens, as it is not at all usual for Mama to make long speeches. And Pastor Unger falls silent too.

'You say your stipend is small,' Mama goes on, 'but think of all the joints of veal and the pike and cheesecakes and tubs of butter that find their way into the kitchen! They count for something as well.'

'Yes, yes,' says Pastor Unger. 'You are surely right, Louise.'

'You and Maria have such a wonderful knack of making your small income stretch a long way,' says Mama. 'We are always saying that we cannot fathom how you do it. Pastor Lindegren and his wife at Halla presumably have roughly the same stipend as you, but they do not have a carriage and horses like you, nor do they keep company with all the gentlemen's families in Sunne and Ämtervik and throw big parties like you do at Västra Ämtervik.'

When Mama has been sermonising in this way for a good while, Pastor Unger pushes away his plate, leans back in his chair and surveys the table with slightly clouded eyes.

'Indeed, Louise, you are quite right,' he says. 'And there will most certainly be no move for me until Gunnarskog falls vacant. But then, you see, I shall feel obliged to apply, for the Ungers have been clergymen there since time immemorial, and every soul in the place knows me.'

'Is that so?' says Mama, getting up from the table. 'In that case we must hope that the rector at Gunnarskog will live for many years yet.'

This last Christmas, when Aline had moved to Västra Ämtervik, Pastor Unger did not pay us his customary Christmas visit, and as we sit around the table at our evening meal, Papa asks Aline how her uncle is. 'He is not ill, I trust?' says Papa. 'He did not come to us before Christmas on the worst day of preparation and disarray.'

'Oh no, he is not ill,' says Aline,' but he had such a troublesome time just around Christmas. You have probably

Selma Lagerlöf

heard, Uncle Lagerlöf, that the old rector of Gunnarskog died last autumn?'

'Oh no, is Gunnarskog vacant?' exclaims Mama. 'Then your uncle and his wife will certainly not grow old at Västa Ämtervik.'

'Oh they will,' says Aline. 'He is definitely going to stay.'

'But that was the only place he ever wanted to move to,' says Mama, 'and he was absolutely sure of getting all the votes.'

Then Aline says it is entirely true that her uncle had wanted to move to Gunnarskog. He had spent much time there as a child, and knew everyone there, and to him it was as beautiful as Paradise. He always had such a lot to say about vicarages and stipends, which gave the impression that he thought of nothing but finding a good parish, but Aline believed that even if he were the incumbent of one of the best and largest parishes such as Sunne or Karlskoga, he would still have applied for the position in Gunnarskog.

'Well,' says Papa, 'why does he not put in an application, then? Is it for the sake of the Västra Ämtervik residents? Perhaps he thinks that considering they have now built him a large vicarage....'

But Aline does not think so. Her uncle had informed his parishioners long since that as soon as Gunnarskog fell vacant, he intended to apply there, so they had known they would have to allow for that when they built the vicarage. But the local people had wanted nonetheless to build a fine and splendid house, to thank him for having helped them in the year of the famine*.

'Yes, that is true, I remember it,' says Papa. 'He took out a loan to provide them with some income and seed for sowing. Yes, he has certainly done as much for them as they have for him. He does not owe them anything.'

'But what has happened now, Uncle, is that the rector of Gunnarskog has been unwell for a number of years and has been unable to perform his duties. For the past four years he has had as his assistant an elderly, married clergyman, acting as the "consistory coach horse", as they call it, working for many years without ever gaining a permanent position.

He is poor, as you may imagine, and has a wife and four children. And you see, Uncle Alfred believes that the assistant clergyman has been hoping to get Gunnarskog, too, as he has served for four years. And he needs it very badly. He does not even have a home, but has been obliged to find lodgings on a farm for his wife and children.'

'Yes, that is a hard knot to unpick,' says Papa.

'My uncle talked about it every day,' says Aline. 'He was terribly torn. Neither Aunt Maria nor I could say what he would do. Gunnarskog attracted him like a magnet, but he did not want to stand in the way of another clergyman, who was old and impoverished. "Mustard has got into the honey," he would say. "It does not taste as sweet any more." But he still made the journey to Karlstad the day before the application period ended, so we thought he was going to put his name forward, after all.'

'I do declare, this is really interesting,' said Elin. 'So, what happened?'

'Admissions closed at twelve noon,' went on Aline, 'and at eleven, my uncle came into the consistory chamber. Apparently, they had been waiting for him in there all morning and as soon as he appeared, the consistory clerk told him to submit his papers. There was only an hour to go. But Uncle Alfred did not produce any papers. He took a seat and chatted to while away the time. When it got to half past eleven, the consistory clerk gave him another reminder. 'Now surely you are not going to let this livelihood fall through your hands, Alfred?' he said. 'Oh, I am very content with Västra Ämtervik,' said Uncle Alfred, and did not move from the spot, but allowed the time to pass.'

'What an extraordinary fellow,' says Papa. 'So there he sat with the papers in his pocket and did not take them out?'

'Indeed he did not,' said Aline. 'When the clock struck the three-quarter hour, the consistory clerk let his impatience show again. He reached out a hand and patted Uncle Alfred's breast pocket. "You have the documents with you," he said. "Out with them then!" Uncle replied that he could not very well come into Karlstad with an empty wallet, and stayed in his seat and spoke of how much Maria liked it at the new vicarage in Västra Ämtervik. "You may be sure she will like it in Gunnarskog, too," said the consistory clerk. "Everyone in the parish is perpetually longing to have you as their vicar and vicar's wife." And he tried to draw Uncle into conversation about Gunnarskog, but without success. And that was how the time passed until the clock began to strike twelve. Then Uncle Alfred stood up, put his hand in his pocket, brought out a bundle of documents and showed the clerk that it contained his application for Gunnarskog. As the clock went on chiming, he lowered his hand until the bundle was almost on the table but he did not let go of it, and just as the final chime rang out, he raised the bundle again and thrust it back into his breast pocket. Then he put on his hat and overcoat without a further word and left.'

'What an extraordinary fellow,' says Papa again.

'Yes. But you know, Uncle Lagerlöf, perhaps it was not all that hard, really. The harder part came later. The people of Gunnarskog had been so certain that Uncle Alfred would apply that they had done nothing about it until then. But when they heard that he had not put in an application, letters of enquiry and regret started to arrive at once. And last week a whole deputation came from Gunnarskog. It was all the most prominent farmers, strong and splendid men. Uncle knew them all and how much their opinions mattered. And they told him that the parish wanted to summon him as the fourth candidate to preach a test sermon. They could guarantee that he would get every single vote, if only he heeded the call. I heard them imploring him and trying to persuade him. And I assure you, Uncle, that it was very moving. They did not go down on bended knee before him, to be sure, but they begged as if their lives depended on it. They so badly wanted a good vicar. Their previous one had been sick and confined to bed for so long that the parish had lost its way, as it were. And I am sure you can appreciate, Uncle, how that affected him. Simply to see the many familiar faces was to be reminded of all those things from the past that he loved, and now to hear in addition that they felt the need of someone to help them take the right path! I do not understand how he could say no.'

'And it was all just for the sake of that assistant clergyman?' Elin puts in.

'Yes. He had applied, you see, and been duly nominated, and Uncle Alfred thought that if he himself did not heed the summons, then perhaps the other man could be elected. The Gunnarskog farmers tried to convince Uncle that they did not want the assistant, but Uncle said that he hoped they would change their minds on that score. No, they would never do that. They had had a sickly rector for long enough. The assistant was not in the best of health either. If Uncle was turning this down for his sake, then he was wasting his time.'

'But he stood firm?' asks Papa, and I can see the little twitches and tugs at the lines under Papa's eyes, which usually mean that he is finding it hard to hold back his tears.

'Yes Uncle Lagerlöf, he did. But the night after the Gunnarskog farmers came to see him, he did not sleep a wink. I heard him pacing his office, back and forth, back and forth.'

'What an extraordinary fellow,' says Papa for the third time.

'I think they ought to make him bishop,' says Aunt Lovisa, at which we all laugh and exclaim how right she is.

We are so pleased that someone we know has made such a noble gesture that we find it hard to tear ourselves away and go to bed.

And I am not the least bit hurt by what Aline said to me when we were out for our walk after dinner. I did not take it too closely to heart at the time, and now I have quite forgotten it. If I could do some deed similar to Pastor Unger's, I think that would count for much more than writing the most beautiful of all the books in the world.

But just think, when I finally do get to bed, I dream that I am trying to write something fine about Pastor Unger! And just as I am really engrossed in my writing, Aunt Maria Unger appears and tells me it would be best for me to stop, because I am not good enough at writing. She has heard this from many people.

And when she says that, I am terribly downcast. I feel as if I could die, and I wake with the tears streaming down my face. I soon realise that it was only a dream, but it leaves me heartsore, and my heart thumps and aches for several hours, although I am not entirely sure of that, for I am lying in the dark and cannot see the time on the clock.

I cannot understand why it should cause me such heartache to hear Aunt Maria Unger say that to me in a dream. I was not at all sad earlier, when Aline told me the same thing in the middle of the day.

I turn onto my right side and my left side, and press my hands hard, hard against my heart, but it thumps and aches just the same. In the end I have the idea of telling my heart that it should not be in such distress, for I am certainly going to write books when I grow up, and I will not allow myself to be frightened off.

And once I have said that to my heart a few times, it starts to calm itself. It stops aching, and I go back to sleep.

The next morning, lying there not quite awake, I tell myself:

'I still simply must write novels when I grow up. It is what I was born to.'

And I feel pleased and happy that it is decided. Until now, before Aline tried to advise me against it, it was just something vague and indistinct, but now it is truly definite.

The Easter Witch

And we so much like it when Easter Eve comes.
In the middle of the afternoon, a couple of the maids will slip out of the kitchen with a bundle of clothes under their arms and go down to the hayloft in the cowshed. They do it as secretly as they can so that we children will not notice anything, yet still we know that they are off to make an Easter witch.

We will always know full well what is going on, because Nursie Maja will have told us. Down there in the hayloft, the maids look round for a long narrow sack, which they stuff with hay and straw. Once that is done, they dress the sack in a dirty old skirt, the shabbiest they could find, and a jumper that is all threadbare at the front and has holes at the elbows. They stuff the sleeves with hay and straw, too, so they look rounded and natural, but they do not care one bit that there is straw sticking out of the cuffs in the place of hands and fingers.

Then the maids make a head for the Easter witch out of an old kitchen hand towel, coarse and grey. The tie it together by the four corners, stuff it with hay, draw eyes, nose and mouth and some strands of hair on it with a lump of charcoal, tie it to the sack full of straw and top the whole thing off with the battered old straw hat that the housekeeper uses in the summer when she has to catch a swarm of bees.

Once they are satisfied with the Easter witch, they carry her from the hayloft up to the main building. They dare not bring her into the house, but leave her in the middle of the front steps and fetch one of the kitchen chairs to sit her on. Then they go to the brewhouse for the oven rake and broom and prop them at an angle against the back of the kitchen chair, for if the Easter witch did not have the broomstick and rake with her, nobody would realise who she was. They also tie her apron string to a dirty cow's horn, which is full of all the magic ointment that witches use when they want to fly to the witches' sabbath on Blåkulla Hill*. They stick a long leather in the horn, and last of all they hang an old postbag around her neck.

Then the maids go into the kitchen and the housekeeper comes into the nursery to tell us that one of those nasty witches who take to the skies every Easter Eve has crashed in the front yard of Mårbacka. 'She's taking a rest at the bottom of the front steps,' says the housekeeper, 'and she's got a right wicked look to her, so it's best you children don't go down there at the moment, not before she's made off.'

But we understand the real intention, so we charge past the housekeeper and down the stairs to get a look at the Easter witch. Papa usually comes out with us, but Mama and Aunt stay indoors, saying they have already seen so many Easter witches in their time.

When we come out onto the steps and see the Easter witch glowering at us with her sooty eyes, we pretend that we are fearful and think she is a real witch on her way to Blåkulla, even though she is propped on a kitchen chair in the front yard of Mårbacka. We are not the least bit frightened of her because we know that she is nothing but a straw doll, but it is all part of the act for us to look fearful, otherwise the two maids who made the Easter witch for us will have nothing for all their work.

Once we have admired the Easter witch from a distance for a while, we generally creep down the steps and approach her slowly and cautiously. The Easter witch stays stock still, however close we come, and eventually one of us plucks up courage and thrusts a hand into the post bag. The old abandoned post bag looks bulging full, and we have been keeping an eye on it the whole time. But whoever puts their hand inside it cannot help giving a little shriek, not of terror but of delight, because the bag is all full of letters. We take out whole handfuls of big letters, sealed with sealing wax. There are feathers on them all, as if they have flown to us, and they are all addressed to Johan or Anna or Selma or Gerda. They are all for us children, and the grown-ups get none.

As soon as we have fished out all the letters, we abandon the Easter witch. We go in and sit down round the table in the dining room and open the Easter letters. And we always enjoy that part so much, because Easter letters are not words written in black ink like other letters, but painted pictures. In the middle of the sheet of paper in each letter there is a brightly-coloured Easter witch or wizard, holding brooms and rakes and horns and other Easter paraphernalia.

And we receive lots of different kinds of letter. Some are the drawings of very young children, but in others the grown-ups have stepped in to help. They are not all particularly beautiful, but we do not care very much about that. The most important thing is to receive a lot of them, because that is something to boast about later, when we get to church and meet our cousins from Gårdsjö.

In actual fact it is not altogether true that there is no writing in the Easter letters. Sometimes they are covered in writing, but it is always in verse. The verses are not anything to get excited about, for they are just the same old Easter rhymes repeated year after year and we already know them off by heart.

And we always pretend to be astounded to find ourselves with so many Easter letters, delivered by the flying Easter witch, but in fact we have all been expecting them to arrive. After all, we ourselves have spent every spare moment in the entire month of March drawing and painting, and we have sent out Easter letters to every big house in the neighbourhood. And we know that they have been labouring in just the same way at the other big houses and that the letters brought by the Easter witch have been made at Gårdsjö or Herrestad or Visteberg or some other estate.

When we have spent some time looking at the Easter letters and comparing them and wondering who has sent them, we remember the Easter witch and go out to the front steps to look at her for a bit longer. But when we come out, the chair is empty and the Easter witch has vanished, along with her rake and broom. And then we pretend that the Easter witch must have been in a hurry to get to Blåkulla and flew off as soon as she had delivered her Easter letters.

And we laugh and say it is just as well that she has gone, for here is Per in Berlin, who is a Finn and has hunter's blood in him, coming out of the office, where he has been loading Papa's two shotguns. He takes up position on the flagstone outside the office door and fires the guns straight up into the air. Naturally we understand that he is shooting at the Easter witches even though we can never see them, but Per in Berlin, being a Finn, can see more than other people, so he surely knows very well what he is doing.

And this year we have painted more Easter letters than usual, because Elin Laurell is not as strict about learning lessons for the next day as Aline was, so we have a lot more time. The Mårbacka nursery has been like a proper artist's workshop with paints and mixing pots on every available surface. It all felt more urgent in Easter week, of course, after Elin left for Karlstad to visit her relations. Papa has been driven to distraction by our begging for all his stocks of fine white paper, and in the end he told us we would have to make do with yellow straw-paper. The nice red and blue paints that we wanted to use ran out in our paintboxes, so we constantly had to run down to Aunt Lovisa and borrow the special paintbox she kept from her days at boarding school in Åmål. The drinking glasses in the nursery were used for washing brushes, all the sticks of sealing wax were used up, Mama spent days on end addressing the letters and we searched high and low for pretty feathers to fix under the seals. Paint brushes are always in short supply, and by the time the last Easter letter is sealed, there is nothing left of them but a few sparse bristles.

Memoirs of a Child

We are all very glad indeed now that it is Easter Eve and the painting is over and we say that if we get as many letters in return as we have sent out, then there will be far too many for one Easter witch to carry with her.

As the clock reaches four in the afternoon, the housekeeper comes in as usual to tell us that there is a wicked-looking witch sitting at the bottom of the steps and that we must take care not to go out while she is still there. And we run straight down from the nursery to take a look at her. Papa comes out onto the steps with us as is his custom and, unusually, Mama and Aunt Lovisa come too. Even Uncle Wachenfeldt, who is here at Mårbacka with us for Easter, staggers out to the front porch.

It is not very nice weather, but cold and windy, and we say that it cannot have been much fun for the Easter witch on her journey here. And as usual we pretend to be scared of her and tread softly and cautiously as we go up the porch steps.

The Easter witch looks just as she always does, so we cannot really be frightened of her. There is straw sticking out of her sleeves as usual. The eyes, nose and mouth and a few strands of hair have been painted onto a grey hand towel from the kitchen. The milkmaid's shawl is thrown around her shoulders, the postbag is hanging round her neck and the dirty old cow horn is tied to her apron strings.

This time I am the one to put my hand in the bag before all the others. But I have no sooner felt the letters between my fingers than the witch jumps to her feet, grabs the feather that is stuck in the cow horn and dabs magic ointment over my face.

But how can that be? How is it possible? I cry out, for I am so dreadfully scared, and run away, but the straw woman can also run, and she comes after me, brandishing the feather, to dab me with yet more ointment. She splashes through the puddles, sending up sprays of water.

But it is not just that I am scared, it is also totally outlandish for a straw witch to move. At the instant she leapt up from the chair, it was as if the world was being shaken to its foundations. And as I run, anxious, confused thoughts are going through my head. If a stuffed old sack can come to life, then presumably the dead can rise up from their graves as well, and there can be trolls in the forest, so there is nothing so gruesome and monstrous as to be impossible.

I run screaming up the steps, for if I can only reach the grown-ups they will surely protect me. Anna and Gerda and Johan rush past me, going in the same direction. They seem as frightened as I am.

But up on the top step, the grown-ups are laughing. 'Dear children,' they say, 'there is no need to be scared. It is only Nursie Maja, you know.'

And then we realise how foolish we have been. It really is only Nursie Maja, who has dressed up as an Easter witch. Alas, alas, why did we not realise it at once! It is very provoking to have let ourselves be scared like that.

And above all it is provoking for the person who has been practising for several years not to let herself get frightened.

But there is no time for feeling indignant, either on my own behalf or on others', because now the Easter witch is at the top of the steps and making straight for Uncle Wachenfeldt to put her arms around him and kiss him. And Uncle Wachenfeldt, who recoils from any ugly woman, spits and swears and hits out with his stick. But I am not so sure that he manages to escape. Because afterwards there are some sooty marks to be seen on his white moustache.

Yet that is not enough to satisfy the Easter witch. She straddles the oven rake and rides off across the yard to the kitchen door. The doves, pecking about for peas as they do, and so tame that nothing alarms them, nevertheless go flapping up to the roof at the sight of her. The cat scoots up the drainpipe and Nero, who is as big as a bear, creeps away with his tail between his legs. But the old housekeeper, she does not run away or lose her presence of mind like the rest of us, oh no, not she. She bustles over to the stove, grabs up the steaming coffee kettle, and with that in her hand she advances on the pestilential creature when it shows itself on the threshold, to scald it with boiling coffee.

Memoirs of a Child

And then, seeing the raised coffee pot, the witch is forced to turn about, and goes riding off to the back yard at the wildest of gallops. The first to catch sight of her is old Brownie, who has just been unharnessed and is placidly making his way to the stable door when he sees the scarecrow mask appear round the corner. Brownie does not hesitate for a moment, but kicks up his legs and runs. His mane streams out, his tail is horizontal, his hooves thunder on the ground, and for as long as the way lies open, he carries on bolting.

By the woodshed, Lars in London and Magnus in Vienna are chopping wood. They stop their work, but it would not do for such stalwart fellows as they are to flee from any hobgoblin in the world. And nor do they move from the spot, but threaten her with their axe hammers, for they know, of course, that faerie folk are afraid of iron. And indeed the Easter witch keeps well away from them, but then she spies a man walking up the avenue. And we think it very strange when we see that it happens to be Olle from Maggebysäter, who in his youth once ran into a coven of witches. He was walking home from a party on Easter night, and on one of the flat fields below Mårbacka he saw them sweeping in close to the ground, a long line of them. And they entwined themselves around him and danced with him on a ploughed field and did not let him rest or catch his breath the whole night long. He thought the witches would dance the life out of him. And now, as he comes abreast of the farmhands' quarters, Olle from Maggebysäter sees a witch like those he met in his youth come bounding towards him.

He does not wait for her to reach him. Old and crippled with rheumatism as he is, he turns smartly around and we see him running up the avenue with all the speed of a boy. He does not stop until he plunges into the forest on the other side of the road.

And we children are now free from our terror and can laugh at that of others. We have been keeping track of the Easter witch's movements the whole time. We have seen the housekeeper threaten her with the coffee pot, we have seen Brownie bolt and Olle from Maggebysäter run off into the forest. We have seen Lars in London and Magnus in Vienna brandish their axe hammers at her, and we have laughed as we have surely never laughed in all our lives.

But the best part of all is when Per in Berlin comes rushing past the front steps, down towards the office. Papa asks him where he is off to in such a hurry and the old man barely gives himself time to reply. But eventually it emerges that he wants to load the shotgun to kill that foul piece of work rampaging round the backyard.

And anybody can see that the old man's eyes are alight with a true huntsmen's relish. For you see, Per in Berlin has had to shoot at Easter witches on at least fifty Easter Eves without ever hitting the mark. Now he finally has the chance of bagging one.

Anna Lagerlöf

I do not understand why Anna keeps saying that she knows she is going to be unhappy.

Just imagine, someone so beautiful and wise, someone so well liked by everyone.

It would be more fitting if it was me, so lame and ugly, who kept saying such things, but it would never occur to me, because as long as there are exciting books to read, I do not think that I or anyone else need be unhappy.

This spring we have been able to borrow *The Surgeon's Stories* by Topelius*, and we read them aloud in the evenings as we sit around the lamp at our work. And I do not understand how Anna can think of sorrows and misfortunes when we have such a delightful book to read from.

Sometimes Anna looks at that picture in the room off the kitchen, the collage of a church and a churchyard wall done by Aunt Anna Wachenfeldt. And when she has contemplated the picture for a while, she always says that she knows she is going to be as unhappy as Aunt Anna.

I do not like her saying that, and I ask her how she can be so sure of it.

'Oh well,' says Anna, 'everyone called Anna Lagerlöf is bound to be unhappy.'

I find this very strange, because Anna is generally so sensible. And even though Aunt Anna was so unhappy that she grieved herself to death, it surely does not mean that the same will happen to other people called Anna Lagerlöf.

Anna is going to confirmation classes with Pastor Lindegren this year, and she is not really her usual self. She has grown so meek and quiet, and it is as if her thoughts were far away.

And she makes nothing like the number of critical remarks about Gerda and me as she generally does. When we are going out anywhere, she helps us do our hair and get dressed, which has always been her task, but it no longer seems to be such a great nuisance to her and we feel she is doing it because she is fond of us.

I think the whole house has grown so peaceful now that Anna is going to confirmation classes. Gerda and I do not shout and sing as we usually do. Nobody has told us not to, but we do not feel it is fitting at the moment.

And the kitchen has been such a noisy place this past year. The housekeeper is starting to get old and decrepit and the maids do not have the same respect for her as they used to, so they contradict her or do not do what she tells them. And then she scolds them, and they answer back, and it is so unpleasant. But all it takes is for Anna to walk through the kitchen, and everything goes quiet. The maids cannot carry on their quarrels with the housekeeper when they see Anna.

As soon as Anna comes into a room, everybody can see that a young confirmation pupil has just crossed the threshold. I cannot explain why, but that is the way it is.

And Nursie Maja has told me that old Per in Berlin has said to her that if he was a dog, he would not be able to bark when that girl was going by.

Naturally we know that Mama has always liked Anna best of all her children, and we are not surprised, for Mama has never found the rest of us as useful as Anna. Gerda only wants to play, and I only want to read, but as for Anna, she likes plain needlework and mending clothes, like Mama. And now that Anna is attending confirmation classes, it is as if Mama is going to be confirmed as well. She reads the Bible and the catechism, just like Anna. And she sits over them in the middle of an ordinary weekday, Mama who is normally always so busy with her sewing that she never touches a book except on Sundays.

Memoirs of a Child

And the other day I came across Papa reading Tegnér's 'The Children of the Lord's Supper'* of his own volition.

Mama has now announced that she does not think it suitable for us to carry on reading *The Surgeon's Stories*, as it is the sort of book that will distract Anna from her confirmation reading. Mama does not mean, of course, that there is any harm in the book, but only that it fills the girl's imagination with so many worldly things. Not that I think even those handsome Counts Bertelsköld can lure Anna's thoughts from her confirmation preparations, but of course we do as Mama wishes.

Hilda Wallroth and Emilie Nilsson are also going to confirmation classes with Pastor Lindegren, and they too are transported, if that is the right word to describe it. And when the three of them are together, everything feels so solemn that one hardly knows if one dare speak to them.

And the confirmation candidates in Östra Ämtervik usually dress in black, but as there are three daughters of the gentry preparing for their first communion this time, Mrs Lindegren at Halla has suggested that they, at least, should be allowed to dress in white. She feels very sorry for the pretty little children, she says, having to go up to the altar rail in heavy, unbecoming black wool dresses. And just think, Mrs Lindegren manages to persuade both Papa and Mama and Uncle Kalle and Aunt Augusta and Mr and Mrs Nilsson, so they decide to depart from old ways and let Anna and Hilda and Emilie wear white!

On the journey to church, Mama sits in the front seat of the carriage and Anna sits beside her, because she is to be confirmed. And Gerda and I sit on the backward-facing seat as we usually do. But today I do not mind at all that I have to travel backwards, because it means I can sit and look at Anna all the way there.

But it is neither her white dress that I look at, nor the filigree brooch that Mama has given her as a confirmation gift, for I am gazing at her eyes.

They are big and deep and hazel-coloured, possibly with some flecks of green as well; it is virtually impossible to say what colour they are. But it is not their colour that strikes me, but how big and still and expectant they are. I would very much like to know what it is that Anna is waiting for. I think she looks like someone standing outside the wrought-iron gates of a great, magnificent palace, longing to go in and see all the grand rooms and wide staircases and vaulted ceilings.

And I feel certain that she would have had her wish fulfilled. It would not have been long before the gates swung open and out came a handsome young cavalier, dressed in velvet and silk, who would have bowed to Anna and announced himself as Count Bernard Bertelsköld and bidden her welcome to Majniemi castle*.

But just imagine, Anna would not have spared him a look or taken his outstretched hand! She would not have entered the gates but would have turned away. For Anna is not standing outside Majniemi castle. She is at the gates of Heaven, waiting to see God and His angels.

When we get to the church, Adolf Noreen is standing on the forecourt and hurries forward to open the carriage door and help us down. And you can see that he thinks Anna looks beautiful in her white dress and filigree brooch. But Anna barely sees him. Her eyes are fixed on something far, far away.

When Anna and Hilda and Emilie come into the chancel in their white dresses, it is as if a sigh runs through the whole church. People crane their necks and turn to see them and one young man even stands up in his pew to get a better view, but of course his neighbours instantly tell him to sit down.

And that day I am actually able to hear Pastor Lindegren's sermon, because Mama and Aunt and Gerda and I are sitting down in the body of the church, right behind the confirmation candidates, so we can catch every word. And I can hear that his words are chosen to make all the candidates yearn to see the gates of the kingdom of Heaven open for them.

And now, some days later, I have heard from Nursie Maja – although I probably should not call her Nursie Maja any more, now that she has been promoted to housemaid – well, she has told me that when Anna came into the church in her white dress and confirmation brooch, she was so beautiful that one of the boy candidates who was sitting on the other side of the aisle fell totally in love with her. But he knows he can never have her, says Nursie Maja, so he does not want to stay in Östra Ämtervik any longer and will leave for America in the autumn.

And Nursie Maja says that he has written a poem in which he says he has to leave on account of Anna. The poem is so lovely, she says, that all the confirmation pupils have copied it down to have as a keepsake. Nursie Maja has it too, and she would certainly show it to me as long as I promised not to show it to the master and mistress or to Anna herself, for then the boy would be so angry with Nursie Maja that he would kill her.

And I think that what Nursie Maja has told me about is so fine that I beg to see the love poem written by Anna's poor fellow candidate. But once I have read it, I do feel a little disappointed, because it is only five lines long, and all it says is:

My name is Erik Persson, Karlstad county is my home,
But when the flower withers I will then have far to roam
Farewell my father and mother
Farewell my sister and brother
And you, O girl in white!

'Yes, but Nursie Maja,' I say, 'there is nothing in there at all about him liking Anna.'

'Oh, but he says "Farewell you girl in white,"' says Nursie Maja. 'Surely that's enough?'

And it may well be that it is enough. At any rate, Nursie Maja can rest assured that I will not show that verse to Anna, because the day of her First Communion is so sacred to her that it is out of the question to talk of earthly love in the same breath.

Uncle Schenson

Uncle Schenson was married to Aunt Johanna Wallroth, who was sister to Mama and Aunt Georgina and Aunt Julia, but she has been dead for such a long time that we children scarcely remember her.

But although Aunt Johanna who was Mama's sister is dead, Uncle Schenson still comes here every summer, just as Uncle Wachenfeldt, who was married to Aunt Anna, comes here every Christmas and Easter.

Uncle Schenson is a schoolmaster in Karlstad, and the day after school ends in the spring, he comes to Mårbacka, and the day before school starts in the autumn, he leaves to travel home again, so he stays here all summer.

When Uncle Schenson arrives, he always has with him a big bag of nuts, and we children like that, but Aunt Lovisa is always annoyed when she hears the nuts rattling in the bag, because she has such bad teeth that she cannot chew them.

'That Schenson is so odd,' she says. 'He has Yhnell's cake shop, the best in the world, on his doorstep yet he brings us the sort of rubbish that not a soul can eat.'

But this is the only thing that Aunt Lovisa dislikes about Uncle Schenson.

Uncle Schenson is not a difficult guest, and he himself is convinced that he is no trouble at all. And it is true that he is content with the meals that we usually eat, but of course there have to be cold cuts on the bread at every meal, and dessert several times a week. And we cannot just serve rye rusks with the afternoon coffee, but have to offer cakes and biscuits. And if we did not put out brandy and cold water every evening, so he could mix himself a drink, he would think that we had tired of him and were trying to hint that he should leave.

Uncle Schenson sets such store by his visits to Mårbacka in the summer that he wants to make himself useful from the first day to the last. As soon as he has had breakfast, he goes out with Papa and 'makes his rounds' as he calls it, into the stables and the cowshed and then out to view the farmhands working in the fields. And having helped Papa to run the farm, he might then happen across Aunt Lovisa, sitting on the steps to top and tail berries or shell peas. He goes over to her at once and offers to help, and it is not his fault if Aunt replies that she prefers to do the job herself, but that it will be finished all the sooner if he will sit down for a while and entertain her with tales from the grand parties at the bishop's and county governor's that he has attended over the winter. Having thus speeded Aunt's tasks to their conclusion for a good while, Uncle Schenson goes to find Daniel and Johan and takes them down to Gårdsjö to bathe. And it is a half-hour walk over Åsberget to Gårdsjö. It is up and down and marshy and stony all the way, and who can say whether the boys would have bothered to go if Uncle Schenson had not taken them with him. When he gets back from bathing at around one o'clock, he knows that he has truly earned his midday repast.

After dinner, Uncle Schenson goes down to the office with Papa for a nap and once he has taken his after-dinner rest he has coffee and then he reads aloud to Mama and Aunt and anyone else who wants to listen. And Uncle Schenson is big and fat and bloated and he reads slowly and often has to clear his throat and reading aloud seems to be a real effort for him, but he really does not want to be a burden to us and is determined to make himself useful.

After the reading Uncle Schenson has his brandy and water and then he generally goes out for a walk with Anna and Gerda and me and any other young girls who are visiting. Uncle Schenson does not come out for walks with us because he enjoys it, but because he wants to be useful and make sure we do not get close to any savage bulls or cows grazing in the meadows. We know that Uncle Schenson is quite nervous of anything resembling a bull or cow, so we realise how kind it is of him to come with us.

And on Sundays, when we have not gone to church, and when both we and Uncle Schenson might well think it pleasant to lie on the grass and read a nice book, he makes a point of reading a sermon out loud to us. I am quite sure that this is a sacrifice on his part, but he presumably thinks he should keep us to a little godliness.

If Uncle Schenson was not convinced that he is no trouble to us but makes himself useful from the first day to the last, he would never come to Mårbacka, for Uncle Schenson is so awfully conscientious and tender-hearted.

We always have to be very careful what we talk about when Uncle Schenson is here. We scarcely dare say of anyone that they are ugly or mean or dishonest, because that makes Uncle Schenson indignant on the other person's behalf. 'You cannot say that of your neighbour,' he says, and raises an admonishing finger.

We always say that Uncle should have been a vicar, teaching people to be good. We cannot fathom why he only teaches algebra and Euclid.

If Uncle Schenson is out in the carriage and comes to an uphill stretch, he will always get down to spare the horses. Sometimes both Papa and the stable hand and everyone else will stay aboard, but Uncle Schenson never does.

And if Uncle goes to a party, he always looks around to see if there is some poor spinster lady or widow nobody cares about, and takes the seat beside her. And he always knows what to say to people like that, the old and the poor.

And Uncle Schenson is big and heavy and definitely not at all interested in dancing, but if he is ever at a dance and sees someone left for a long time without a partner, he presents himself to her at once. And he takes a few turns about the floor, waltzing at a slow and cautious pace, and people laugh a little, but they still think it noble of him.

In Karlstad, Uncle Schenson has a small house of his own in a nice riverside location, where he and his family live. We are always welcome to stay there when we have business in Karlstad, and every time we are due to arrive, Uncle is down at the station to meet us, and every time we are due to leave, Uncle comes with us and buys our tickets. And then he gives us half a pound of sweets as a parting gift. He never forgets.

I remember once, when Mama had to take me to Karlstad for a school examination. And we stayed with Uncle Schenson as usual, and we were comfortable in every way, because Uncle Schenson has such a nice, pleasant little home there in Karlstad. And I could really see for myself how kind Uncle Schenson was, because he had his old mother living with him, and she was so old that she could not get up but had to spend all her time in bed. Uncle also had his sister living there, Aunt Matilda Schenson, who ran the household, and two poor cousins, who acted as housemaids for him. And Aunt Matilda and the maids certainly made themselves extremely useful, so perhaps it was not just kindness that prompted him to give them a home, but he also had another family member ...

Uncle Schenson has three children, Ernst and Claës and Alma, and they had their rooms on the upper floor of the little house. And once, as I was going up the stairs to get to Alma's room, I saw a face looking down at me over the banister rail. And it was nobody I knew, nobody I was expecting to see in the house, so I was taken aback. And I saw whoever it was up there raise a fist and threaten me, and the eyes in its unfamiliar face were so wild that I felt as if they were on fire. And a moment later I saw a slim figure vanishing like a shadow into the darkness of the attic.

I was not entirely sure that I had not seen a ghost, and you are not supposed to speak of ghosts at the moment you have seen them, so I said nothing about it until Mama and I were on our way home. And then Mama told me that the figure I had seen was Uncle Schenson's sister, who was not right in the head. She was no threat, said Mama, but she was shy of other people. And I thought how kind-hearted it was of Uncle

Schenson to give a home to his poor sister, who was not right in the head.

And sometimes Mama will tell us a little about Aunt Johanna, who was Uncle Schenson's wife. Mama says she was beautiful, but she was not like other girls.

Grandmother was forever concerned about her. What she liked best of all was driving horses and looking after them, and when she was a child she had a billy-goat that she used to drive all over Filipstad.

And Aunt Johanna was never fearful or shy when she was little, but would strike up conversations with the farmers who had brought their goods to sell in the market square, and sometimes they would let her sit with them when they drove home, way out of town, so Grandfather had to send people out to search the roads for her. And she made friends with all those wild iron hauliers who worked out of Uncle's yard in Filipstad. And Grandmother could hardly be happy to see her daughter on one of their rough sleds in the company of a bunch of tipsy fellows readily sharing out the coarse bread and pork from their food boxes.

It was virtually impossible to get Aunt Johanna into the habit of normal female tasks, but she was all the quicker at helping in Grandfather's shop. 'If only she had been a boy,' says Mama, 'and could have gone into trade and sold syrup and herring, she would no doubt have been rich and happy. But as it was, she caused us nothing but worry.'

Grandfather and Grandmother tried sending her to a boarding school in Södertälje, but it did not work out well. At the school she produced a picture of a Swiss landscape, made of nothing but stones and moss and mirror glass, and admittedly it was very attractive, sighed Mama, and has hung on the wall of the Schensons' house to this very day, but that was the limit of what she learned. The picture was no sooner finished than Aunt Johanna ran away. And it proved impossible to persuade her to go back, because she had discovered that a boarding school was a place where you learned nothing but cheating and lying, and she wanted no part of it.

And once we have heard how bold and plucky Aunt Johanna was, we cannot help feeling surprised that she married Uncle Schenson, who is cautious and solemn and afraid of horse-drawn vehicles and nervous of what he can say about people. We have asked Mama many times how those two came to marry, but Mama has never told us.

We are not certain of anything, but we often say that we simply cannot believe Uncle Schenson and Aunt Johanna were happy in their marriage. They were so unlike one another, when all was said and done. And one thing we definitely do know is that Aunt Johanna carried on driving horses and looking after them, even once she was married.

Uncle Kalle at Gårdsjö has a horse called Fly, which he uses to pull his gig when he goes out on his own, because the horse is so fast and wild that no one else dares to ride with him. Aunt Johanna was certainly the only one who dared entrust herself to Fly, apart from Uncle Kalle, that is.

And on one occasion when Fly had taken Uncle Kalle into Karlstad, Aunt Johanna asked to borrow the horse and gig to go out for a spin. And she invited Aunt Nana Hammargren, who also lived in Karlstad at that time, to join her. But Aunt Nana will never forget that ride as long as she lives. Fly set off at such speed that you could barely see its hooves touch the ground; its eyes were blazing and the chips of ice that it kicked up from the ground flew into their faces like sharp nails. And all the while, Nana thought that Fly was bolting and was convinced she would never get home alive, but Aunt Johanna just sat there with the reins slack in her hand – for there was no way of reining in Fly, who would simply have jumped out of the shafts – enjoying herself immensely. 'Isn't it glorious, Nana?' she said. 'Fly is my life. Have you ever seen such a horse?'

But as to whether Uncle Schenson and Aunt Johanna were fond of each other and happy together after they married, that is something we have never found out.

This year, on the other hand, we children are wondering whether Uncle Schenson could marry Aunt Lovisa. It certainly seems to us that he has had her in mind for several years now, and now we have learned that his old mother has died and one of his cousins is going to America, so perhaps he thinks he will have a little more space at home and be better able to afford to marry.

We have our suspicions that Aunt Lovisa's thoughts are also turning in that direction. At any rate, she takes more trouble to prepare nice meals for him than ever before. And Aunt Lovisa and Uncle Schenson, they ought to suit one another terribly well. They are both the type who like to have life and merriment around them, while they themselves sit quietly. And think how many big parties Aunt Lovisa would be able to arrange! She would get to invite both the bishop and the county governor. And think of all the grand gatherings she would be able to go to! She would never have time any more to sit and brood on sad things.

And think how nice it would be for her to go by the title of 'Mrs' and be permitted to take food at parties at the same time as the older ladies instead of like now, when she has to wait for even the young wives to help themselves first!

And think how attentive and kind Uncle Schenson would be to her, and what a stately pace they would go at when they travelled by carriage, and what steady, sensible old horses they would pick out at the coaching inns!

Aunt Lovisa would have liked a vicar best of all, but Uncle Schenson feels almost like a man of the cloth. He is clean-shaven, and he goes to church every Sunday, and all the clergymen of the diocese treat his house as a refuge when they come in to Karlstad.

We really cannot think of any two people who would be better suited to entering into matrimony together than Uncle Schenson and Aunt Lovisa, and we think Mama and Papa feel the same, and we are awfully curious to see how things will turn out.

And it so happens that Alma Schenson has been at Gårdsjö all summer, but now she has come to spend a few days with us, because she was missing her papa. Alma is only a young girl, no more than eleven years old, but she is so nice and so used to wrangling with boys, for she has two brothers herself, and

Uncle usually has plenty of schoolboys lodging with him, as well. And it is quite remarkable how much all the boys like her, young as she is. They will never leave her alone. Sometimes they are so unkind to her that they make her cry, but it is my belief that they really like her, all the same.

But Alma does not care about the boys at all, she only likes her papa. It is probably because her mama is dead that she has become so terribly fond of him. She likes nothing better than to sit on his knee and stroke his hand. Uncle Schenson does not need to say a word to her. She is content simply to be near him.

And we like our papa too, of course, and say he is the nicest father on earth, but it is still not the same thing.

It is as if Alma would die if she did not have her father's affection.

And if Alma thinks there is anyone her father is fonder of than her, she will be heartbroken, and she will hate that person so much that she wants to kill them.

And I do not think Alma would welcome a stepmother, though not because she would be afraid of the stepmother treating her badly, but because she would be afraid of Uncle Schenson liking the stepmother more than he liked her.

We generally talk to Alma about everything, but we have made no mention to her of Uncle Schenson marrying Aunt Lovisa. We think it would be best for Uncle to tell her about that for himself.

But one day Nursie Maja is in the nursery helping Alma to do her hair, because we are expecting visitors, and Nursie Maja asks Alma how she feels about getting a stepmother.

And Alma starts up out of her seat, pulling her hair out of Nursie Maja's hands, and turns to confront her.

'What are you talking about, Nursie Maja?' she demands, in such a harsh, thick voice. It is not a bit like her normal one.

And this seems to scare Nursie Maja. 'Well, maybe it's nothing. It's just something folk are imagining, I daresay,' she says.

But Alma questions her sternly. 'Is it Aunt Lovisa you are thinking of, Nursie Maja?' she says.

'Well Miss Alma, you could never hope for a nicer stepmother,' says Nursie Maja, trying to coax her back into a good mood.

But it is impossible to put Alma in a good mood now that the question of a stepmother has come up.

She picks up an erasing knife that is lying on the table. It is small and harmless, but Alma waves it in front of Nursie Maja's face as if it were an axe for chopping wood.

'Papa can marry Aunt Lovisa or whoever he likes,' she says, 'but he knows what will happen if he does.'

Alma has such attractive blue eyes with long black eyelashes, they are simply lovely, everyone says so. But at that moment, as Alma stands there brandishing the knife at Nursie Maja, I see something very curious. There is the same look in Alma's eyes as in those of the deranged aunt I saw on the stairs in Karlstad.

'You're not going to stab anybody now, are you, Alma?'

'No-o-oh, I am not,' says Alma, 'but I shall walk into Klarälven river. And Papa knows it.'

And although Alma is only a young girl, we know she is in earnest. And we realise that Uncle Schenson will have to forego marriage. Otherwise, his sweet little daughter would descend into madness like his sister.

So that is what he does. When Anna has returned to Gårdsjö, he becomes a little less obviously polite to Aunt Lovisa, and she no longer makes him as many delicious sweet dishes.

Other than that, everything is just as before, as far as we children can tell.

The Pond

1

And although I am thirteen, I well remember the old duckpond that was at Mårbacka when we were young.

It was small and round, and every summer it was so full of tadpoles that it was a mass of black. Towards autumn it would be overgrown in something green that covered it like a lid, and we were almost glad of it, because at least then we did not have to see the tadpoles.

The water in the old duckpond was so cloudy and muddy that it was no good for rinsing out the laundry, and we could not bathe there, either, because of all the horse-leeches, for if you get a horse-leech on you it will never let go but sucks all the blood out of your body. The housekeeper says they are even more dangerous than the big medicinal leeches she keeps in a water carafe on the kitchen windowsill, ready to bleed anyone who gets a toothache that makes their face swell up.

I cannot remember us ever finding anything to enjoy about the pond in the warmer months, but when it froze in the autumn, it was a different story. We were in such high spirits the morning Nursie Maja told us the ice was safe that we could barely contain ourselves while we pulled our clothes on.

Papa came down in person to bang on the ice with his stick and make sure it could take our weight, so we would not suffer the same fate as King Ring and Ingeborg* on their way to the feast, and we hunted out our old ice skates in the attic storeroom and ran to the stable hand so he could sharpen them and replace any straps that had worn through.

And we were terribly keen on skating when we were young. We did not care that we only had a little pond to skate on. And when it snowed, towards Christmas, we had an awful job to keep our skating rink clear. We kept on sweeping and shovelling, right up until the big Twelfth Night blizzard blew in. Then we had to give in and go tobogganing instead.

And sometimes we heard people remark to Papa that it was strange that such an aesthete as he could be content with the duckpond as it was and did not dig a ditch and drain it. It served no useful purpose, they said, in fact that rank smell coming from it on the hottest summer days could even be harmful. And it was so close to the road that no one coming to visit Mårbacka could avoid seeing it. Even Aunt Lovisa, who otherwise clung to keeping things as they were, would tell Papa that the pond was an eyesore and spoiled the whole farm.

We children were so worried whenever anyone spoke to Papa about getting rid of the duckpond. For we did not care that it was full of tadpoles or did not smell very fresh in summer. All we could think about was our skating. There is not much fun to be had in November and December, let me tell you, so we fervently wanted the pond kept there for us to skate on.

And I cannot remember the course of events very clearly, but certainly a good long time passed before Papa did anything about the duckpond. He finished building the cowshed and he laid out the garden in a different way but he left the pond as it was. And we children thought, of course, that it was for our sakes he had decided not to drain it. There was no one else who derived any pleasure from it, after all.

But eventually one summer Sven in Paris and Magnus Engström set to work down by the duckpond. We were dreadfully downhearted of course, because we realised that Papa had been obliged to give in to Aunt Lovisa and all the other people who wanted to get rid of the pond.

Memoirs of a Child

But we could not really work out what Sven in Paris and Magnus Engström were up to. They carted in rock and gravel and made them into a bank, only not right beside the pond but a little way off. What in the world was that bank for?

It soon became clear that there would be no more skating, anyway, and I remember we would say that it was really bad of Aunt Lovisa to talk Papa into taking out the pond, and that Papa could not be as fond of us as we had previously thought, as he had found it in his heart to rob us of our greatest pleasure.

And we asked Sven in Paris and Magnus Engström what the point was of that big bank of stones they were building, and they said that the point of it was to deal with that sludgy old hole where there was nothing but tadpoles and horse-leeches.

And we could barely bring ourselves to look at the embankment, but against our wills it grew and grew, until it finally seemed to be finished. Then Sven in Paris and Magnus Engström set to work removing a layer of turf from the ground around the pond, and once that was done the ditching and draining would presumably start.

One morning, just after we got up, we saw all the grown-ups making their way down to the duckpond. It was not only Papa, but also Mama and Aunt Lovisa and Uncle Schenson and the housekeeper. We realised at once that they must be about to empty the duckpond and we so disapproved of the whole business that we declared we would not go and join them to view such sorry proceedings. But then our curiosity must have got the better of us, for it was not long before we found ourselves down at the duckpond, watching like everybody else.

And we got there just in time, for on the southerly edge of the duckpond Magnus Engström and Sven in Paris were standing barefoot with their trouser legs pushed up way above their knees, spades raised, ready to break through the banks of the pond. Papa counted: 'One, two, three,' and they started to dig. Their spades flashed until the earth had been shovelled aside and the pond water was flowing out in a little stream.

It purled and bubbled as it ran. We thought it had such a merry look to it but we said that if only the water had known this was the end for the old duckpond, it would not have embarked on its journey with such delight.

It made rapid, roguish advances into the area south of the pond, where the turf had been taken off, filling every little hollow, making a detour round every little rock, but always finding its way forward. Sometimes it stopped, as if exhausted, but reinforcement soon arrived from the pond and it advanced again. Eventually the pond water reached the embankment, and there it had to stop. It could not continue straight ahead, but had to spread sideways along the base of the embankment.

Sven in Paris and Magnus Engström kept on digging. The pond water flowed with greater and greater force. Soon they could abandon their digging, for the water was making its own inroads. Just like a barrel that has sprung a leak on one side, it overtopped the pond all along the southern edge. And many little rivulets found their way to the embankment and began to spread out.

But soon the pace slowed. The water was left in pools and puddles. We children thought that it no longer seemed in such a hurry to leave its old haunts. But then Sven in Paris and Magnus Engström breached the eastern bank of the pond, and then things proceeded faster. We could hardly believe that there was so much water in the duckpond. It spread out to the south and the east over an area that was three times bigger than the old pond, and covered it all.

And we children were so dreadfully stupid. We stood there the whole time feeling upset and angry that it was the end of our old pond and it did not dawn on us.

But finally we realised that the duckpond was not being emptied at all. Instead it was expanding, growing many times larger than it had been before. If it was to be that size, then we would have an awfully big skating rink. It made us quite dizzy to think of it.

We watched and were amazed. We did not want to show any pleasure until we were really sure, but soon we could be in no doubt. Nobody had any intention of draining the pond.

Imagine how happy we were! We had been standing apart from the others, but now we ran to join the grown-ups. We heard Papa explain that he had thought it more advisable to enlarge the pond than to get rid of it. The water in it would be cleaner and better, once it was bigger. They would be able to use it to rinse the laundry, and if there was ever a fire, it would be good to have such a big pond to fetch water from.

And all the grown-ups, Mama and Aunt Lovisa and Uncle Schenson, praised Papa and told him he had made a really successful job of it.

And neither Papa nor anyone else said a word about skating. But we children, we were not deceived. We were completely convinced that it was to give us more room on the ice that Papa had embarked on the whole venture.

And later in the summer, when the visitors – the Hammargrens and the Afzeliuses and Mrs Hedberg and Uncle Kristofer and Aunt Julia – came to Mårbacka, they were so taken aback to see the new lake at Mårbacka which had replaced the old duckpond. And in the mornings Papa would take Uncle Hammargren and Uncle Oriel and Uncle Schenson and Uncle Kristofer down to the lake with him and show them that he had dug a drainage ditch running right through the embankment, with a sluice gate in it that he could close to stop too much water running out. He also took them to the forest and showed them the digging and ditching he had done up there to channel all the forest water down into the pond.

And they thought it was all first-rate, of course, and above all they praised the big stone drainage pipe Papa had installed under the road, so the water from the forest could reach the pond. And Papa was so happy. I do not think he had received as much praise for anything else he had done as he did for those excavations.

And one evening Uncle Schenson and Aunt Hedberg went out for a stroll at dusk and when they came back, they claimed to have seen a strange glow hanging over the pond. It could not have been moonlight, for the moon still had not risen into the heavens, but nor was it a reflection of the sunset, because a large cloud was covering the sun that evening. And even though the evening meal was on the table, all the visitors, and Papa of course, went rushing off to the pond to see the glow.

When they came back, some said it was probably the glint of an anchovy tin that was lying at the bottom of the pond; others thought it must be luminescence in some decaying wood that had somehow been thrown into the water, but Mrs Hedberg was unwilling to accept either of those explanations. She insisted that what she had seen was a bluish phosphorescent shimmer, rising out of the water, and that it was quite plainly supernatural and mystical.

And we children were down at the lake as well, but we could not see anything the least bit remarkable. We were almost inclined to think that Mrs Hedberg had invented it all.

But the grown-ups derived an awful lot of entertainment from the mysterious shimmer. Every evening they went in solemn procession down to the pond to look at the phosphorescent glow shining up from the water. And some saw it, and others did not, and there were endless discussions. In the end, Uncle Oriel proposed that the new lake at Mårbacka be called Phosphorescence, and everyone was in agreement.

And this peculiar glow coming from the Mårbacka pond became the talk of the whole district, and when Papa's birthday came and cantor Melanoz was called upon as usual to pen verses in Papa's honour, the pond featured there, too.

It was a long poem, sung to the same tune as Mrs Lenngren's 'I recall the lovely time'*. It was Messrs Schullström and Gustav Asker and Mrs Jacobsson, sister to Messrs Schullström, who performed it, and it was so excellently moving and witty but I cannot remember any of it except the lines about the pond:

> Such love of beauty is needed indeed
> to make a lake so pleasant.
> Now let this bog once choked with weed
> be famed as Phosphorescence.

2

After that I cannot remember anything of note happening to the pond until the following spring.

But then Nursie Maja came into the nursery one morning and announced that Mårbacka lake had gone and the old duckpond was back. She would say no more but told us to go and see for ourselves as soon as we were dressed and could go out.

And we had felt so superior, of course, about having a lake at Mårbacka like they do at Gårdsjö and Herrestad, so we positively threw ourselves into our clothes and ran out. And then we saw with our own eyes that Nursie Maja had told the truth.

It was right in the middle of the spring gales, you see, and just the day before, the ice had melted on Mårbacka lake. We had never seen it looking as splendid as when it has thrown off its covering of ice. The water came right up to the top of its banks, and there were real waves. Volumes of water were flowing down into it from the forest and the sluice gate had let through, so much that we were almost tempted to move the water-driven hammer there, the wooden one Johan had made for us, which we normally had in the stream where they did the laundry.

But it must have poured with rain overnight, and the pond had got so full that it burst through the embankment that Sven in Paris and Magnus Engström had built the previous summer. We were astonished to see that the water had had the force to take big rocks with it and throw them down in the field. It had carried the gravel even further and some little willow saplings that Papa had planted on the embankment were no doubt on their way down to Lake Fryken.

It was a real scene of destruction. The whole area that had been covered by the majestic swell was now bare ground. There was nothing left but mud and a few puddles of water. The only thing left intact was the old duckpond.

There it lay, just as small and round as ever, within its secure old margins. It was neither larger nor smaller than before, but we had the distinct impression it was looking a little bit smug, confident that it would now be back in favour.

But of course it was impossible for Papa to let everything go back to how it was before. After all, he had won more plaudits for his improvements than he ever had for any of his other projects. The cantor had written verses about it, the wider family had taken an interest and Mrs Hedberg had seen that strange bluish glow hovering above the water of the pond. He was pretty much obliged to rebuild the embankment. Nothing less than the honour of the farm was at stake.

And although there was all the spring farm work to be done, Papa could not make his peace with starting it until he had repaired the embankment. That meant carting rocks and clay and gravel to the pond and levering, mortaring and filling instead of harrowing and sowing. And Lars in London and Magnus in Vienna, they shook their heads at these new orders, but old Per in Berlin, who was a Finn and understood the secrets of nature, he said straight out that it would all be wasted effort, for it was clear that there were those living in the old pond who really wanted to keep it as it was, the way that had been familiar to them since time immemorial.

But the embankment was built, and topped with turf, not just gravel like the last one. And it was planted with two rows of little willow saplings, which would send their long roots down between the rocks and stones and help to hold them together.

And it was a sturdy piece of work, and it only took a few showers of rain to refill the pond with water, and when the visitors came in August, the lake at Mårbacka glittered and shone just like the previous year. The only difference was that Mrs Hedberg could not detect any bluish phosphorescent glow above the water. It must have been washed away in the great spring destruction.

The next year, Papa was terribly careful when the time came for the ice to thaw. He walked along the embankment every day to check whether there were any cracks where water could seep out. And whenever a single drop of water appeared on the outer side, he summoned labourers to reinforce the embankment with stone and clay and gravel.

And if it rained one night, Papa got out of bed and went down to the pond to keep watch there, in case anything happened.

And the whole household was in such a state of anxiety about the pond. Nobody could stop worrying until summer came and all the spring storms and gales were over.

I am quite sure there were little cracks in the embankment every spring, so it had to be shored up and repaired, but it was not entirely washed away until the year Papa slept in damp sheets and went down with pneumonia.

Mama did not have time then for thinking about the pond and patching up the cracks. And the ice melted so early that year, and it was Easter, and things were not at all easy.

The stable hand came to the door late on Easter eve to report that the water had started seeping out under the embankment and Mama said that that was a calamity, and he should try to find somebody to help us.

But this was impossible, of course, because it was Easter, and every home had made sure to lay in some schnapps, and nobody really cared about that pond, which was artificial, after all, and had only existed on the farm for a couple of years.

And the result was that the water was left alone to wreak its havoc for all of Easter Day, and the next morning the whole embankment was strewn about the field just like the last time. And the whole bottom of the lake was bare ground, except for the old duckpond. It squatted there within its banks, as round and secure as ever, winking and glittering as if it was delighted to be king of the castle once again.

But when Papa was well enough to get up and heard that the embankment had come to grief once again, he was so downcast that we almost thought illness would reclaim him. The first thing he did once he was able to take charge of the farm again was to have the embankment built for the third time.

He was definitely not best pleased that he was obliged to attend to the embankment once more. There were many urgent spring farming tasks to be done and our workers were exhausted by constant labour on the pond, which had no useful function at all. But there was nothing else they could do, for Papa said that the honour of the farm demanded that the Mårbacka lake be maintained. It was quite impossible for Papa, after all the praise that had been heaped upon him, to go back to the old duckpond.

And who should turn up just as all the day-labourers were toiling with rocks and stones down by the pond but Uncle Wachenfeldt! He had somehow heard about Papa's illness and had come to enquire how he was.

Uncle Wachenfeldt pulled up his horse when he saw work in progress on the new embankment, and shook his head. Then he drove on to the foot of the front steps and addressed Papa before he had even climbed down from his cariole: 'If you carry on filling your embankment in that fashion, Erik Gustav, you will find yourself rebuilding it every single year.'

'Is that right, Wachenfeldt?' replied Papa. 'Hah, you always know best, don't you?'

'You will never get it to hold if you carry on using loose gravel,' said Uncle Wachenfeldt. 'You need to put it into bags, like they do when they build defences in wartime.'

Well, Papa followed his advice anyway, and ever since then, the embankment has held firm. And we are all so glad about that, because spring was always such a dreadfully anxious time while we were waiting for it to break.

3

Soon after Papa had secured the embankment, he went to Strömstad, and no doubt his thoughts kept returning to his pond at home all the time he was down by the sea. He probably thought of all the ways it fell short in comparison with Kattegat. At any rate, he had not long been home before he embarked on more improvements.

He again planted out two rows of willow saplings on either side of the embankment and had a little gravel path laid between them, so there would be a waterside promenade just like the one at Laholmen in Strömstad. And he told us children that once the willows had grown, he would build a pavilion in the south-east corner of the pond, because that was where it was most attractive. And when he was old, he wanted to sit in that pavilion in August, when the moon shines, and see the trees he had planted reflected in the water.

And I do feel sorry for Papa, because those willows grew, right enough, but everything else he tried to do to make the pond beautiful and special was dogged by bad luck.

And when Daniel and Johan are at home over the summer, Daniel spends a lot of his time helping Aunt Lovisa with her flowers. He enjoys watering and weeding like a proper gardener, and Aunt is so glad of all the help he gives her. But Johan is more interested in carpentry and wood turning. And when Papa came home from Strömstad, Johan suggested that he could make some kind of boat to use on the pond. And Papa had been out sailing every day in Strömstad, and he felt that the Mårbacka lake was lagging too far behind Kattegat, for as long as it remained without some rowing boat or other craft, so he immediately gave Johan permission to attempt it.

And the first thing Johan produced was a little raft, two ells square, and he fixed four empty beer kegs beneath it to keep it afloat and make it fit to carry a really heavy load. Then Johan added a steamboat engine made from an old spinning wheel and an old stove damper. And the damper was positioned under the raft and would act as a propellor, and the spinning wheel would be fixed on top of the raft and Johan would stand at it and turn it. And the moment he turned the wheel, the propellor would start to rotate down in the water, and the raft would speed off across the water, so that Johan could cross from one side of the pond to the other, whenever he wished.

And we were all so pleased with Johan's invention and thought what good fortune he would enjoy in being able to travel about the pond on his raft, and we wondered whether he was going to be a new John Ericsson*. But there must have been some error in Johan's calculations, for however hard he spun the wheel, he could not make the raft move. And that was the end of that.

But down there in Strömstad there were many other things active on the water beyond boats and ships. There were also mallards and eider ducks, and on that score, Papa thought he could mount some competition. So he sent for some geese from a place in Västergötland, and one day seven young birds were delivered to the jetty at Herrestad, and the stable hand had to go and collect them.

And everyone said what splendid geese they were. They were not at all small, but almost full-grown, and Aunt Lovisa thought it was nice to have geese back at the farm, as there were in her parents' day, and the housekeeper told the story of that gander that flew away with all the wild geese* one spring when Mrs Raklitz ruled the roost at Mårbacka, and returned in the autumn with a wife and nine fully grown offspring. We children were not very satisfied with the geese because they were not white but grey or grey-speckled, but the grown-ups said they were no less good for all that.

The geese were to be kept closed up in their pen in the cowshed for a week, so they could get used to their new home and would not run away and get lost once they were let out, but on the eighth day they would be allowed out for some exercise. And they were gentle and well-behaved, they did not run after us and peck at our skirts the way geese generally do, but as soon as they were let out, they went to the nearest field and grazed the grass, as if they were cows or sheep.

We children yearned to see them swimming in the pond, but it was a long way from the cowshed to the pond, so Papa thought that on their first day, the geese should stay down near the cowshed, so they could get used to their surroundings. The next day, said Papa, we would be able to let them out for a swim in Mårbacka lake.

But there is also a little pond in the area in the yard in front of the cowshed, for the cows to drink from when they come home from grazing, and we were so impatient to see the geese from Västergötland swim that we were bold enough to drive them over to the little pond. And we had always thought that geese would be happy to see the tiniest little pool of water and would flop down into it at once, but these geese simply would not go into the cowshed pond. So we concluded that they must be so refined and spoilt that a dirty cowshed pond was not good enough for them. Things would go better on the morrow, when they could swim in nice, clean water.

And the next day we drove the geese up towards the house, to the proper pond. But those fine Västgötland geese did not seem to understand how much better it was than the cowshed pond. They went up to the edge of it and quacked and pulled at the grass, they walked round the whole lake, but did not look at the water. They did not so much as dip their beaks in it to take a drink.

And Uncle Schenson said that the Västgötland geese must have grown up on a farm where there was no open water. They had not learned to swim when they were little. They had no idea that they were water birds.

We tried to accustom them to the water by throwing seed and breadcrumbs into the pond so that they would swim out and get them, but they just tried to get away. They were more scared of the water than our hen turkeys.

And I remember that we once surrounded the geese, all the girls and boys there were at Mårbacka, and drove them down towards the pond. And when they got to the water and saw that there was no escape, they stretched their little wings and flew in mortal dread across the pond to the other bank. And I am sure they felt very fortunate to have saved themselves from drowning, because swimming was completely beyond them.

So it is fair to say that Papa was unlucky with his plans for enhancing the pond and that there was good reason to feel sorry for him.

But Papa is not the kind to give in that easily.

He must have thought that as he could not get any boats, or any geese to swim on the surface of his pond, he might have better luck creating life and movement down below.

He therefore arranged with some young lads who lived over by Gårdsjö lake to catch some live baby fish for him. And every Sunday, when the boys were off school, they came over to Mårbacka with big jars full of little roach and perch. Papa released them all into the pond, and then we children and Papa spent the whole week throwing breadcrumbs to the fish.

But it was so curious that despite Papa releasing so many little fish into the pond each Sunday, nothing was to be seen of them.

They never came up to top of the water, and never made little leaps out of the pond to catch mosquitos the way fish usually do at dusk. They simply vanished. But they could not be dead, either, for they would have floated up to the surface in that case.

So Papa worked out that they must be making their escape through the drainage ditch, so he put in a kind of grille, which would allow the water to keep flowing, but keep the fish inside.

The next Sunday, when the boys from Högbergssäter brought their roach and perch, the grille was in place and Papa was sure he would be able to keep his fish. But his pleasure was short-lived, for the next morning the surface of the pond was covered in little dead fish. They were a sorry sight, floating there so pale and bloated with their bellies sticking up in the air. And thinking of them the evening before, flicking their little fins and swimming about, so hale and merry, it was almost enough to make you weep.

And we children said to each other that Papa would surely have to give in. It was obvious now that we could not have fish in the pond.

But a few days later we heard Papa asking Sven in Paris, who had ranged about these forests all his life, if he knew of any tarn where there were carp.

Sven in Paris scratched his head and racked his brains, and finally he said that when he was a little boy, he and his father had once caught carp in a faraway tarn, up in the Gårdsjö hills. 'We dint catch 'em with hooks, though,' he said. 'We put in a kneading trough wi' a layer o' dough in the bottom, and the minute we let it down into the water it was brimful o' fish. They were big and fine and shone like gold, but they weren't worth the eating. When we got 'em home, Ma scarce wanted to cook 'em. She said they only tasted of mud, and she wasn't far wrong.'

But the following Sunday, Papa sent Sven in Paris to that faraway tarn in the Gårdsjö hills to fish carp for him. And he did indeed take with him a kneading trough, a lump of dough and a brass pot to carry the fish in.

And it was all undertaken with a kind of secrecy. I do not think either Mama or Aunt Lovisa knew what errand Sven had been sent on. We children were the only ones who knew.

We hung about waiting for the whole of Sunday, but there was no sign of Sven in Paris. We thought he had not been able to find the carp tarn, and had given up the whole venture and gone back home.

On Monday, Sven in Paris came to the farm at five in the morning as usual, and he went to the cowshed and helped the dairymaid to rub down the cows and let them out to pasture. He said not a word about carp to anyone.

Once Papa had finished breakfast he went down to the cowshed, and there he immediately ran into Sven in Paris who came along, pulling a barrow.

'Well then, Sven,' said Papa, 'did you find the carp tarn?'

'I did 'n' all,' said Sven in Paris, 'though I had to run round the forest all day Sunday.'

'But didn't you get any carp, then?'

'I dint get any worth having. It was only small fry as come into the tray to eat dough. The big 'uns must've been asleep at the bottom of the tarn.'

'So you didn't bother bringing them with you?' said Papa.

'Nope, they were nothin' worth bringin' along.'

'But what about the brass pot and the bread tray?'

'I put 'em in the hands' quarters when I come by this mornin'.'

And I am sure Papa must have felt that he was attended by remarkably bad luck, but he remained as calm as usual. He gave Sven in Paris a *riksdaler* for his trouble and asked us children to go down to the hands' quarters to collect the brass pot and kneading tray and take them to the kitchen.

But when we got to the hands' quarters and found the brass pot, it turned out to be full of water, and swimming around in the water were lots of little yellow fish, the prettiest you could possibly see.

We dashed off to Papa as fast as our legs would carry us and showed him the fish, and he was so happy and said they were proper carp. Why Sven in Paris had not admitted to having brought them was beyond us all, but he always had a strange way about him, Papa said.

We released the carp into the pond, and Papa and we children were the only ones who knew they were there, for Papa had asked us not to tell anyone. 'We shall see how it goes, first,' he said.

The grille was across the drain, so the young carp could not swim out, but we were very worried that they might meet the same fate as the perch and roach from Gårdsjö lake. But none of the carp were floating dead on the pond the next morning.

A couple of times a week, Papa would take us up to the storehouse and we would fill our aprons with rye, which we had to throw into the pond as food for the carp. We never caught sight of any of them and we were almost sure they had managed to escape somehow, but we still did as Papa bade us, of course.

Sometimes when we were all having dinner, Papa would happen to get annoyed that we had nothing but meat and bacon, day after day.

'You must bear in mind that Schenson lives in Karlstad,' he would say to Aunt Lovisa on those occasions. 'He lives only a stone's throw from the River Klarälv and is used to eating fish every day.'

Papa only said that because fish was his own favourite food, but Uncle Schenson was anxious that Aunt might think he was dissatisfied with the Mårbacka fare, and tried to make light of the matter.

'I suppose we will have to wait to dine on fish until we can catch them in Mårbacka lake,' he said.

Papa fell silent at that, for he did not want either our aunt or Uncle Schenson to know anything about the carp.

But we were expected to keep on throwing rye into the pond until it finally froze over. And once it was frozen, Papa would come out onto the ice every day and make sure an airhole was kept open, so the carp could breathe.

When winter was over and summer returned, we had to start going up to the storehouse with Papa again to get our aprons filled with rye that we were to throw into the pond. And that is how we have gone on for several years now. We never see so much as a fishtail, and we think it is a real shame to waste so much good rye to no purpose whatsoever, but we do it anyway.

4

Just think, it is Papa's birthday and we have no idea what to do! Jansson, who has been down to the jetty to fetch the salmon we ordered from Karlstad, has come back to tell us that the steamer has brought no fish.

The housekeeper and Aunt Lovisa, and Mama too, are quite beside themselves. They are at such a loss that they are obliged to go out to Papa, who is sitting on the steps with Uncle Schenson, and tell them what trouble we are in.

'How can we hold a party for up to a hundred people,' says Aunt Lovisa, 'when we have no salmon?'

'Do you not think it would be best to send to Gårdsjö and ask them to bring some pike from the fish cage?' suggests Mama.

'Yes, perhaps there is nothing else to be done,' says Aunt Lovisa, 'but it is simply a disgrace that we have nothing to put in front of people but a couple of starved fish-cage pike.'

'Well, some fish from Mårbacka lake would certainly not come amiss now,' says Uncle Schenson.

And when Papa hears this, he simply cannot contain himself any longer. He thinks the moment has come to reveal his secret.

'Do not worry, Lovisa!' he says. 'There will be fish for supper here, and we shall have it for you within the hour.'

Then Papa puts on his hat and goes to find Daniel and Johan and sends them over to Halla with a message for Pastor Lindegren. And we know, of course, that Pastor Lindegren thoroughly enjoys fishing and that the boys have been out on long fishing trips with him several times, but we cannot really see how that will help us in our current predicament. He certainly will not have a fishing line set out today. It will be impossible for him to get any fish before tomorrow morning, and the party will be over by then.

But a little while later we see Pastor Lindegren and the boys walking along the road. The boys are struggling with a heavy bundle of drift net and Pastor Lindegren is carrying quite a big bag net over his shoulder.

And they come down towards us and stop by the pond.

Then we all hurry over there, those of us who live here and all our visitors too: the Hammargrens and Afzeliuses and Mrs Hedberg and all the cousins, who have come to celebrate Papa's birthday.

Uncle Lindegren stands out on the little jetty in the northeast corner that they use for washing the clothes, and lowers his net into the water. He moves it cautiously back and forth, but when he lifts it out it is completely empty.

And then all the guests say, of course, that this is what they expected. What fish could you expect to find in a pond? 'Nothing lives in here but frogs,' says Uncle Schenson.

But Pastor Lindegren does not give up. He unfurls the bunched-up drift net and Johan and Daniel take off their shoes and wade with it from one side of the pond to the other. Then they lower it in and drag it some distance across the bottom of the lake.

And all at once, the water comes to life. It bubbles as if it has come to the boil, and there is splashing, as if large bodies were darting to and fro in the depths, and suddenly a big, shiny, golden-yellow fish throws itself up into the air.

This makes Pastor Lindgren so eager that he can hardly control himself. He shouts out to Daniel and Johan, and they raise the net above the surface. And there is a whole row of shimmering gold fish hanging in its mesh, glinting and sparkling in the sunlight. It is as if they have fished up nuggets of gold.

'What do you say now, Schenson?' asks Papa. 'I think those frogs are going to prove good enough to eat.'

And Pastor Lindegren stands there so noble and proud, but there is someone beaming even more broadly, and that is my papa. At last he has redress for much humiliation and many spiteful remarks. Now he can once again hear himself congratulated and lauded, just as he did when the pond was newly dug and went by the name of Phosphorescence.

But Aunt Nana Hammargren and Aunt Georgina Afzelius are standing a little apart from the others, talking as the carp are taken out of the net. They must not have noticed me there close beside them. Or perhaps they think a little girl like me does not understand anything, because that is how the grown-ups always think.

'You know what, Georgina,' says Aunt Nana, 'I do not like this. It always used to be the case, that when we came to Mårbacka, Gustav was always keen to show us all his improvements and works. When he had bought more land to extend the property or erected new buildings or laid out the garden or planted oaks and Lombardy poplars. In those days there was always something useful or attractive to admire, but now all we ever hear about is that tedious pond.'

'I must tell you, Nana,' replies Aunt Georgina, 'that Louise is very worried about Gustav. "He is not well," she says. "He has not been well since he had that bad case of pneumonia, three years ago."'

'Yes, and you know what, his hair has gone grey at a remarkable speed,' says Aunt Nana meditatively.

'And he has lost weight.'

'But what has his illness got to do with the pond?'

'Well, you see, Louise thinks Gustav is no longer able to do anything properly. But he presumably wants some project to keep him busy, so he can convince himself he is getting things done, and that is where this pond comes in.'

'My poor brother!' says Aunt Nana.

It is very unfortunate indeed that I happen to hear this on the seventeenth of August, the very day when we always have such a lovely time. My heart aches and causes me so much pain. It will most assuredly ache for the rest of my life.

Agrippa Prästberg

And now they are dancing in the dining room, but my heart is aching so badly after what I heard that morning that I would not want to dance, even if someone were to ask me. I take myself out to the front porch instead, where the old gentlemen are sitting at a big, round table with their steaming glasses of toddy in front of them, and listen to them telling stories.

I do not know how they come to be talking of that old reprobate Agrippa Prästberg, who comes here every spring to mend the kitchen clock. I enjoy it much more when they tell tales of the notable people who lived in their youth, but now that the subject of Prästberg has come up, I do not doubt that they will spend a good long time on him.

It is peculiar, the way all gentleman are so taken with Agrippa Prästberg. He scares me whenever I see him, for he has a big nose that is crooked in three places and his beard sticks out like a brush, and he has luridly yellow eyes. He never says a kind or polite word to a single soul but just rants and swears, wherever he goes. To me he seems like an old wolf.

Prästberg claims to have been a drummer with the Värmland Rifle Corps, and Papa must see him as a former comrade-in-arms, and always indulges him. Papa surely knows as well as the rest of us that Prästberg has no idea how to mend clocks, but he lets him stay for several days, even so, and fiddle about with the kitchen clock.

And the thing is, Aunt Lovisa will never let him handle the clock in her room and Mama has told him expressly that he must not so much as glance at the new clock in the dining room, but as for the kitchen clock, he has already broken that, and it will not go any more and has stopped once and for all. And when Prästberg turns up in the spring and asks for work, Papa lets him have another try at the kitchen clock. He takes it to pieces, greases the parts with neat's-foot oil, files and hammers the wheels and puts it back together again. He makes this operation last at least three days, and in the process creates a huge mess in the kitchen with all his tools and grease, and makes life absolutely intolerable for the housekeeper and maids. When he has finally finished and hung the clock back on the wall, the pendulum generally swings for as long as it takes Prästberg to get back up to the road and then it stops, and nobody touches it until Prästberg appears to mend it again the next spring.

But it is not only Papa who likes Prästberg. It is plain how eager all the gentlemen in Östra Ämtervik are to tell tales of him to Uncle Oriel and Uncle Hammargren and the other visitors, who have never heard of him before.

But they only tell the usual old Prästberg stories that I have heard a thousand times.

There was a time when Prästberg was living in a little cottage down by Östra Ämtervik church, but he mistreated his wife so badly that people there thought he was going to kill her. And it was worst of all at Christmas, with schnapps to hand at every turn. One year, Messrs Schullström, whose shop was right next to Prästberg's cottage, took pity on the poor old woman and wanted to make sure she had a peaceful Christmas for once. On Christmas Eve they sent for Prästberg and presented him with a thick letter bearing a big seal, with a feather stuck under the seal, and told him that an express letter had arrived and that he, as a servant of the Crown, would have to take it down to Captain Belfrage in Karlstad. So Prästberg set off for Karlstad, ploughing on day and night in worsening weather, and he was not back until the third day of Christmas. But by then he had found out that the letter contained nothing but straw and sawdust, and he was so mortified at letting himself be duped by Messrs Schullström that he would no longer stay in Östra Ämtervik. So then his main haunt became Sunne, where he hung about the small shops and ran errands for the shopkeepers when it suited him.

Another topic of conversation for the Östra Ämtervik gentlemen is the peculiar living quarters that Prästberg has devised for himself. He had the notion of begging semi-rotted logs and planks that were lying around uselessly on farms, and from this collection he fashioned himself a raft, which he launched into Fryken lake. On that raft he then built himself a hut, where he lives every summer. The hut has a floor and a ceiling, a window and a door, and it lacks neither a stove nor a bed, nor a lathe nor a carpentry bench. There is plenty of space around the hut, so Prästberg can sit out there and fish in the lake for his dinner. He has a flat-bottomed rowing boat tied to the raft, so he can row ashore whenever he wants, and what is more he can move his raft at will, so that when he is tired of living near the eastern shores he can tow it over to the west, and when he is bored with those shores, he can bring his house back to the eastern edge. And once when we were on the steamer to Karlstad, I saw Prästberg's hut in a pretty little bay, and I did not feel at all sorry for him, living out on the water. I thought it looked very nice. I would very much like to have a houseboat like that to live in.

Cantor Melanoz has thought up such a good name for it. He has dubbed it Moses.

And when the gentlemen visitors hear that, they burst out laughing and shake their heads at the cantor.

'Oh Cantor Melanoz!' they exclaim. 'How can a cantor and elementary-school teacher come up with something so ungodly? What will our clerical friends round the table say about that?'

But the cantor does not look the least bit troubled.

'Let me tell you, gentlemen,' he retorts, 'that Prästberg's Moses is a very pretty sight floating there, reflected in the lake. Even the daughter of an Egyptian king might find it appealing. And it is counted among the attractions of the district. Last summer there was a man from *Värmlandstidningen* here, and he did a drawing of it and wrote a long article on the subject.'

'*Skål*, Melanoz!' says Papa. 'Do not let these Stockholm gentlemen do him down. He can stand up for himself! For that is something he is good at.'

And with that he raises his glass in a toast with the cantor, because he likes him enormously and always says that if the fellow had had as much learning in his youth as boys get nowadays, he would have invented a flying machine or made a trip to the moon.

'But as we happen to be talking about Moses,' says the cantor, 'perhaps I could tell you the story of something that happened, let me see, seven or eight years ago?'

Yes, they are very happy for the cantor to tell that tale. And it makes for good listening, because it is a Prästberg story that I have not heard before.

'I do not know how it came about,' says the cantor, 'but all the praise heaped on Moses must have gone to old Agrippa's head, because he decided to stain the raft red. He went round the farms and borrowed reddle and a boiling pan and a brush, and one day he started his preparations. Moses was moored close to Sunne deanery, just below Sundsbro bridge, so everyone who crossed the bridge could see what was going on, and that was probably what he intended.

'Oh, it's *that* story,' says Papa, sounding less than pleased. 'Can't you choose another, Melanoz?'

But the cantor continues, and does not let Papa's question put him off.

'I said just now, that even an Egyptian princess would find Moses attractive, and I have to admit that I have felt very drawn to it myself. But Moses still has its best friends and admirers among the children. As soon as they see it out on the lake, they gather on the shore and cast longing looks in its direction, because they are never allowed on board. And now that Moses was to be painted red, groups of them crowded onto Sundsbro bridge to watch.'

'Come on now, Melanoz, hurry up!' says Papa. 'It is almost time to go out and see the illuminations.'

'But you see, Lieutenant,' the cantor goes on, 'the unfortunate thing was, that just as Prästberg was busy painting, a message arrived from Rydberg, the shopkeeper at Lerbrobacken, sending Prästberg off round the parish to sell fish. It was urgent, for Mr Rystedt had caught so many fish on his lines that morning that he scarcely knew what to do with them, and what with it being a warm day they would soon spoil if they were left too long. And however important it was to get Moses painted, Prästberg did not dare to refuse the shopkeeper, for Rydberg's shop was his principal refuge in the winter time. So he put down his paintbrush, rowed ashore and set off to sell fish.'

'Oh dear!' says Uncle Oriel. 'I hope he chased away the crowds of children first?'

'You may well ask. No, he did not. He probably counted on the children having enough respect for him by then not to dare to touch his property. But of course, now that their treat had been snatched away from them, they were bound to be impatient. They had hoped to see Moses all painted by the evening, but it had come to nothing. And after a while, one ill-starred rascal came up with the suggestion that they should help Prästberg to paint Moses. It was not out of mischief, but simply because they liked Moses and wanted to see it smartened up. And once the idea was in their minds, they wasted no time on further thought but set off into town right away to find themselves some reddle brushes. Some places gave them to the children for nothing, and perhaps they stole them from others, and before long a whole gaggle of them were equipped with brushes. It was easy enough to get a boat and row out to Moses, and then they started their painting.'

And just as the cantor gets to this part of his story, Johan and Daniel and Teodor Hammargren and Ernst Schenson come running past, because it is time for them to start lighting the coloured lanterns, and the dance is over. And a throng of girls and young gentlemen, deprived of their dancing, emerge onto the steps and stand listening to his tale. And I think everyone finds it entertaining except for Papa, who would have preferred the cantor to desist.

'The children's initial intentions were certainly good,' says the cantor. 'They threw themselves body and soul into the painting and Moses was not very large, so they soon got it done. But by the time they had made the hut as red as a rose from the roof to the base, the children had started to find painting such fun that they very much wanted to carry on. There was enough reddle boiled up to cover a two-storey house, and they had the brushes. As anyone knows who has done any painting in their young days, once you get a taste for it, you feel like daubing paint over everything you see.'

'I really think you have made enough excuses for those children now, Melanoz,' says Papa. 'Let us move on.'

'Ah,' says the cantor, 'it may well be that I am making excuses for them, but someone has to, you know. The first thing they painted was the raft the hut stood on, and that was harmless enough. Then they painted the roof and the chimney, and that did not really matter, either. But you see, they were so much in the swing of it by then that they seized on the idea of going into the hut to paint the walls and ceiling and floor, and that overstepped the mark. Reddle is not suitable for the interior of a house because it never really dries properly but continues to come off on other things. And the worst thing was that they were so carried away with painting that they decided to give a coat to the carpentry bench and the bed and the lathe and the chair and the table and all the tools and household utensils. The Lieutenant always likes to claim that I have a weakness for children and try to excuse them as far as I possibly can, but that is not the case here. I am saying that it was very naughty of them and that I feel sorry for Prästberg and would not have wanted to be in his shoes when he came home and saw the mess the youngsters had made.'

'Well then, what did he do?' asked Uncle Oriel, laughing as he did so. 'For shame, imagine coming home and finding your spoons and glasses and cups and bedclothes all smeared with red paint! Those children got a good telling-off from him, I hope?'

'Well, judge advocate*, in fact they did not. Old Greppa was so dispirited when he saw the way his property had been treated that he simply lay down in his rowing boat, which was the only one of his possessions that had not been painted red, and stayed there, unmoving, taking no action at all. But there was someone else who was angry in his stead... Yet I do not know if I am permitted to carry on?'

The cantor falls silent and looks at Papa, and Papa says resentfully, 'Huh, now that you have gone so far, I suppose you might as well tell them everything.'

'Well then,' says the cantor, 'the person who got angry was Lieutenant Lagerlöf at Mårbacka. As soon as he heard what had happened, he decided to go to Sunne to give those young scoundrels a good whipping. Mrs Lagerlöf tried everything she could think of to make him desist. She said that it had happened in Sunne, where he had no authority to speak. She was sure he would be the one to get a whipping, rather than the children. But the Lieutenant considered himself to be an old comrade-in-arms to Prästberg. He felt someone had to come to the poor fellow's defence, and off he went.'

Now it is completely dark outside, and I can see the first lanterns glimmering out of the darkness, as the boys run around, setting them out. And all at once the sky turns such a deep blue, and the tall rowans standing below the circular flowerbed in front of the house look deep black. And it is so quiet, and not at all cold. And the very moment the cantor says it was Papa who went to Sunne to give those children a whipping, I feel my heart aches a little less. For I do not care one jot about Prästberg, but it is still nice that Papa wanted to help him.

'Yes, off he went,' continues the cantor with a smile, 'but it so happened that as he drove past the deanery at Sunne, the dean and Miss Eva were standing outside, having just returned from their morning walk. And the Lieutenant has always liked Professor Fryxell a great deal, so he jumped down from his carriage and went over to bid them a good morning. And they immediately invited him to come in with them and talk awhile. And Professor Fryxell always has so many interesting things to say, and he has known the lieutenant ever since he was a boy, and I would go so far as to say that he has a soft spot for him. So he always feels well disposed when he meets him, and they had many different subjects to talk about. But after an hour had gone by, the lieutenant remembered why he had come to Sunne, and leapt up and said that he had to go.'

And I feel so sorry for Papa, because this is a torment to him. He squirms in his seat. He cannot endure having the cantor give this account of him.

'But Miss Eva Fryxell has noticed that her father Anders is enjoying Lieutenant Lagerlöf's company,' says the cantor, 'and she asks him not to leave them in such haste. Can he not stay to dinner? And when the lieutenant declines and says he has urgent business, she wants to know what it is. And in the end the lieutenant is obliged to tell her all about it. And the professor hears it, too.'

'Oh goodness,' cries Uncle Hammargren. 'He of all people!'

'Yes, you may very well say that,' says the cantor, 'for as I have already told you, the professor is fond of the lieutenant. When he heard the Prästberg story, he took the lieutenant by the hand and led him into his study, where the big desk stands in the middle of the floor and the rest of the room is crammed with books and documents. For my humble part, I can never come into that room without feeling I am in some holy temple and far from all things petty and pitiful, and Lieutenant Lagerlöf undoubtedly felt the same way. And then the professor pulled open one of his desk drawers and showed the lieutenant a big bundle of letters and newspaper articles.

'"Let me show you something, Erik Gustav," he said. "In this drawer I have collected everything that was written about me at the period when I was publishing volumes twenty-one to twenty-nine of my history, the ones on the subject of Karl XII*. They did not stint on the drubbing they gave me, I can tell you. I would almost say that their attacks on me were worse than what the children meted out to Prästberg, because they painted me in a bad light and tarnished my reputation and were aimed at me personally, not just at my boat. My dear Erik Gustav, we have always been friends, to be sure, but you did not come hotfoot to give my assailants a thrashing."

'The professor spoke in a friendly manner, with a glint of mischief in his eye, but one can well understand that the lieutenant felt awkward. He tried to excuse himself by saying that Professor Fryxell was a man who could defend himself.

'The professor laughed at that. "No, Erik Gustav," he said. "That is not how the land lies. The fact of the matter is that we Swedes, you beyond all doubt and I to a certain degree, we like adventurers and daredevils, the likes of Agrippa Prästberg and Karl XII. And that is what impels you to come here and give those offending Sunne youngsters a good hiding. But stop and consider, Erik Gustav! Do you think that man deserves Lieutenant Lagerlöf as his knight and protector? We up here in Sunne view him as a real public nuisance. And you, a man of reputation and competence..."'

Papa can contain himself no longer. 'Watch your step, Melanoz!' he says, rapping the table with his knuckles.

'Yes, yes, Lieutenant,' says the cantor, 'I am almost done. The only part left to tell is what happened afterwards.'

And I think it is just as well that Papa rapped on the table, otherwise the cantor would probably never have stopped talking about Professor Fryxell, because he loves him. And that is no more than right, after all, for Professor Fryxell is the one who helped him so that he, just a boy from a poor farming family, has now become a cantor and elementary-school teacher.

'Well it was plain, of course, that the Lieutenant would have to concede,' went on the cantor. 'He had to promise to stay to dinner, and not only that, but to go home without getting himself into any more scrapes on Prästberg's account. It is not that easy to stand your ground against a giant figure like Professor Fryxell, let me tell you. You cannot avoid feeling small and insignificant when faced with him, even if you generally think yourself a capable fellow. So I can well understand the Lieutenant yielding, but I understand that he must also have had a slight sense of dissatisfaction in the depths of his soul and felt that he had let down his comrade-in-arms. And the professor could not avoid noticing it.'

Then Papa raps on the table again.

'Yes, yes, Lieutenant,' says the cantor. 'There are only a few words left now. Well, after dinner the professor took the lieutenant out into the garden with him, and they descended the broad set of steps that led between the beautiful terraces down to Lake Fryken. And when they reached the lowest terrace, which juts out over the water, what should they see before them but Moses and the little rowing boat with Prästberg lying in it, grieving as he has grieved ever since the day that misfortune befell him? "There you see, what I told you is true," the lieutenant hastens to point out. "He can no longer live in his house."

'"Yes, I see," says the professor. But then he goes right out to the balustrade and looks down onto Moses. "What do you say to this reddle now, my dear Erik Gustav?" he asks.

'For Professor Fryxell is one to keep his eyes peeled, and he sees at once that Moses is not red, but rather streaked with grey. The water of the lake, on the other hand, is red for some distance around.

'So the professor leant out over the balustrade and called out to Prästberg: "Listen, Prästberg!" he said, "did you not put any rye flour in the reddle when you boiled it up the other day?"

'Prästberg was on his feet and standing bolt upright in the boat in a single bound.

'"Well I'm damned," he shouted. "You are right, Professor! I forgot to add any rye flour!"

'He knew as well as anybody that it is vital to mix rye flour into the reddle – otherwise it will not adhere, and just washes off like chalk – but he was no doubt in such a hurry to get Moses painted that it slipped his mind.

'"Now that was a stroke of luck for you, Prästberg," said the professor. "You will be able to move back into your house again soon."

'Then the professor turned to the lieutenant. "Let us first of all go and speak to those two charitable daughters of mine, Louise and Matilda," he said. "They keep track of all the children in the area, and they will soon know who got up to this piece of mischief. And then the culprits can be given the task of scrubbing Moses clean both outside and in, for they do deserve some kind of punishment, and I think this will teach them more than any thrashing. And then Prästberg will get his house back, and you can go home with your duty fully discharged, my dear Erik Gustav.'"

Then Papa raps on the table a third time.

'I know, I know,' says the cantor. 'I am to dispense with the part about you thanking Professor Fryxell, so I will leave my story there.'

And then the cantor stands up, toddy glass in hand.

'Lieutenant Lagerlöf, sir,' he says. 'I think we are all very glad that you went up to Sunne that time to help your old comrade-in-arms. I propose that we give three cheers for Lieutenant Lagerlöf.'

And everyone gives three resounding cheers, and once that is done, we see that the illuminations are ready, with all the coloured lanterns put in place. And the flowers in Aunt Lovisa's beds and borders have become as translucent as flowers of glass, and over in the shrubbery the leaves are tinged with blue and yellowy-white and pink and all manner of colours. And the night is still and warm, and something strangely delicate and fragrant comes flowing through the air to fill our hearts with joy.

And positioned on the sandy path at the bottom of the steps, Schullströmmar and Askar sing:

'Who does not our brother recall?'*

At the Jetty

And we have all come down to the jetty at Herrestad, bringing the covered carriage and the open carriage and a loaded cart, because Uncle Schenson and Ernst and Claës and Alma are leaving for Karlstad, and Uncle Oriel Afzelius and Aunt Georgina and Elin and Allan are leaving for Stockholm.

Just as the carriages were about to depart from Mårbacka, Papa said there was room for a couple of us children to come along for the ride, if we felt like it. And that is how Gerda and I came to join the trip to the jetty. And we did not have very comfortable seats on the way there, but we know that on the journey home we will get a front seat in the open carriage, and that is really why we have come along.

Papa always wants to make sure that the visitors get away in good time when they are catching the steamer. For that reason, we started on the farewell breakfast at nine o'clock, the carriages left at ten, and now, at eleven o'clock, we are here at the jetty.

We can be absolutely sure that we will have to wait here for at least an hour, because the steamer, the *Anders Fryxell*, never gets to the Herrestad jetty until noon. Uncle Schenson and Uncle Oriel were not all that pleased about having to leave so early, but Papa said that you never knew what might happen along the way. The horses could go lame, or the wheel rims could come off, so it was always best to allow plenty of time.

And as soon as we get down to the jetty, we naturally go out to the far end of it and look north for the steamer. But nobody sees the faintest sign of it, and nor do any of us expect to.

Then Aunt Georgina goes over to sit on a flat rock among the trees above the jetty, and Uncle Oriel throws himself down in the moss beside her, stretches out with his hat over his face and tells us not to forget to wake him when the steamer arrives, Uncle Schenson takes a seat on the rock next to Georgina for some conversation, but Aunt does not think much of the idea.

'You know what, Schenson, you might just as well lie down for a nap like Oriel,' she says. 'I shall stay awake and tell you when the steamer is coming.'

Ernst and Claës and Alma and Elin and Allan and Gerda and I, we take a little tour of the grounds at Herrestad. We go and look at Engineer Noreen's lovely pavilion, which is now being left to rot away because the Noreens no longer live at Herrestad, but in a little place near the church, called Eriksberg. We also go to Bear Cavern, and show our cousins the marvellous blackberry bushes, which are the only ones in the district.

We walk as slowly as possible because we know, of course, that we have a whole hour to fill, and we sit down under the spruce tree with branches growing out over Bear Cavern and talk as usual about how it would be if the bear was still down there and tried to climb up to us.

But as we are sitting there, a fellow comes running by and shouts to us that the steamer has already left Sunne. It is just putting in at Rottneros jetty and could be here within half an hour.

So that, of course, makes us run down to the jetty in a hurry. We go right out to the end of it again and spy out for the steamer, and sure enough we think we can see a plume of smoke and something dark, moving towards the land, way up to the north west. And now we are all so pleased and relieved that Papa was eager to send them off in good time, because otherwise they could have arrived too late.

Uncle Oriel and Aunt Georgina and Uncle Schenson look to make sure that they have gathered up all their trunks and cases and baskets, and Aunt Georgina gives instructions as to what each person is to carry when it is time to go aboard. They know, of course, that the boat will not be here for half an hour, but I have to say that things are always a bit unpredictable where the steamer is concerned. Sometimes there are such winds and gales that it cannot put in at Herrestad jetty, and sometimes it has big lighters to pull, so it is delayed and does not get to Fryksta station in time. So that is why everyone is so happy and eager, now that they know it has already got as far as Rottneros.

'It is really good to know that we will soon be underway,' says Uncle Schenson. 'It is probably a little rash to leave the return journey until the last moment like this, but it is so hard to tear oneself away from dear Mårbacka.'

'Is it tomorrow that your school starts again, Schenson?' asks Aunt Georgina.

'Tomorrow at ten,' replies Uncle Schenson. 'I expect you think it strange behaviour on my part, Georgina.'

'That is what I think about all men,' says Aunt Georgina. 'Oriel does just the same thing. He returns to his professional duties in Stockholm the day after tomorrow, and we will not be home until tomorrow evening. If it were me, I would make the journey at least a week in advance. Just think of all the things that might happen!'

'Yes, but now we can see that the boat is coming,' says Uncle Schenson. 'And that is the only unreliable element, after all. Then we have the railway.'

'Yes, let us hope that everything goes well,' says Aunt.

But she definitely remains anxious, because she goes up to the farm steward and addresses him.

'Do you not think the boat seems to be taking a very long time at Rottneros?' she asks.

'You know what, ma'am, I think it'll be there a good while longer yet,' says the steward, and laughs. 'Yesterday there was a bunch of Karlstad gentlemen on the boat, on their way to pay a visit to the estate owner at Rottneros. And who's to say whether they'll have finished their big breakfast by now.'

'The estate owner at Rottneros?' says Aunt quizzically. 'Who is it that owns the place these days?'

'His name's Wall, Gustav Adolf Wall*,' answers the steward, 'a man you can count on in any weather.'

'Oh yes,' says Aunt Georgina, 'I remember now, I heard something about him. But the steamer has to keep to its timetable, surely, even if Mr Wall is giving a farewell breakfast?'

'Ho ho ho,' laughs the steward. 'You clearly haven't had any dealings with Wall, ma'am. If the steamer captain was to dare depart from Rottneros without Wall's guests, that would be the last time he stood on the bridge of the *Anders Fryxell*.'

'Is that so?' says Aunt Georgina. 'Well in that case I think I shall go and sit up in the trees again.'

Aunt goes back up the hill and sits down on the same flat rock as before. Uncle Schenson and Uncle Oriel soon follow her. Ernst and Claës and Elin and Allan stay down at the jetty, but Alma and Gerda and I go to sit on the rocks with the grown-ups.

'I heard you asking the steward who the owner of Rottneros was, Georgina,' says Uncle Schenson. 'It is remarkable to meet someone who does not know all about G.A. Wall.'

'Oh, so you think him that prominent do you, Schenson?'

'Unquestionably the leading man in Värmland,' says Uncle Schenson. 'He has given Rottneros works an incredible shake-up. New constructions every year. And he does not only think about the practical benefits. They say the house has been renovated too, and looks fit for a prince. And the garden and park are excellently maintained, as well. I have often thought of going there while I was at Mårbacka, but it cannot be done, because the two families are not on socialising terms.'

Uncle Oriel has been silent ever since we left home, but now he puts in a few words.

'It is quite right of Lagerlöf not to socialise with G.A. Wall.'

'Naturally they do not have the same level of wealth,' says Uncle Schenson, 'but Wall is certainly not arrogant, despite that.'

'That confounded rogue!' says Uncle Oriel. 'Bankrupt within five years!'*

'But Oriel!' objects Uncle Schenson. 'He was wealthy even before the war, and they say that these current excellent booms in business have made him terribly rich. He is buying up all the old working estates and properties in the whole of Sunne. I have been told that he already owns Lövstaholm, Bada, Torsby, Kristinefors, Stöpafors and Öjervik.'

Uncle Oriel is lying on the mossy ground with his hat over his eyes. He does not remove it even as he replies. 'Oh, so he's a property speculator as well. Bankrupt within four years!'

'Now listen, Oriel,' says Uncle Schenson, who really does seem to be running out of patience. 'I can assure you that the man is no adventurer. He is said, for example, to be exceptionally considerate to his workers. Just think of this: every working household at Rottneros has a pig and a cow to slaughter in the autumn. And in the famine of 1868, when they were reduced to eating bark bread in some parts of Frykdalen, the smiths at Rottneros could eat their fill of white bread and pork.'

Now Uncle Oriel actually does take off his hat, and props himself up on one elbow.

'Oh, a spendthrift too,' he says. 'Bankrupt within three years!'

And we three children, Alma and Gerda and I, we simply do not know what to make of Uncle Oriel. We know that estate owner Wall is as powerful as if he were in possession of Aladdin's lamp. He only needs to wish for something, and it is his. We think that Uncle Oriel is just trying to provoke Uncle Schenson, because it has to be said that Uncle Oriel, who is so awfully clever, does sometimes like to tease people.

Uncle Schenson will not be cowed, but tries to continue defending G.A. Wall.

'You are forgetting what a reputation that man has,' he says. 'He has been elected a Member of Parliament, you know.'

'A jack of all trades!' exclaims Uncle Oriel. 'Bankrupt within two years!'

'No, Oriel, now you are being too harsh,' says Uncle Schenson. 'People have the highest expectations of him and his abilities. He intends to resuscitate the old project to link the two lakes, Fryken and Vänern, by a canal.'

'Oh, a canal builder, to boot!' cries Uncle Oriel. 'Bankrupt within the year!'

Uncle Schenson makes no reply. He takes out his watch instead.

'It is almost one,' he says. 'I think I shall go down to the jetty to see if the steamer will be here soon.'

Uncle Schenson goes halfway down the hill, but then he turns round.

'Oriel, you have not taken into consideration the fact that if things go as you say, then not only Wall will go under, but the whole of Fryksdalen.'

'Can I help that?' asks Uncle Oriel. 'That is the way things are always bound to go, because people cannot learn to tell the difference between sensible folk and birds of ill omen.'

'But what proof do you have?' persists Uncle Schenson.

'Dear Schenson,' says Uncle Oriel, 'what proof would I need? I am many years older than you, and I have seen more of the world than you or anybody here in Värmland. And I know, see, that when a fellow lays on big breakfasts lasting so long that other people have to sit around waiting for hours, and risk not reaching their destinations in time, then that fellow is getting close to his fall. You mark my words!'

And I cannot really tell whether Uncle Oriel is joking or in earnest, but I cannot get his words out of my head the whole way home.

The Well

We are sitting on the steps up to the verandah at Mårbacka – everyone thinks we ought to start calling it the verandah instead of the porch or the front steps as we have up to now, because that sounds too old-fashioned – and we are saying to each other that it is very dull that Aunt Nana Hammargren cannot tell us an entertaining story this evening, as she usually does. Aunt Nana has stayed a little longer at Mårbacka than the other guests so she can spend some peaceful time with Papa and Mama and Aunt Lovisa, and that is so nice. And we have had glorious weather the whole time she has been here, so we have been able to sit out until eleven in the evening, and she generally sits down on the steps with us children and tells us one tale after another.

And we all think that Aunt Nana has such a remarkably lovely voice. It is impossible not to cry when she tells us a moving story. Aunt Nana is beautiful herself, too, and she is so happy, because she and Uncle Hammargren go so well together and are so fond of each other. We often say it is a shame for Aunt Nana that she has only the three boys and no girl, but she is most certainly perfectly content with things as they are.

And we were sure that Aunt Nana would tell us stories this evening, too, but she suddenly started to feel ill this morning. She was entirely well to start with, but then the post and the newspaper came, and she started to read *Värmlandstidningen*. And she had hardly cast a glance at it before she said she had a very bad headache and wanted to go up to her room and rest for a while. I could not fathom how anyone could get a headache from reading *Värmlandstidningen*, so I went through it from beginning to end, but there was plainly nothing in there except all the usual things.

Since then we have not set eyes on Aunt Nana, so we understand full well that she will not be telling us any stories this evening, and we will have to make our own entertainment.

But then we get a pleasant surprise! Aunt Nana comes out onto the verandah and says she is feeling better. She immediately sits down on the steps with us children, because it is to keep her storytelling promise to us that she has come down, she says.

And it is almost dark, of course, but I do think that Aunt Nana looks pale and her eyes are as red-rimmed as mine were when I went to the ball at Sunne. Yet her voice is even more lovely than usual. And everything she tells us, even the parts that are meant to be funny, sounds curiously moving. And I do not think the story she tells us is anything particularly remarkable, but I find myself having to fight back the tears as I listen.

Aunt Nana's Story

It was in my parents' time that this took place, and it was the middle of summer. The housekeeper, the same Maja Persdotter who still toils here to this day, was sitting in the kitchen, crushing salt in the brass mortar, when a man came in at the door and asked for the regimental paymaster. The housekeeper answered that he was away, which was true, and then the man asked whether he could speak to Mrs Lagerlöf.

'She's not well,' said the housekeeper, and that was true, too, for Mama had had toothache all day and was lying on the sofa in the room off the kitchen with a poultice to ease the pain.

Once the stranger had been informed of that, he should by rights have left, but he did not seem to understand the fact.

He went over to the long seat that stood beneath the kitchen counter, just as it does now, sat down and stretched out his long legs across the floor.

'I wonder whether Missus Lagerlöf is so sick that I couldn't have a word with her, if I was to wait a bit,' he said.

Then the housekeeper asked him what his business was with her master and mistress.

He said he was a well-digger. He had heard tell that there was no good water at Mårbacka, so now he had come to dig a proper well. His name was Germund Germundsson and he claimed that the name was well-known all over Värmland, because he had dug wells at almost all the properties in these parts and found good water, so he knew people remembered him with gratitude.

But the housekeeper at Mårbacka had never heard mention of him or his great fame, and now that she had a chance to examine him more closely, she thought to herself that if she had her way, he would get no work from her employers. He was a massive sort of man and tall, too, but his head was small and very tapered at the top. His eyes were deep-set and sharp, his nose stuck out like the beak of a bird, and his chin was big and powerful. This was an individual she wanted out of the house as soon as possible.

'We've had a whole heap of well-diggers here, in the regimental paymaster's time and before,' she said. 'They pranced around with rowan twigs looking for water on every hillside, but we didn't ever get better drinking water for all that.'

'Poor fools, they were, who didn't know what they were doing,' said the well-digger. 'I'm different. You could at least go in to Mrs Lagerlöf and let her know I'm here, eh?'

But the housekeeper did not want to do that. She knew better than anybody that the water was of poor quality at Mårbacka. They only had one well, and it had water in it all year round, even in the worst droughts, although the water was not really clear, but cloudy and a reddish colour. It could not be used as drinking water, which had to be fetched every day from a spring, a long way from the farm. But she would rather carry drinking water long distances than have anything to do with such a vagrant as Germund Germundsson.

'You needn't think you're going to be let in to see the mistress,' she said. 'She's got toothache and I've just been in to give her a poultice, so I expect she's sleeping now.'

'All right then, s'pose there's nowt else for me to do but wait till she wakes up,' said the well-digger.

So saying, he casually crossed one leg over the other and rested his back against the counter as if to make himself really comfortable. The housekeeper began crushing salt in her mortar again and a good while went by before anyone said a word.

'What are you grinding?' asked the well-digger after a few minutes.

'Salt,' said the housekeeper.

'Ah, so that's why you're so harsh and bitter,' said the stranger.

The housekeeper held her tongue. She did not want to bandy words with some unfamiliar joker, and silence descended on the kitchen again.

But shortly afterwards the kitchen door opened and two maids came in, carrying a tub of water. They had drawn the water from the well, and now as usual they were bringing in the full tub on a carrying pole balanced on their shoulders. It was a heavy burden, and they must have felt it in their backs as they set the tub down on the floor and then lifted it onto its cross-shaped wooden stand.

As soon as the maids had the tub in place, the well-digger got to his feet and went over to look at the water, which was darker and cloudier than usual because it had just been drawn from the well.

'What the devil is this bucket of mud?' he exclaimed, and spat straight into the water.

That was the worst thing he could possibly have done. It was bad enough that he had spoiled the water, so the maids would be obliged to carry in a new tub, but spitting in the water like that, as I'm sure you understand, children, was every bit as bad as trampling on a slice of bread.

The maids were furious, and they bore down on him to drive him out of the kitchen, one wielding the carrying pole and the other the big copper scoop that always hung at the edge of the tub.

'Out with you!' they shouted at him. 'What's your business here anyway? You've no manners or common decency.'

But the man fought back, and there was uproar in the kitchen. And naturally it was not long before the door to the next room opened and Mama appeared in the doorway.

'What in the world are you all doing out here?' she said.

Everything suddenly went quiet. The stranger turned swiftly away from the maids and greeted Mama quite politely.

'It's not as bad as it looks,' he said.

'That brute spat in the water tub,' shrieked the maids.

'I had to make a bit of a rumpus to be sure you'd wake up, missus,' said the well-digger, 'but it'll all be set to rights in no time.'

With that he grasped the handles of the tub, lifted it and carried it with outstretched arms right across the kitchen and into the open air. There he emptied out the tainted water onto the flat rock just beyond the threshold.

Mama and the housekeeper and the two maids looked on without saying a word. They were dumbstruck to see how strong he was.

But there was a better sight to come. Germund Germundsson gripped the water tub by one handle and swung it as easily as one would a beer glass, and bore it down to the well and began filling it with water. When Mama saw this, she sent the cook down with the carrying pole, but he refused any help. He grasped the handles again and carried the full tub in front of him across the stable yard and into the kitchen, and set it down on its stand.

Well, once he had performed such a feat, his honour was restored in everyone's eyes and it was obvious that he would be allowed to dig as many wells at Mårbacka as he had a fancy to. One does not readily turn down a fellow who could have lifted the roof off the house if he had taken it into his head to do so.

As soon as Mama had promised Germund that he could dig the well, he asked her where she wanted it dug.

'Presumably it has to be in a place where there is water in the ground,' said Mama, 'but it would certainly be useful if it could be close to the washhouse, because that is where the most water is needed.'

'If you want the well near the washhouse, Mrs Lagerlöf, then that's where it shall be,' said Germund.

The next day, he did indeed start digging just outside the washhouse. No one had seen him going round with a divining-rod or making any other investigations. It was as if he felt himself to be the master of the veins of water in the ground below and could command them to move in whatever direction he wished.

He did not want any help with the digging itself, but he asked for a couple of boys with wheelbarrows to cart away soil and gravel. He worked at such speed that the boys had never had to labour so hard in all their lives. They had scarcely emptied one barrow before the other was full and waiting to be emptied. He had measured out an area that was at least sixteen ells square, and it was no small task to dig it out. But before evening he had worked his way so far down into the earth that not even his head was visible above the edge of the hole.

Mama always said that during the time Germund was digging the well, she found it hard to sit sewing indoors, because she was terribly interested in seeing whether he found any water. And besides, she found it fascinating to watch him work because she could never have believed that a man could have such strength and stamina.

The well-digger was well satisfied with the ground where he had chosen to dig. He said all the indications were that he would strike a vein of water soon. He had not come across any stones or layers of hard, compacted ground, but had hit dry gravel as soon as he was through the topsoil. And once he got the bottom of the gravel, he would reach the water. He was certain of it.

But the gravel layer was deep and Germund had to carry on digging the next day, too. He could not make such quick progress as he had done on the first day, either. He had to enlist help to build a platform, where a couple of hands could stand and receive all the gravel that Germund flung up to them, and then shovel it out over the edge of the well shaft. Soon, not even that was enough. The shaft was so deep that they had to rig up a hauling system with long ropes and two barrels going up and down in much the same way as when they bring up the ore from mines.

As evening drew in on the third day, Mama was starting to get quite worried. Germund was digging deeper and deeper into the ground, but there was no sign of any water. If she had known that it was going to be such a protracted process, she would certainly not have dared to authorise it on her own initiative. She had hoped to be able to surprise Papa with the water when he came home, but now she was afraid that she would be left shamefaced for having embarked on something that she could not pull off.

One day it rained, and the rain poured in from all sides and down into the shaft. But that was what they call surface water, most definitely not spring water. It had to be bailed out, and it took them a good long time to get the well dry again.

The well-digger laboured on and on. They had to bring the tall fire ladder that was normally propped against the wall of the main house and lower it down into the shaft so that he could climb up and down. Soon even that was not long enough, and they had to lash it together with a couple of other ladders.

And the worst of it all was that they were in the middle of harvest time. The hay was dry and would have to be brought in, and the rye was ripe and would have to be cut. Mama did not know what to do, what with all her day-labourers being fully occupied with work on the well, so that everything else got put off.

She suggested to the well-digger that he might stop, but he would not hear of it. She asked whether he ought to try in a different place, but that was equally badly received. She was at her wits' end with him. She sensed that he would be capable

Memoirs of a Child

of any act of spite whatsoever if he was forced to give up a task that he had grown so attached to.

One day Mama noticed that the rye was starting to turn brown. This was a sign that it was so ripe that the grain would soon be falling from the ears, and there was no time to lose in harvesting the crop.

Papa was not that far away. He was up at the Kymsberg estate in Gräsmark where he was the manager, and Mama could very well have sent for him. But she did not want to do so until it was absolutely necessary. It would have been a blow to her pride, I expect, to be forced to admit that she could not cope on her own.

In the midst of her distress, she had a good idea. She went down to the well-digger and asked him to come up out of his hole so that she could talk to him.

He came up the ladder, so covered in mud and grit that she could barely see what he looked like underneath.

Then Mama told him that the rye had to be cut the next day and asked if he would be prepared to help in that task.

Germund threw his head back, thrust out his chin and gave a slight sneer.

'Well, I've cut rye in my time, sure enough,' he said. 'But I don't rightly think it's proper work for me.'

'But rye is something we all have to live on,' said Mama. 'No matter how much water we get from your well, Germund, it will be no use to us if we have no bread.'

At that the well-digger gave her a pointed look from his dark eyes, but he smiled quite indulgently. He must have found it amusing that a woman dared to tell him the truth.

'Well then, let it be as you wish, ma'am,' he said. 'But I want the longest scythe you've got on the farm and enough binding girls so I don't have to stand about waiting.'

Yes, Mama promised him all that.

In the evening the well-digger inspected all the scythes on the farm. He was so dissatisfied with them that he actually took back his promise to help with the rye harvest. You couldn't offer a grown man scythes like that. They were nothing but children's toys. Mama had to send Little Bengt out in the middle of the night to fetch a smith, who made a scythe that was two ells long.

The next morning, Mama was up at four when the farm folk went to work because she was afraid that Germund would raise further objections. And it was just as well she was on hand, otherwise he would have found a way to wriggle out of the job.

Germund arrived at the same time as the other harvesters, carrying his scythe over his shoulder. He was at the head of the group, of course, and he was the first to start. But once he had swung his scythe a couple of times, he turned round and glared at the binding maids. And the troublesome fellow was finding another excuse to get out of the job.

'What's the meaning of this?' he said. 'Am I only getting two binding girls? I might as well go back to bed in that case.'

'Those are the two best binding girls we have here at Mårbacka,' said Mama, but the well-digger just stood there shrugging his shoulders.

'Ah, if that is the only thing you lack, Germund,' said Mama, 'then I shall get you a binding girl who is accustomed to picking up after two men. Perhaps that will be enough for you.'

'Well yes, mebbe that's the sort I need,' responded Germund.

Mama went home and into the kitchen and asked the housekeeper to show what she was made of and teach that arrogant fellow to have a little respect for the working people of Mårbacka.

And Maja Persdotter, who could keep up with binding the sheaves of two harvesters, set off at once to the rye field, but Germund proved prodigious enough to keep both her and the two other girls fully occupied.

A rye harvest was brought in at Mårbacka that day, the like of which had never been seen before. Because when the other harvesters saw the way Germund was wielding his scythe, they first stopped and stared and then went at the rye as if in a fit of fury, and the stalks fell to the ground as if flattened by torrential rain. They reaped the whole field in a single day.

This was a great relief to Mama, of course. With the rye cut, she thought she could let Germund carry on with the well for a few days more. But it was soon brought home to her that as long as Germund remained at Mårbacka, there would be no end to trouble and anxiety.

On the very day of the rye harvest, an unfamiliar young woman approached the farm. She came up the front steps and into the hall, but then she turned aside into the kitchen.

There she found Mama, because the housekeeper and all the maids were busy with the rye, so it had fallen to Mama to prepare the evening meal.

Mama took one look at her as she opened the door, and wondered what manner of person she could be. She was dressed as a gentlewoman, all right, but the clothes were threadbare and so ill-fitting that it was obvious they had not originally been made for her. She was perhaps around twenty years old, thin and delicate, but at the same time she had the big, rough hands of someone used to physical toil. She was not exactly beautiful, yet nor could she be called ugly, for she had clear, rosy skin and a nice roundness to her cheeks. When Mama wanted to describe her, she always said she was one of those people you do not notice, and find difficult to recognise, until you have seen them many times.

'I would very much like to speak to Mrs Lagerlöf,' said the newcomer.

'Mrs Lagerlöf?' said Mama. 'Well, you have found her.'

Then the girl came closer to her. 'I am Johanna Octopius, daughter of the dean at Brunskog,' she said, and held out her hand to take Mama's.

As Mama shook hands with her, she tried to remember what she knew of Dean Octopius and his family. Mama was a vicar's daughter herself and related to all the other clergymen's families in Värmland, so she thought she ought to know those Octopiuses as she did all the rest.

'Dean Octopius of Brunskog? He is dead, is he not?' asked Mama.

'Oh yes, he certainly is,' replied the girl. 'To my great grief and loss, both Father and Mother died many years ago.'

Now it all came back to Mama. She remembered that Dean Octopius and his wife had died at more or less the same time, leaving behind them a little girl who was said not to be quite like other children. There were no relations who could take the child into their care, so the poor lass was left in the home of their father's successor like some kind of Cinderella. She got her food and some cast-off clothes, and helped out with what she could, although it was not much. She was not an idiot, far from it, but nor could you say she had normal powers of comprehension and sense.

So it was this Johanna Octopius who had now come to Mårbacka, Mama realised at once, but what in the world was she doing there?

Johanna Octopius was not slow in explaining her business. She wanted to ask Mama whether she could stay at Mårbacka for a few days.

'It would not be impossible, I suppose,' said Mama, 'but first I want to know why you wish to stay here with me.'

The poor girl was not remotely self-assertive. She spoke so quietly that her words came out in little more than a whisper. She was shy and unforthcoming, and was probably not at all prepared for a question like that. She just stood there without any idea how to answer. She blushed deeply, and pulled on one of her fingers until its joints made a cracking sound.

'It is not very easy to answer that,' she said. 'I was told to come here.'

'Is there someone here that you want to see?'

The girl looked even more distressed.

'I have never been able to lie,' she said. 'I do not want to answer the question of whether there is someone here that I very much wish to see. But anyway, that is not the reason I am here. I have come because I was bidden, so I would be on hand when I was needed.'

Mama could hear from her answer that the poor girl had a screw loose, and it made her feel very sorry for her. She thought it best to let the girl stay at Mårbacka until there was an opportunity to send her home again. 'All right then, you may stay, Miss Octopius,' said Mama. 'For now, go into this room beside the kitchen and rest, while I prepare the supper! I have neither a housekeeper nor my maids at home today. They are all out binding the rye.'

When Johanna Octopius heard this, she said she was not at all tired, and offered to help prepare the meal.

Mama saw at once that she was doing everything wrong, but she was willing. She brought in wood and made up the fire. She was terribly willing. But she so oversalted the porridge that it was inedible and the whole panful had to be thrown away. And as for the new batch, she let it burn.

When the time reached eight o-clock and the labourers came in to eat, Johanna Octopius was standing by the stove, ladling the burnt porridge into a big bowl. The well-digger came first, and he cursed when he saw her. Johanna Octopius uttered no curse, but she dropped a whole ladle of porridge into the fire, so there was an even more acrid smell of burning than before. They did not exchange greetings, nor say a single other word.

The next day, the housekeeper reported to Mama that the well-digger had told Little Bengt that the vicar's mad daughter had fallen in love with him when he was digging a well at Brunskog vicarage. To start with, he had felt a little flattered that a better sort of person had taken a liking to him, but she soon became so hateful to him that he could not stand the sight of her. Yet still she followed him wherever he went. He started to think that killing her would be the only way to get rid of her.

Well, Mama had suspected at once that there was some kind of love interest behind the mysterious visit, and now that she was sure, she immediately ordered Little Bengt to get ready to drive Miss Octopius home to Brunskog.

Then she informed the girl and tried to explain to her how inappropriately she was behaving. Did she not see how very shameful it was to run after a man who wanted nothing to do with her? Lastly, Mama made it clear that she would have to return home and that there was no point her coming back.

Johanna Octopius made no response at all. She yielded, like the weak reed she was. She took her seat in the cart and let herself be driven away from Mårbacka without offering the least resistance.

But when Little Bengt had gone an old quarter mile or so, a harness peg came loose, and he had to get down and fix it back in place. It was done in an instant, but Johanna Octopius used that moment to jump out of the cart and make off into the forest. She did it so easily and quietly that the farmhand did not notice until she was a long way in among the trees. He certainly ran after her and tried to catch her, but he could not leave the horse for long, and she got away.

Creeping off and disappearing, running away like water between your hands, that was the only thing she had any skill in. She must have been perfecting the art all her life.

Little Bengt had to turn back and go home, and Johanna Octopius did not show up all day. Mama wondered whether she had done herself harm because Mama had spoken so sternly to her, and the thought made her feel quite miserable.

But the next morning the runaway came into the cowshed and asked for milk, which they gave her. The dairymaid surreptitiously sent word to Mama, but when Mama got there to talk to the girl, she had already gone.

The well-digger was in a rage. One side of the well had collapsed, and the whole shaft was filled with gravel. Whenever that Crazy Hanna showed up, things went awry for him. He had never killed anyone in all his life, but if that girl carried on persecuting him, he would have to get rid of her some way or another.

Mama was convinced there was going to be an accident. She had had that feeling ever since Germund first entered her house. She wrote to the dean in Brunskog to ask him to have the girl fetched home, but she got nowhere. Then she tried to catch the girl so she could keep her locked up, but she was on her guard and ran away as soon as she saw anyone. And in any case, Mama could scarcely have compelled her to give up going her own way.

One day Mama saw Johanna Octopius slip across the yard to the well-digger's hole and stand on the edge looking down into the deep shaft. Germund was digging at the bottom, but he must somehow have been aware of her standing there, because he soon emerged at the top of the ladder, shouting and cursing her. She fled at once, as he tried to pelt her with loose stones. He chased her away like some filthy cur. But Johanna Octopius was not to be deterred, and went on sneaking around the farm as before.

And then a morning came. They had by now been through all the accidents that could happen when a well was being dug, and the shaft was so deep that anyone standing at the bottom could see the stars moving across the sky, although it was broad daylight up at ground level.

Yes, to repeat, a morning came when a man charged into the kitchen, all out of breath.

'Water,' he yelled, 'water!' And he ran back out again.

Mama and the housekeeper and all the maids went running out after him, and soon they were all at the edge of the well, peering into the depths. And what did they see down there but the glint of water!

It is a special occasion when you find water at your farm like that. Mama had had a difficult time, after all, and no doubt she had wished more than once that she had never started the excavations, but now that the water had come, she thanked God with all her heart for this great gift.

Then she asked where Germund was.

'He's still down there,' answered one of the men. 'Expect he wants to check if it's a proper vein o' water he's found.'

They called to him, but there was no answer. One of the men was about to climb down to see if anything had happened to the well-digger when he came into view on the bottom ladder.

He climbed very slowly, not at all at his usual speed. He felt around with one hand for each rung of the ladder and kept the other clasped to his eyes.

'He must have got a bit of sand in his eye,' they said to themselves.

When he got to the top of the ladder, he reached out his hand. A couple of men ran forward to help him, but it was virtually impossible to get him onto solid ground. All he had to do was extend one foot and take a step, but he did not dare.

'Dear Germund, we are so pleased that you have found water at last,' said Mama.

'But that water came at a high price, ma'am,' said Germund. 'Summat came at me down there, just as the water broke through. It flew into my eyes like smoke. And now I can't see a thing.'

They finally got him onto firm ground, and he threw himself straight down on the grass, keeping his hands pressed to his eyes. The others stood in silence, waiting. None of them liked him, but it would be terrible if he had lost his sight.

After a while he sat up. 'Still the same darkness,' he said. 'I'm blind. It's all up for me.'

Mama tried to calm him, saying it would soon pass. She thought he had been down in the dark for too long and was not used to the daylight.

'Na-a-ah,' he said, 'It's burning like fire. My eyesight's been burned away. I'm blind. What'll become of me?'

With those words he leapt to his feet, raised his arms in the air and made to throw himself into the well. The men ran up to block his path, but he threw them aside.

'Let me be!' he roared, 'I want to die down there.'

It was awful. The men could not hold him, but in the struggle he had lost his sense of where the well was, so he went in the wrong direction.

He charged round, shouting and cursing. His hands grabbed at the air as if trying to catch someone.

'Show me where the hole is!' he shouted. 'Or I'll squeeze the life out of the first person I get hold of.'

He made all the noise and commotion of a madman. But no one came to any harm because people ran away from him and he, strangely enough, never came anywhere near the shaft.

He threw himself down in the grass once more. His whole body twitched and jerked. His fists clenched, and he broke out in wild threats over and over again.

As he lay there in such a violent rage that no adult man would risk going near him, half-crazed Johanna Octopius came creeping up. She arrived in her usual unobtrusive way. Nobody noticed her until she was right at his side.

Mama wanted to rush over and warn her, but it was too late. She had already laid her hand on his.

'That is enough of your cursing,' said the girl in the same quiet, gentle voice as usual. 'I am here to help you.'

Everyone expected Germund to put his hands round her neck and throttle her. And he did indeed burst into wild and wicked laughter, but he inflicted no harm on her.

'I am here,' she said again. 'There were those who knew this was going to happen, and they have sent me here. I have come into this world for nothing other than to help you.'

There must have been something about her that had a soothing effect. He took her hands and put them over his burning eyes.

'You Crazy Hanna!' he said. 'You Crazy Hanna!'

But it was clear from his tone that it was meant kindly.

'It doesn't matter that you are blind,' she said. 'I have eyes for you.'

He was so helpless and distressed that it felt comforting to know there was someone who was fond of him, whether he was blind or sighted, weak or strong, evil or good, poor or rich.

Mama stayed close by. She was not altogether sure how this would end, but then she heard Germund say:

'Your hand is doing my eyes good.'

Then Mama relaxed. She walked away and gestured to the others to leave them alone, too. She understood, you see, that a great miracle had occurred. Love had not proved misguided. It had been God's intention from the start for the two of them to belong together.

*

Here, Nana falls silent and we thank her so much and say that the good drinking water at Mårbacka definitely deserves its own story.

'You are truly remarkable, Nana,' says Aunt Lovisa, 'for being able to remember so many of Mama's old stories. I certainly recall her saying that the man who dug the well went blind, but as for his name and all those other details, they had completely slipped my mind.'

'Indeed you are remarkable, Nana,' says Papa too. 'But are you sure the girl's name was Octopius? It sounds so peculiar.'

Aunt Nana gives a little laugh. 'You are quite right, Gustav. She had an entirely different name, but I did not want to give her real one, so I invented another.'

'Really? Well yes, that is what they do, those women, the real storytellers.'

'But,' says Mama, 'what made you tell that particular story this evening, Nana? I do not think I have ever heard it before.'

'Oh,' says Aunt Nana, taking her time to answer. 'It is not so easy to explain. I have heard so much talk of the pond these past days, so perhaps that was why...'

Then Elin Laurell puts in a question. 'Do you mean, Mrs Hammargren,' she says, 'that we should always trust love to show the right way? Should we not question or scrutinise, but simply follow?'

Aunt Nana is silent for a long time before she answers.

'Let me just say, Miss Laurell,' she says, 'that I believe it shows us the right way, but it takes great courage to obey it, and that is what we lack.'

And Papa generally stows away all the old copies of *Värmlandstidningen* in the little cupboard at the back of the desk, and the next day he asks me to put away the paper that Aunt was reading just before she got her terrible headache. But as I am folding it up, I see two round blotches on the front page, as if teardrops have landed there and dried. And I think that the newspaper and the headache and the story are all connected somehow, but I cannot work out how. And I am so young that nobody is willing to tell me. I shall simply never know.

At Fair Time

And there has been so much to do, so much to do, ever since Aunt Nana Hammargren left us. There has been the harvesting of the hops, and the killing of the bees*, and the picking of the apples, and the big autumn wash and the crispbread baking, all within in a few days. And we have dipped long wax tapers and brewed small beer and grated potatoes for potato flour and made a whole cask of cider. I hardly know how Aunt Lovisa and the housekeeper and maids have had time for it all, but we children have been in the kitchen to help whenever we have any free time, of course.

There has been sheep slaughtering, too, and we have culled some of the doves, because we have over a hundred of them to feed every day, and we think that is too many. But the day of the dove cull is always so difficult, because it puts Papa in such a bad mood. He knows that we have to keep the numbers down, but he so much enjoys watching the doves. He would much rather the hawks ate them than us.

And everything has to be done in September, because then it is not long until the big Åmbergshed fair that opens in Sunne on the first Friday in October and carries right on into the following week, so all those little tasks have to be out of the way by then. And the whole house also has to be swept and scrubbed, and all the inner windows have to be put up, so that on Fair Eve – which is what we call the day before the fair opens – everything is as spick and span as at Christmas or Easter.

And for me, a Fair Eve like that feels pretty much the most special day of the whole year. It is quiet and peaceful everywhere and there are new rag rugs on the floors and the copper pans and coffee kettles are a burnished red and it is so lovely and warm with double glass in all the windows and everyone is so expectant and good-natured.

Papa has had a lot to get done in September, too. He has had Inspector Nyman here and they have been down in the office, settling the accounts for the whole year. And Papa has brought home big bundles of money from the bank in Karlstad and now, on Fair Eve, he pays all the people who work for him what they are due. Lars in London is the first of all the day-labourers to step into the office, followed by all the others in turn. Then come the farm foreman and the stable hand and the boot boy and the boy who has looked after the sheep in the fields, and after them the housekeeper and housemaids and farm maids, and finally it is the governess's turn to be paid. No, the last of all to come in are us children, and we each get a *riksdaler* to spend the next day at the fair.

And the housekeeper never takes any money. She just asks Papa to put it into her savings account, but the maids come out of the office flushed and beaming with fine new banknotes in their hands and they devote the whole evening to working out what they will be able to buy at the fair. And the most sensible of them ask Mama or Aunt Lovisa for advice, and Nursie Maja confides in Mama that she plans to buy a pair of black gloves to wear when she goes to church. But Mama says she should not do that, because gloves are terribly dear, and she will look smart enough if she buys herself a pair of the black string variety.

And towards evening the road starts to get so busy. It is the fair-goers from far away, farmers from Ransäter and Ullerud, and even from Råda and Ekshärad, who have set off in good time. They are on foot or in their wagons, jostling for position, and they have almost all brought horses or cows or goats or sheep that they want to sell. And that is the most enjoyable part of it. We do not take much notice of the people, because they are simply walking or riding along the road in an ordinary way, but just look, the billy goats and rams and little bullocks and young horses, they seem to find the walk very amusing, and get up to all sorts of mischief.

And we children and Elin Laurell have gone up to the end of the avenue to watch the fair-goers and we have already been standing there for quite a long time when Papa comes to join us. And then things get very interesting, because Papa starts talking to all those passing by. He asks them where they have come from, what they are asking for their livestock, and all manner of things. And one man says that he has a splendid young horse that he thinks the lieutenant ought to buy, and an old woman weeps, telling him that the whole grain crop on her smallholding has been ruined by the frost, so she is obliged to sell this pretty heifer, which she been struggling to keep for two years, to make money to feed herself and her children over the winter.

And the rogues and tricksters come along in their small carts, bringing with them long strings of horses that they hope to exchange at the fair. And their horses look so showy and spirited, but Papa says you should never swap horses with tricksters because they give them something, arsenic perhaps, that makes them look splendid on the first day, but then they fall flat, like a few bits of wood nailed together.

And it is the first time that Elin Laurell has been at Mårbacka at Åmbergshed time, and it so surprises her that we celebrate it as if it were some important festival, but she also finds it very diverting, because she has never experienced anything like it before. And then she says to Papa that it seems remarkable to her to think of fairgoers passing this way for so very many years. And the owners of Mårbacka would have stood here and conversed with them, just as Papa has been doing this evening. 'You know what, Uncle Lagerlöf,' she says, 'it makes me feel as if I have been transported several hundred years back in time.'

'It may well be that it makes you feel that way,' says Papa, 'but let me tell you, Åmbergshed fair is nothing now, compared to how it was in my youth. Back then, an evening like this at Mårbacka would have been like a night at an inn. Kjellin, a dealer from Åmål, husband of my sister Karolina, would come here with several cartloads of wares and stay with us, along with all his stallholders, and they would spend their nights here for as long as the fair lasted, which must have been at least a week. And one after another, acquaintances of my father's would roll up here and ask for lodgings for the night, for they had nowhere to sleep but the carriage they were travelling in. And what was more, there was a sort of association of the gentlemen of Fryksdalen, and its members took it in turns to treat all the travelling gentry to a meal in an old building in the middle of the fairground, which was known as "the Saloon". And I may say that it put Mama to a great deal of trouble when it was her turn to provide the food. Let me tell you that the leading merchants of Karlstad, Filipstad, Kristinehamn and Åmål travelled round to fairs in person in those days, and they expected a generous spread and nothing but the finest. But nowadays, now that we have the blessed general stores, all the enjoyable old ways have gone.'

And we are starting to freeze because we have been fixed to the spot in the avenue for so long, so we turn north and take a little walk to warm ourselves up. And Papa comes with us, because he knows he must not stand about, outside in the autumn chill. And he and Elin Laurell walk along chatting about the old Åmbergshed in all its glory. And he tells little stories, and we have a really good time.

But just as we come to the long, dark hill north of the vicarage, Papa stops.

'That's very odd,' he says. 'Elin, you were just saying how all of us who have lived at Mårbacka must have walked here on an evening like this and talked to the fairgoers. And this very instant I could distinctly see my father, just as I saw him standing on this road one Fair Eve. Although now I come to think about it, it was not Fair Eve, no, but it was a day that had something to do with the fair.'

Papa takes off his hat and rubs his hand across his brow as if to polish up his memory.

'Now I remember how it was,' he says. 'We had come out, Papa and my sister Nana and I, to watch the fairgoers, because it was what he always did, as I do now. But it was not Fair Eve, and it could not have been the first day of the fair, either, because naturally he would have gone into Sunne to make his purchases. No, it must have been the evening of the second day, when a lot of people had finished their business at the fair and were going back home.'

'Did this happen when you were a little boy, Uncle Lagerlöf?' asks Elin Laurell.

'Oh no, I was into my twenties, and so was Nana. I cannot recall why I was at home that autumn. I was normally away on my surveying trips, but I suppose Papa was getting older and needed help with settling the accounts, because his business affairs were much more complex than mine. Anyway, when we had been up at the top of the avenue watching the wayfarers for a while, we started to feel the chill and turned north for a little walk, just as we did today. And Nana was beside Papa, holding his arm. She and he were always such good friends. She was certainly his favourite among all the children.'

'She was quite a beauty, wasn't she?' said Elin Laurell.

'Oh yes, she was. But she was funny and cheerful, too, and the old man so much enjoyed her company. But let me see! Yes, this must have been in the early forties, because Nana was neither married nor engaged. I remember that very clearly, because our parents had told me that they felt concerned for her. The vicar over at Halla was so old that he could no longer perform his duties, so he had taken on a curate, a handsome young man, and now both Papa and Mama thought they could detect him turning his charms on Nana, and her seeming quite partial to him. And the old folk would not have been against such a match in itself, for the curate was a gifted man with good preaching skills, but on more than one occasion they had heard people refer to his liking for strong drink, and it would not be desirable to give their daughter to a man like that.'

'Indeed not,' says Elin.

'It is peculiar the way things can suddenly come back to one,' says Papa. 'I cannot exactly say what we were talking about as we walked along here, Papa and Nana and I, but I know what we were thinking about. We were undoubtedly all three wondering whether the curate was back from the fair. Papa had seen him at the fair the first day and had thought he seemed drunk even then. And we knew full well that he had not come home the night before, so we had him very much in our minds as we approached the vicarage, and were wondering whether he was safely back home or still at his revels up in Sunne. But naturally we all kept our thoughts to ourselves, it being a sensitive subject.'

'That cannot have been a very enjoyable walk, Uncle,' says Elin Laurell.

'No Elin, it certainly was not. I could see that Nana was very uneasy and not able to joke and chat to Papa and me with her usual ease. I came to her aid as best I could, but the conversation did not flow readily. And then we stopped and exchanged a few words with some passer-by, for Papa had lived at Mårbacka for forty years, so everybody knew him. Eventually we walked on past the vicarage, and came to a stop just here on the hill.'

As Papa says this, he looks about him and points his stick up at the tall, dark spruces edging the road.

'It was dark and dismal there in those days, as it still is today,' he says, 'In fact perhaps even more so. I do believe there were taller trees here then, and the road was narrower and steeper. But as we reached this point, a cart came into sight round the bend in the road down there. We recognised the vicarage horse at once and we could see that the vicarage hand was in the driver's seat. We realised what errand he had been sent on. He had surely been sent up to Sunne by the vicar's household to find the curate and bring him home. It was Saturday evening, you see, and they had to take him in hand so he could sleep off the drink by the next day.'

'I must say, Uncle, that this is starting to get quite thrilling,' says Elin.

'Thrilling!' says Papa. 'You all have such strange words nowadays. For me it was a horrible moment when I saw that the hand was alone in the cart, so we could only surmise that he had not been able to find the curate. Nana turned deathly pale and my father the regimental paymaster looked sterner and more scornful than I have ever seen him. But you know what, just as the cart went past us, Papa caught sight of a dark figure lying in the bottom of the cart, asleep, and he gestured to the driver to stop.

"So you found him then, Ola?" he said.

"Yes sir, I've got him here. But look at the state of him!"

'And as he said it, Vicarage Ola leant backwards and lifted the hat that was covering the curate's face. We were standing right alongside so we could not avoid seeing him, but Nana instantly averted her eyes, and she might well have run off if Papa had not taken her by the wrist and kept her there. "Look at him," he said, pulling her closer to force her to look at the curate, who was flat on his back in the cart, bloated, ruddy-faced, dirty and so utterly changed that we could barely recognise him. "Look at him!" Papa said again. "It is for your own good to do so. I pity any woman who weds such a man!" I do not for a moment think that Nana obeyed him. She kept her eyes lowered until Papa let go of her hand and signalled to the hand to drive on.'

'How absolutely terrible,' said Elin Laurell.

'It certainly was,' says Papa. 'But you must remember that one of Papa's daughters was married to Wachenfeldt and he did not want Nana, whom he liked above all the rest, to go the same way. But Nana was angry and saddened, and the whole way home she walked a few steps ahead of Papa and me and did not say a word. And Papa looked stern, but also a little gratified, you could see. He no doubt thought it was a good thing that Nana's eyes had been opened.'

Then Papa falls silent and we turn and head back home.

Elin walks beside him, and they are still talking about the same subject.

'It is curious, Uncle,' says Elin. 'I thought Mrs Hammargren was so happy with her husband. I would never have imagined her being taken with anyone else.'

'Perhaps things were not so serious between her and that curate, either,' says Papa, 'or her grief was not long-lasting, at least. It was at fair time, and Kjellin from Åmål was staying with us, and Father and Mother arranged that he would take Nana back with him to her sister Karolina, to stay in Åmål over the winter. And down there she got to know Tullius Hammargren, who was a teacher at the boys' school, and she was engaged to him by the time she came home in the spring.'

Elin asks no more questions, but I am impatient to know the most vital thing of all.

'But Papa, what happened to the curate?'

'Well, well,' says Papa, sounding a little surprised. 'Little pots have big ears, do they? Actually, things went badly for him. He drank, and he mourned, and he is said to have ended his days in an asylum. I do not know exactly what happened, but some people say he went out of his mind because Aunt Nana wanted no more to do with him.'

And there is something rather special about knowing that a person has been driven to madness out of love for one of my aunts. I wish I could ask so much, so much more, but I do not dare.

And now, afterwards, I have asked Elin if she will enquire of Papa what it was that Aunt Nana read in the paper that day last summer, and why she told the story of the well on that particular day. But Elin says she will not. She thinks being inquisitive is not at all nice.

Earthquake

And when the time reaches noon and it is the end of lessons, we always run down to the bedroom to see Mama as she sits sewing at the little table under the window. We admire her work, and she asks us whether we learnt our lessons well and whether we have worked hard and behaved ourselves, and of course we always answer that we have.

Today I am a little quicker than the others at putting my books back on the shelf and cleaning my slate, so I reach the bedroom a few minutes before Gerda and Anna do.

And when I open the door, I see that Mama is not seated at her sewing table as usual, but pacing about the room in a fit of weeping.

It is not the sort of weeping that might mean she has received word of a death, but rather she is weeping as if she were not only sad but also angry and despairing and utterly beside herself. She has her hands clasped over her head and is letting out piercing cries of 'I will not let him! I will not!'

And I stop in the doorway, unable to take another step. I would never, ever, ever have believed that Mama could weep like that. It is as if the floor has gaped open in front of me. The whole house is lurching up and down.

If Papa or Aunt Lovisa had wept in that desperate way it would not have been so bad, but to see Mama! Mama could not be weeping like that unless we were facing ruin. Mama is so prudent. Mama is the one we rely on.

Papa is sitting at the desk, his eyes following Mama. He looks distressed, but nothing like Mama. He tries to say something reassuring, but Mama is not listening.

When Papa sees me at the door, he gets up, comes over and takes me by the hand. 'Let us go and leave Mama to calm herself,' he says, ushering me into the dining room.

There, Papa takes his usual seat in the rocking chair, and I stand beside him.

'Why is Mama crying?' I ask.

Papa says nothing at first, but then he must realise that I am so frightened that it would be too cruel simply to tell me it was something that I would not understand.

'Uncle Kalle was here this morning, and he told us that he is planning to sell Gårdsjö.'

And it is dreadful news for me too, because I so much like Gårdsjö and my cousins there, and it has always been my second home. But I still cannot understand why Mama is taking it so hard.

'You must not forget how attached Mama is to Gårdsjö,' Papa says in explanation. 'It was quite something when your grandfather bought an estate, you know. It was at his merchant house in Filipstad that he made all his money, of course, but becoming an estate owner earned him a completely different standing, and his wife and daughters too.'

I say nothing, because I simply do not know what to say.

'Father-in-law had to travel up to Gårdsjö a few times a year to attend to estate business, you know,' Papa goes on, 'and he would generally bring his eldest daughter with him. That was how we met, your mama and I.'

I realise that Papa is trying to tell me how many of Mama's happy memories are linked to Gårdsjö, but it was not like Mama to weep so readily at fond memories of any description.

'And when we got married, we lived at Gårdsjö for the first few years, until your grandfather died and we could move to Mårbacka.'

I just shake my head, as a sign that I do not understand a thing.

'You can surely see how upsetting it must be for Mama to know that your uncle wants to sell?'

Well yes, naturally I can see that, but I have no comprehension of the bigger picture.

'Why has Uncle Kalle got to sell?' I ask.

'He says that he is losing money every year that he carries on living there. The forge closed down a long time ago, and he cannot make a living from the farm alone. Mama thinks he should be able to manage, with the sawmill and brickworks and watermill, but he feels the income is not to be relied on. He says there are bad times ahead.'

Hearing Papa say that, I recall that conversation between Uncle Oriel and Uncle Schenson, down by the jetty. I remember that Uncle Oriel thought the whole of Fryksdalen would collapse.

I close my eyes, and in my mind I see the earth shake and one manor house after another collapse to the ground. There goes Rottneros, there goes Skarped, there go Öjervik, Stöpafors, Lövstafors, Gylleby, Helgeby; Herrestad has already fallen and Gårdsjö is teetering on the brink. I begin to understand what is frightening Mama.

As I am standing there with my eyes closed, Papa takes my hand.

'Now listen, my Selma!' he says. 'You go into the drawing room, open the bedroom door a crack, and see whether Mama has calmed down!'

And I do, of course, but I cannot help wondering why Papa does not go himself.

I know Papa really hates it when anyone is in tears, but he surely ought still to try to comfort Mama. I sense that he was actually quite glad to see me come to the bedroom a little while ago, so he had an excuse to leave. Papa is really rather helpless when it comes to some things.

And now, as I stand alone in the drawing room, I understand why Mama was reduced to tears.

I think of Aunt Georgina, who said Mama was anxious because Papa was sick and no longer able to carry through a project. Mama knows that the bad times are coming, and

Mama has put her hopes in Uncle Kalle and imagined he would provide her with support and help now that Papa no longer can. But now he wants to move away, and Mama will be left on her own and have no one to turn to.

When I open the bedroom door I see that Anna is there now, and she has made Mama lie down on the sofa and is spreading a shawl over her.

And so I think that Mama is in good hands and I go back to Papa in the dining room.

And when I open the door, it seems to me that I have never noticed before how grey-haired and old and shrunken he is. And so strangely helpless.

And I wish I was grown-up and clever and learned and powerful and rich, so that I could help him.

NOTES

All translations are my own unless otherwise stated.

16 *going to gymnastics*: these 'gymnastics' would perhaps be described today as physiotherapy or exercise classes, and were held at the Orthopaedic Institute. Its head at that time was Herman Sätherberg, who was very actively involved in the development of this therapeutic exercise regime. In *Mårbacka*, the very young Selma suffers unexplained paralysis to her legs and is for a time carried everywhere by her nurserymaid Kajsa Uphill, until she suddenly regains the use of them during a summer bathing holiday at Strömstad, arranged by her father with a view to improving her health. The deformed and sometimes painful hip she has had since birth, though much improved, still intermittently impedes her mobility and in the interlude between *Mårbacka* and this book, she has been sent to stay with Stockholm relatives so she can attend therapeutic gymnastics.

16 *my visits to the Royal Opera House and the Dramatic Theatre*: Lagerlöf writes Dramatiska Teatern. Its full title is Kungliga Dramatiska Teatern, the Royal Dramatic Theatre.

16 *'Lilla Sessan'*: the Little Princess. This refers to Princess Lovisa, daughter of King Karl XV (reigned 1859-72) and his queen Lovisa/Louise, who came from the Netherlands.

17 *the Leja shop*: the firm of Joseph Leja was one of Stockholm's largest retail businesses and was run by the family of Joseph Sachs, who in 1902 went on to found the Nordiska kompaniet

(NK) department store, still a fixture in central Stockholm today.

17 *kalospinterokromatokrēne*: from the Ancient Greek, 'a fountain illuminated in colours'. This elaborate water feature was said to have been constructed in the mid-nineteenth century, possibly as some kind of academic joke. The effect was achieved by paraffin lamps shining through coloured glass onto the fountain.

17 *Saint George and the Last Judgement in Stockholm Cathedral*: see note to page 62.

17 *Nösselts General History for Women*: this multi-part work, translated from the German and published in Swedish in 1861-2, is referred to in a number of Lagerlöf's works including the short stories 'Dunungen' (Baby Bird), and 'Två spådomar' (Two Predictions). In the latter, a seminal text from 1915 on her childhood reading and early writerly ambitions, Lagerlöf writes: 'We have worked our way through all seven parts, but the most comprehensible to me is the first part, with all the myths and legends. My joy is unbounded when Odysseus comes home and shoots the suitors dead, but I prefer to skip over the parting of Hector and Andromache, because I can never read it without weeping.' Published in her volume *Troll och människor* (Trolls and Humans), 1915, p. 211.

18 *on heathens who have not the law*: Lagerlöf's 'hedningarna', which is from Romans 2:14-15 and appears in the longer version of the Evangelical-Lutheran catechism, is here translated as 'heathens'. In many editions of the English Bible over the years, however, it has been rendered as 'Gentiles'.

18 *skilling*: this was a small copper coin, minted until 1855. Forty-eight of them made up one *riksdaler*. The term was later used more generally for coins of small denominations.

19 *Oceola*, sometimes spelled *Osceola* was an undistinguished but popular adventure novel by William Mayne Reid, published in 1858, its protagonist a heroic native Indian. In her short story 'Två spådomar' (see note to page 17), Lagerlöf admits it is not the kind of book normally found at Mårbacka and says

she does not know how it got there. She describes opening it at random at a scene in which the beautiful young heroine, a plantation owner's daughter, is caught unawares by a threatening alligator when she is bathing. The young Lagerlöf is then hooked, keeps returning to read the next few pages, and thinks about the story and characters day and night. *Troll och människor* p. 212.

20 *Per in Berlin*: the cosmopolitan names of the labourers' dwellings are explained in *Mårbacka* in the chapter 'Land of Hope': 'They had Lars in London, Sven in Paris, Magnus in Vienna, Johan in Prague, Per in Berlin, Olle from Maggebysäter, the stable hand and the farm boy. And Lars in London, Sven in Paris, Magnus in Vienna, Johan in Prague and Per in Berlin were not foreign in the least, but day labourers at Mårbacka. The fact of the matter was that it had amused Lieutenant Lagerlöf to name the tied cottages on his land after the leading cities of Europe.'

21 *a quarter of a Swedish mile*: known as 'en fjärdingsväg', the old Swedish quarter mile is equivalent to 2672 metres or 1.66 English miles.

25 *sympathy patience*: Swedish *sympatipatiens* was a competitive game of patience for two players.

27 *Lasse-Maja*: Lars Larsson Molin (1785-1845) was a notorious Swedish thief whose nickname Lasse-Maja came from his habit of disguising himself as a woman. He was active in the Stockholm-Örebro-Västerås area and was frequently arrested and sentenced to long periods in prison. He wrote an autobiography in the form of a novel, which proved very popular and made him even more widely known.

33 *A Life of Love by Johan Mikael Lindblad*: *Kärlekens liv* was among many titles published by Johan Mikael Lindblad (1817-1893), who was a clergyman in the south of Sweden, author of improving works and sermon collections, and was also a prolific writer of hymns.

36 *twelve brothers who were turned into wild swans*: in the Hans Christian Andersen story 'The Wild Swans' (Danish: *De vilde svaner*) the heroine Elisa is saved by her brothers at the last

moment from being burned at the stake as a witch. Andersen
adapted a folktale which was popular in a variety of retellings
across Europe and he would also have been familiar with
variations on the theme in the Brothers Grimm's collections.
In common with other Andersen stories such as 'The Steadfast
Tin Soldier' and 'The Little Mermaid', it features an upstanding
central character who commits him or herself to silence for
some form of noble motive and is misunderstood or sacrificed
(Wullschlager (2004), p. 428).

36 *The Woman in White*: Wilkie Collins' novel, initially a magazine
serialisation, came out in book form in 1860. It was published
in Swedish as *Den hvitklädda qvinnan* (translated by Thora
Hammarsköld) in 1861.

38 *My Rose in the Forest*: *Min ros i skogen* was a one-act comedy
originally written in German by Wolfgang Müller von
Königswinter under the title *Sie hat ihr Herz entdeckt*. It was
adapted into Swedish by Oscar Wijkander and was widely
performed in Sweden from 1867 onwards, and into the 1870s.

41 *Dr Piscator's pills*: Dr Piscator is the family doctor and lives in
the nearby town of Sunne.

42 *A Capricious Woman*: *En nyckfull kvinna*, written in 1848-49, is set
in upper-class circles in Stockholm. It was published in New
York in an English translation by Elbert Perce as *A Whimsical
Woman* in 1854. Emilie Flygare-Carlén (1807-92) is however
best known for her novels set in the seafaring communities of
Sweden's West Coast, notably *Rosen på Tistelön* (1842; *The Rose of
Tistelön*).

44 *Astrachans*: an early apple variety.

52 *acts the part of Erik XIV*: a performance of *Erik XIV* at Lieutenant
Lagerlöf's birthday party is described in the final chapter,
'The Seventeenth of August'. The play is a tragedy in five acts
by Johan Börjesson (1790-1866), a priest, poet and dramatist.
Published in 1846, it was reportedly one of the first modern
historical plays in Sweden.

58 *Frithiof and Sven Duva and Sandels*: *Frithiofs saga* (1820-25) by the poet Esias Tegnér is a cycle of 24 poems based on an Old Norse saga about the Viking Frithiof or Fritiof. In this idealised image, the bold, plundering Viking ultimately atones for his misdeeds. Sven Duva is the protagonist of *Fänrik Ståls sägner* (*The Tales of Ensign Stål*), a cycle of poems by the Finland-Swedish author Johan Ludvig Runeberg, published in 2 volumes, 1848-60. Sven is a somewhat simple-minded orphan boy who enlists at fifteen and displays greater loyalty and bravery than some of his officers. Sandels is a general in the poem cycle and is at one point accused of cowardice, but subsequently drives back the enemy and wins his men's praise.

62 *the dragon that St George does battle with in Stockholm Cathedral*: 'Saint George and the Dragon' is an impressive medieval wooden sculpture by Bernt Nolke. It was installed in 1489 in Storkyrkan, also known as Stockholm Cathedral.

65 *Professor Fryxell*: Anders Fryxell (1795-1881) was a historian, educator and clergyman. He was dean of Sunne from 1836 and was elected to the Swedish Academy in 1840. He was a good friend to Selma Lagerlöf from her childhood onwards. In her speech at the unveiling of a Fryxell bust in Sunne in 1910, she recalls being awed by him as a child when he, already mature in years, preached at Östra Ämtervik church. She praises the succinctness and accessibility of his sermon compared to anything she has heard in church before, and his readiness to talk to the children afterwards. (Söderlund pp. 35-36.)

67 *the Siege of Paris*: this siege lasted from September 1870 to January 1871 after French emperor Napoleon III's surrender at the Battle of Sedan in the Franco-Prussian war. The new French Third Republic did not accept the German peace terms and the Germans besieged Paris in order to end the war. It is no coincidence that this is the war that is said to be casting its lurid red glow on Mårbacka; it was after this war that Värmland's times of prosperity came to a rapid end and people began to leave.

68 *exiled empress*: Empress Eugénie de Montijo was the Spanish wife of Napoleon III and mother of Napoleon-Eugène-Louis Bonaparte. Concerned about continuing the family line, she

began taking an active role in political affairs. She supported French opposition to a Prussian candidate for the vacant Spanish throne, a controversy that precipitated the Franco-Prussian War of 1870.

68 *two riksdaler*: the *riksdaler* was the currency of Sweden from 1777 to 1873. The two riksdaler was a silver coin issued from 1855 onwards.

75 *leather-cloth*: Swedish *läderklot*. This was cloth coated with waterproof varnish on one side and intended to imitate leather.

75 *copal varnish*: copal, or gum copal was a natural tree resin, hard but soluble, which was imported to Europe from such places as the former Belgian Congo, the Philippines, Madagascar and South America for use in varnishes. It was in widespread use until the mid-twentieth century, by which time synthetic resins had become more durable.

75 *bugles*: ornamental, tube-shaped glass beads.

78 *Kille* is a Swedish variety of the card game Cuckoo. The Swedish pack has 42 cards, all of the same suit, and each card is duplicated. The 21 different cards include harlequin (kille), cuckoo, hussar, pig, horse and flowerpot.

79 *Mrs Hwasser at the Dramatic Theatre, when she is playing the Queen and addressing a lackey*: Ebba Charlotte Elisa (Elise) Hwasser, 1831-94, was one of the leading actresses of her day. She played many Shakespearean roles and was a noted Ibsen actress. It is hard to say which queenly role Selma Lagerlöf saw her perform. Her list of roles at the Royal Dramatic Theatre includes Mary Stuart in plays by both Schiller and Björnson. Alongside her leading parts in history plays and tragedies she also however enjoyed success in comedies such as Eugène Scribe's *A Glass of Water*, in which she appeared as Queen Anne in 1860. This was probably a more likely play for the young Selma to be taken to see.

84 *Der Bazar*: this illustrated fashion journal was published from 1854 to 1933 and included sewing patterns, needlecraft

instructions and even features on hairstyles, cosmopolitan lifestyles and interiors. It inspired many other titles including the US fashion magazine *Harper's Bazaar*.

87 *Kristina Nilsson*: Kristina or Christina Nilsson (1843-1921) was a Swedish operatic soprano who studied for four years in Paris and went on to build an international singing career, appearing in concert tours of Sweden, France, Germany, Britain, Russia and the USA.

91 *moist snuff*: *snus*, or smokeless tobacco, inserted in portions behind the top lip, was reportedly first introduced into Sweden in 1637, initially among the aristocracy. The *Oxford English Dictionary* has dated the earliest use of *snus* as a word in English to 1916.

92 '*Now from the temple down unto the strand, of aiding hands is knitted swift a chain*': the burning of Balder's temple in Esias Tegnér's *Frithiofs saga* (see note to page 58) catches Selma's imagination. This English quotation is taken from *The Saga of Frithiof: a Legend*. Translated from the Swedish of Esias Tegnér by Oscar Baker. Publisher: Edward Bull, London, 1840.

92 *feather and fan stitch*: called *fjällstickning* in Swedish, this lacy crochet work is known in English as feather and fan pattern, sometimes also as old shale stitch.

99 *Erik Bøgh*: Bøgh (1822-99) was a prolific Danish songwriter, also active as an author, playwright and journalist.

99 *the 'Gluntarna' duets*: this is a famous song cycle for two voices and piano written in 1847-50 by Gunnar Wennerberg, who composed the music and also wrote the lyrics. It is based around student life at the University of Uppsala and the two characters featured in the duets are 'glunten' (the student) and 'magistern' (the master).

99 *Emilie's Throbbing Heart*: 'Emilies Hjertebanken' was a vaudeville number by Danish poet, playwright and literary historian Johan Ludvig Heiberg, which premiered at the Royal Theatre in Copenhagen in 1840.

100 *The Visit of the Countess:* the poem 'Grevinnans besök' from 1800 was one among many deliciously sharp and satirical poems by Anna Maria Lenngren (1754-1817). Its subject is a class-conscious parson's family that puts itself at the beck and call of a visiting noblewoman.

113 *Miss Broström:* this ill-used spinster's story is told in the chapter of the same name in the first part of the Mårbacka trilogy *Mårbacka* (1922).

116 *Field Marshal Klingspor in The Tales of Ensign Stål:* see note to page 58. Klingspor is described as a majestic figure with two chins, one eye and barely half a heart.

119 *Tegnér:* The poet Esias Tegnér (1784-1846). See note to page 58.

128 *the year of the famine:* this very probably refers to 1867. Wet conditions in the provinces of Dalarna and Värmland in that year caused the harvest to fail, leading to severe hunger among the rural poor and spurring widespread emigration to America.

134 *Blåkulla Hill:* in Swedish folk tradition, the Thursday before Easter was believed to be the day when witches flew off on broomsticks to the legendary island of Blåkulla (literally, Blue Hill) to feast and dance with the Devil.

141 *Topelius:* the works of Zacharias (Zachris) Topelius (1818-98), written mainly in Swedish, are classics of Finland's national literature. *Fältskärns berättelser* (poems written in five cycles, 1853-1867; translated into English as *The Surgeon's Stories* [translator unclear] and published in Chicago 1883-1900) is one of his best-known works and owes much to the narrative techniques of Walter Scott, depicting both kings and ordinary people and the tensions between them. There are also supernatural, magical elements.

143 *The Children of the Lord's Supper:* Esias Tegnér's 'Nattvardsbarnen', written in 1820, was translated by Henry Wadsworth Longfellow under this title. The poem has an idyllic rural setting and culminates in scenes of a confirmation.

144 *Majniemi castle*: this is a recurring setting in the second cycle of Topelius's *Fältskärns berättelser*.

155 *King Ring and Ingeborg*: in the chapter 'The Ride on the Ice' in Esias Tegnér's *Frithiofs saga*, King Ring and the beautiful Ingeborg were warned by a stranger (a disguised Frithiof) that the ice was not safe, but did not heed his words. Their sleigh fell through the ice and they were saved from drowning only by the quick actions of the stranger, who pulled it out of the water.

160 *I recall the lovely time*: see note to page 100. Anna-Maria Lenngren's 'Pojkarne' (The Boys), 1797, also known by the opening words of its first line, 'Jag minns den ljuva tiden' (I recall the lovely time), was written to a tune from Gluck's *Almide*, which had premiered ten years earlier.

165 *John Ericsson*: this Swedish-born American engineer and inventor (1803-1889) developed a steam-powered warship and a screw propellor.

166 *that gander that flew away with all the wild geese*: the housekeeper's story can be found in the chapter 'The Gander' in *Mårbacka*. The story and its reappearance here also, no doubt deliberately, reference the framework narrative of Lagerlöf's enduringly popular work *Nils Holgersson's Wonderful Journey Through Sweden* (1906-07).

181 *judge advocate*: Melanoz addresses Uncle Oriel by his Swedish title *auditörn*. A judge advocate was an experienced official working within a division of certain armed forces dealing with judicial or legal matters.

182 *the ones on the subject of Karl XII*: Anders Fryxell's *Berättelser ur svenska historien* (Stories from Swedish History) was published in 49 parts from 1828 to 1893.

185 *'Who does not our brother recall?'*: 'Vem är som ej vår broder minns?' from *Bacchi tempel* (1783) by songwriter, composer and poet Carl Michael Bellman (1740-95).

189 *Gustav Adolf Wall*: Wall (1821-81) was a multiple estate owner and an entrepreneur, and later entered politics.

190 *Bankrupt within five years*: Rottneros estate did indeed go bankrupt and dragged many of the smaller estates around Lake Fryken down with it in the process, just as Selma Lagerlöf (with the benefit of hindsight) has Uncle Oriel predict.

209 *the killing of the bees*: bees were often killed in the autumn before the honey was harvested. This practice is known to have persisted in southern Sweden into the eighteenth century, and in Värmland clearly even longer. Methods may have included drowning the bees, and stunning them with sulphur fumes before burying them, but accounts are sparse. This brutal practice was only sustainable because wild bees were numerous and swarmed readily. For further details (in Swedish) see: blog.svd.se/historia/2012/06/25/historisk-biodling/.

Translator's Afterword

Ett barns memoarer (*Memoirs of a Child*), written in 1930, is the second part of Selma Lagerlöf's trilogy about her own childhood. The opening part, *Mårbacka*, was written eight years earlier in 1922, and she concluded the series in 1932 with *Dagbok för Selma Ottilia Lovisa Lagerlöf* (Diary of Selma Ottilia Lovisa Lagerlöf). The three parts are sometimes subtitled *Mårbacka I-III*. The trilogy is often loosely termed autobiographical, but that is a rather problematic name for what is undoubtedly a work of fiction, as I argue below.

Mårbacka is the name of the farm in the province of Värmland on which Lagerlöf grew up, a property which the family later lost through bankruptcy. Later, when she was an author with an international reputation and a significant income, Lagerlöf bought it back and had the house rebuilt into a grander dwelling that she considered more fitting as her legacy. I have written in greater detail about these aspects in my Translator's Afterword to the Norvik Press edition of *Mårbacka* (2016), to which I refer interested readers.

In the intervening eight years Lagerlöf had turned to other writing despite periodic urging from her publisher Bonniers to continue her autobiographical series. She had been working on several Mårbacka-related stories even during this time and some of them were integrated into *Memoirs of a Child*. Nevertheless, the book is skilfully constructed to create a consistent, artistic whole. There is some overlap in content between the two books, but in broad terms the second book succeeds the first chronologically. The period covered by *Memoirs* is spring 1868 to autumn 1872, when Selma Lagerlöf was aged between ten and thirteen.

In terms of narrative perspective however, it is a striking departure from the first volume of the Mårbacka series. It is told in the first person, although Selma often speaks for her sisters, too, employing a collective 'we'. The reader is thrown so breathlessly *in medias res* that one kindly reader of my draft enquired whether some text had gone missing at the start. 'And we are so pleased that we have such a kind-hearted governess here at Mårbacka', begins the book, and it is a pattern that is built up at the start of many other chapters to create an almost incantatory effect, with various opening sentences of the 'And we so much enjoy' variety. It is a technique that owes much to oral storytelling, which I will discuss further below. It also plays its part in announcing that this is a child's perspective, imitating the sort of 'Aren't you lucky to have...' remarks that adults tend to make.

Finding Multiple Voices

Lagerlöf the accomplished writer – as she by then was – is supremely confident in *Memoirs* in conjuring up a whole mini-universe and writing about it in her own unique way. In correspondence with her friend and fellow author Sophie Elkan about their calling, she expressed this as a kind of blessing both poetic and organic: 'To inhabit an idea or a character for an extended period brings such happiness! To be filled by a world – like a tree.' (Edström, p. 19)

In her essay 'I jättens fotspår' (In the Footsteps of Giants) in the late collection *Höst* (Autumn), 1933, Lagerlöf recalls the crucial decision she took in carving out her own distinctive style during the long genesis of her first novel *Gösta Berlings saga* (*The Saga of Gösta Berling*): 'I decided to write in an intensely personal way, with all my dreams and follies, even though I believed that in doing so I would have to abandon hope of my book finding any readers' (p. 59).

Afterword

Lagerlöf once said 'I never succeed in writing any book until I have made several attempts to find the language it wants to speak' (quoted by Niklas Rådström in his acceptance speech on recently winning the Selma Lagerlöf Literary Prize). In *Mårbacka* she had striven for some time to find this language, eventually hitting on a naïve voice, imagining herself as a child narrating her memoirs to her younger sister Gerda. It took her some years to set her mind to writing the continuation that became *Memoirs*, but once she had done so, it flowed readily. A large part of the novel was produced in what she called 'ett författarraptus', a state of creative rapture, almost a paroxysm of writing, which extended into an easy-flowing, if exhausting, production period (letter of 4.10.30 to Henriette Coyet, bosom friend of Lagerlöf's old age, cited in Palm, p. 592).

But she sets herself the extra goal of creating a duality of perspective. Events are seen through the eyes of a child – albeit a knowing and verbally advanced one – but simultaneously through the prism of a mature and successful writer's consciousness. Lars Ulvenstam (p. 9) terms this 'double exposure' and Elin Wägner (p. 365) says that Lagerlöf was fascinated by the challenge of trying to resuscitate her world of ideas and experiences from sixty years before without bringing into play what she had subsequently learnt of life. The work is a reckoning between the child and the septuagenarian, and she found they had more in common than one might have thought, according to Wägner.

Edström (pp. 533-34) goes further, writing of the reader as a 'co-creator' whose job is to supply additional information about adult behaviour and psychology. Beneath the idyllic surface of *Memoirs* with its parties and summer holiday visits there is a seething world of adult problems. The reader has to fill out and interpret what the child's eyes see. Edström's example is the chapter 'The Kiss' in which Selma, having played detective to find out why Aline has left her position of governess at Mårbacka in such a hurry, still does not understand the underlying reason. There is also a very early example in the chapter 'Bible Interpretation' that is my own favourite: Selma uncomprehendingly observes the lower half of Nursie Maja's Sunday afternoon tryst with her admirer on the steps up to the stable loft.

The dual perspective means that Selma is often placed in the role of wise old head on young shoulders. In places, Lagerlöf has to resort to frankly somewhat creaky narrative devices to give the child the required access to adult concerns and views. One of her favoured techniques is to choreograph the 'overhearing' of adult conversation. In the chapter 'Agrippa Prästberg', for instance, she perches on the verandah steps as the gentlemen sit over their toddies and hears them tell a fresh anecdote about colourful ne'er-do-well Prästberg in which her father plays a less than flattering role; in 'The Pond' she is party to her aunts' whispered exchange about Papa's increasing inability to complete any project; and as time hangs heavy on their hands in 'At the Jetty' she overhears the grown-ups' various views on entrepreneur G.A. Wall. All of these examples underline the ways in which the locally-rooted, patricentric life of Selma's childhood is unravelling. But the chronology is flexible; she sometimes allows herself to rearrange or loop back on time to suit her own narrative purposes, such as in her depiction of her father's increasingly perceptible decline into alcoholism and ill health.

Lagerlöf's original Swedish readers largely saw the book as a fact-based memoir. This is unsurprising, since the late-nineteenth century recession in Värmland and its impact on hundreds of local families cast a long shadow and most readers (not just Swedish) would also have been aware of her (well self-publicised) life story. But fictionalising is absolutely central to Lagerlöf's writing project. Storytelling is her means of interpreting, and coping with, the world. Helena Forsås-Scott argues persuasively that instead of explaining herself and the heroes of her stories when she writes her memoirs between the ages of 64 and 74, Lagerlöf ensures that they are all turned into fiction (p.148).

By the time the author wrote her autobiographical trilogy, she had already co-opted individuals from her childhood world into her fictional works in various guises, only to then bring them back as embroidered versions of themselves in *Mårbacka* and *Memoirs*.

Ulla-Britta Lagerroth stresses Lagerlöf's insistence on imbuing the account with her own personality: 'A strong personality speaks out of these texts – not only talking about how that personality was formed and developed, but also manifesting itself as an authorial personality in the writing' (p. 12).

The Power of Books And Personal Tenacity

Simultaneously, Lagerlöf is devising and polishing her own creation myth, about her own genesis as an *author*. She mythologises her childhood, providing guidelines for posterity on how to view her route to becoming a writer. In this ostensibly autobiographical work, she is consciously creating a 'konstnärsroman', a portrait of her development into an artist. In *Memoirs*, as in the preceding *Mårbacka*, Lagerlöf presents her childhood as a time steeped in storytelling, but in this second part she widens her focus to include the young Selma's insatiable appetite for books, and the importance of Mårbacka as a place where reading is valued. Fresh novels – not all of them of any literary merit – are sought-after objects that are obtained from the lending library or passed around among acquaintances. The essay 'In the Footsteps of Giants', written much later in life, is again an illuminating source: Lagerlöf claims a particular debt of writerly gratitude to Thomas Carlyle's *Heroes, Hero Worship and the Heroic in History* (1841), and she also provides a list of other authors she read in her youth: Dickens and Thackeray, Daudet and Flaubert, Ibsen and Bjørnson, Lie and Kielland, Turgenev and Tolstoy, Hans Christian Andersen and J.P. Jacobsen. It is a list that has clearly been designed to impress, although it strangely sidesteps all the Swedish-language literature she so avidly consumed, and includes only male writers. *Memoirs* is full of references to the work of Anna-Maria Lenngren, Emilie Flygare-Carlén, Tegnér, Runeberg and others.

As early as 1908, in her short story 'En saga om en saga' (A Tale of a Tale, in her collection *En saga om en saga och andra sagor*), she writes of Mårbacka as a house that had once been a vicarage, which had seemingly left a lasting mark, because it now seemed like a place 'where people had a greater fondness for books and reading than in other places' (p. 8). And the story continues, shedding light on how the child Selma began to view the tales of her own home as just as suitable for a book as her pastiches of *A Thousand and One Nights* or Walter Scott or Runeberg's Fänrik Stål. And it was only on leaving the place for the streets of the town and her teacher-training course that she was suddenly struck by the fact that the Värmland world from which she came had equally compelling material to offer her (p. 13).

Memoirs is a conscious evocation of a life in which fiction and the imagination are omnipresent in young Selma's life. In the chapter 'The Church Visit', for example, she and the other girls all have daydreams and ruses for passing the time during boring church services. Her own, naturally, involve imagining a catastrophe in which she can come to the heroic rescue of the community, a story inspired by a scene in Tegnér's *Frithiof's Saga*. It is a classic work to which she returns in the key chapter 'The Pond', invoking the scene where the sleigh carrying King Ring and Ingeborg goes through the ice in order to inject some extra heroic romance into Papa's ritual annual testing of the pond ice to determine if it is safe for the children to skate on. This second volume of the Mårbacka trilogy shows us in a charming variety of ways how books can supply almost anything in terms of heroic wish fulfilment, although when young Selma superstitiously tries – and tragicomically fails – to restore her father to health by penitently reading the Bible from beginning to end, the power of even this Book of Books is called into question.

Lagerlöf is also at pains in *Memoirs* to emphasise the crucial role played by self-discipline and dogged perseverance in her progress towards becoming an author and making a career out of her writing. Ulla-Brita Lagerroth identifies the starting point in this process of character formation and moral and emotional education as Selma's dethronement, described in *Mårbacka*, from the privileged position of youngest child and indulged invalid. She continues: 'This narrative rhythm: advancement–fall, self-overestimation–subjugation runs through the entire trilogy in many ways.' In *Memoirs* we repeatedly see Selma crushed before she doggedly picks herself up and carries on.

Scholars have rightly devoted a good deal of attention to the vivid scene in the chapter 'The Game of Cards' in which Selma does battle with the demon of her own anger, following her frustrated outburst at the card table. The association of Selma with heroic roles is nowhere more evident than in this psychological battle with her own powerful emotions. Her anger assumes the form of a fearsome creature, 'a huge, horrible head with gaping jaws and spikes on its forehead, rising up out of the depths'. It has 'a dark, scaly body with a big, jagged crest along its back' and is 'much bigger and more terrifying' than the dragon that she saw locked in combat with St George in the statue in Stockholm Cathedral. But Selma determinedly forces the monster back down into the depths and resolves never to waken it again.

From the heights of her mature success, it suits Lagerlöf to create her own origin myth, stressing the importance of sheer personal determination in achieving goals in life, but she is also at pains to reveal the debt she owes to the home environment that put so many books within her youthful reach, and to the many other writers whose work sparked her imagination.

Performance And The Stylistic Impact of Oral Storytelling

Almost as central as books to young Selma's home life and social circles are play-acting and other forms of enactment. The children stage plays – inspired in part by her own theatre and opera visits in Stockholm – and domestic evening entertainments are provided in the summer 'visiting season'. The annual apotheosis of all this fiction-making occurs at Papa's grand August birthday party, where he is ritually lauded in songs, speeches and verse by his friends and neighbours.

Theatrical performance adds another dimension to the importance of oral storytelling that emerged in Mårbacka as a formative component in Lagerlöf's creative writing and continues to be seen here in the tales related by Aunt Nana Hammargren and others, and the prohibited scary ghost stories told by the maids. Reading at Mårbacka was not necessarily a solitary activity. It was often a communal one, for example in the evenings when Selma's mother would read while the girls sewed, or as a reward for completing some needlework task.

Reading aloud was only a step away from oral storytelling, a transitional position between storytelling and solitary reading. It still required elements of performance, even if the words were not the reader's own. By the time Selma Lagerlöf wrote the Mårbacka trilogy she was an internationally acclaimed author who had been in demand for many years to give readings from her work. She had put considerable effort into learning to read aloud compellingly, and became adept at using readings to test the artistic effect and stylistic assurance of a work before it was published. (Vinge, 2005.)

The additive language and avoidance of complex sentences are important in oral storytelling. Lagerlöf creates a slightly hypnotic effect in places, with a childlike relish for repetition. One frequent example is the repetition of the girls' names: 'Anna and Emma Laurell and Gerda and I', the sort of list which has echoes of, say, a nursery rhyme or folk song refrain. In the chapter 'The Vow' in which Lieutenant Lagerlöf returns from a work trip with a life-threatening case of pneumonia, the repetitions are taken to extremes in the scene in which Selma's mother hears the children recite their prayers at bedtime, each girl concluding with one for the preservation of the Lieutenant. The scene is one of mounting tension as it moves towards the moment in which Selma is unable to utter that prayer, an omission which leads to her heroic vow to atone by reading the Bible from cover to cover. There is also something endearing about this child who has to tell a story

Afterword

properly, literally, and should not cut corners. It adds to the intensity of Selma.

We can find echoes of folktales and fairytales with their formulae and frequent multiples of three or seven. Lagerlöf was a keen reader of tales, from *A Thousand and One Nights* via the brothers Grimm, Laboulaye and Perrault and – as we see in Selma's borrowing of its idea of atonement in *Memoirs* – to Hans Christian Andersen's 'The Wild Swans'.

At various points in the chapter 'The Pond', Lagerlöf anthropomorphises the water. When the new pond is first being filled, the water has 'a merry look' and makes 'rapid, roguish advances', but when disaster strikes and the banks of the new lake repeatedly fail to withstand the gales of the season, the muddy, algae-covered old duckpond assumes a mischievous, I-told-you-so air. The first time, the children have 'the distinct feeling that it was looking a little bit smug, confident that it would now be back in favour'. And the following year, it 'squatted there […] winking and glittering as if it was delighted to be king of the castle once again'.

On the publication of *Memoirs* one reviewer declared that this was a specifically Andersenesque device which Lagerlöf had copied. She wrote to her trusty Danish translator and friend Elisabeth Grundtvig in no uncertain terms: 'Is that really true? Have not others done the same before him? […] I would rather say that there is an entirely ancient story style that we have all learnt from, living and dead authors alike' (Palm p. 587).

The end result in *Memoirs* of this language marinade is a consciously constructed, multi-layered style that nevertheless comes across with the requisitely naïve and childlike tone. Lagerlöf also shows great ingenuity in seeing with the younger Selma's eye and describing things in unexpected ways, as a child might. There are many examples, such as her account of the children's fascination with the dark regions of the forge at Gårdsjö and Selma's memorable description of the parquet floor in Uncle Noreen's new pavilion in the park at Herrestad: 'And it had such a splendid floor of short blocks of wood at angles to each other, so we felt as if it was going up and down in waves, and we were really nervous about dancing on it.'

The Chill Winds of Change In Värmland

Memoirs is a deliberate broadening out of its predecessor *Mårbacka*, which is very much centred on relationships, interactions and traditions at the farm itself, with a whole section entitled 'Old Buildings and Old People' and chapter headings such as 'The Raised Storehouse', 'The New Cowhouse 'and 'The Garden'. *Memoirs*, while still firmly rooted in the domestic world of Mårbacka, encompasses the whole district around Lake Fryken where the Lagerlöf family had their wider social circle. There are chapters named after the nearby manors and estates but also others that take us a little further afield: 'The Church Visit', 'The Sunne Ball', 'At the Jetty' and 'At Fair Time', and local outings and personalities, or their visits to Mårbacka, are at the heart of the book. The descriptions of Gårdsjö and Herrestad, where Selma's aunts, uncles and cousins lived, focus initially on the houses themselves, which Selma covets and wishes the more modest Mårbacka could emulate. But here and in descriptions of other formerly grand estates in the district, Lagerlöf provides detailed depictions of the grounds and the infrastructure of small forges and other small-scale industry, and does not disguise the fact that some are falling into disrepair. Engineer Noreen's once lovely pavilion, now being left to rot away because the family no longer lives at Herrestad, is a very visible case in point. Economic collapse afflicted this part of Värmland when it could not compete with new industrial processes and larger-scale production elsewhere. Painfully aware of this collapse and its impact on her own family, who were ultimately forced to leave Mårbacka, Lagerlöf ropes the whole area into her narrative of decline, which culminates in the final chapter 'Earthquake'. Selma's childhood world cracks wide open when the uncomprehending girl witnesses the disintegration and tears of her normally wise, unflappable mother Louise at the news that Louise's brother is to sell Gårdsjö and move away:

> I close my eyes, and in my mind, I see the earth shake and one manor house after another collapse to the ground. There goes Rottneros, there goes Skarped, there go Öjervik, Stöpafors, Lövstafors, Gylleby, Helgeby; Herrestad has already fallen and Gårdsjö is teetering on the brink. I begin to understand what is frightening Mama.

This is the dramatic culmination of a growing sense of threat running through the entire book, caused by an undercurrent of fear of, and resistance to, future change. Lagerlöf drops many hints of the way things could change, or are already are changing. The chapter 'Maja Råd' about the visiting dressmaker includes various examples. Maja Råd herself appears to the young Selma to be unchanging, almost as if she were made of wood. She is as unwilling to discard her old-fashioned crinoline as she is to acquire a sewing machine. The speed of her hand-sewing could always match a machine, she claims, and we are given to believe that she is without equal in the smooth tailoring of a fitted bodice. But the winds of change are blowing. The German fashion magazine she subscribes to is full of pictures of new styles, even if she cannot understand the German words, and although she is never one to gossip, her 'harmless' chat at coffee time includes news of 'who is dead and who is leaving for America'.

Although the main thrust of the chapter about the ill-fated pond concerns Lieutenant Lagerlöf's increasing incapacity and decline, it too has a comment to make about progress and change. When Papa, always eager to make improvements to his lake, gives Selma's brother Johan permission to devise a wheel-driven raft for boating, comparisons are drawn with Swedish-American John Ericsson who has developed a steam-powered warship and a screw propellor. But symbolically enough, Mårbacka's attempt to compete comes to nothing when Johan's raft refuses to move.

The looming threat of change is at its most evident in the elegiac chapter 'At the Jetty'. The familiar ritual of waving off the gaggle of relatives on the steamer after the summer holidays at Mårbacka for the journey back to the city is wholly disrupted by the entitled behaviour of up-and-coming entrepreneur and new Rottneros estate owner Gustav Adolf Wall. Money talks, and the Lagerlöf relations find that the steamer timetable can be brushed aside by a man of means holding an extravagant farewell breakfast for his associates. But Wall is destined to overreach himself, as foreshadowed in the conversation on the jetty between Uncle Schenson and Uncle Oriel about the businessman's wide-ranging plans and extravagant outlay, and Oriel's speculations as to how long it will be before he goes bankrupt.

Sweden in the period covered by the book was on the cusp of various other changes that do not appear in the narrative. Lagerlöf chooses to end her tale before bankruptcy forces the Lagerlöfs to forfeit their beloved Mårbacka, a step which manifests itself most harrowingly in the auction sale of all their possessions, as Anna Bohlin has pointed out (p.62). Lagerlöf originally planned to conclude her autobiographical trilogy with an account of the upheavals experienced by her own family and other manor-house families in this part of Värmland, but she ultimately found the prospect too emotionally draining, and focused instead on the fine detail of her Stockholm visit the winter after *Memoirs* ends and the next step in her own emergence as a writer.

Another major change on the horizon at that time was the emancipation of women and their gradual expansion into employment outside the home. In life at Mårbacka in the first two parts of the trilogy, women's work is essentially domestic and family-based. The only other women's roles we see in *Memoirs* are those of domestic servant, farm girl, visiting dressmaker and – two characters who play a major part in the narrative – governess. The life paths open to girls of Selma's social standing and generation were largely limited to marriage, a paid position as a governess/teacher, or remaining at home as a maiden aunt to assist in the household, as Aunt Lovisa does.

This is not to imply that the women in the book come across as cowed and powerless; in fact the pattern of home life as Lagerlöf portrays it is one of a rather domineering paterfamilias repeatedly outmanoeuvred by the women of his household, who have their way of arranging things for the greater good of the family members and staff. This pattern, which we have already seen in *Mårbacka* in the near-perfection of the chapter 'The Smelt Season', is evident here on several occasions, especially in 'The Marseillaise', and really only fails in the heart-wrenching scenes of 'The Ball at Sunne', where Selma's tearful pleas not to go to the ball fail to persuade her father.

Male authority continues to hold sway on the wider stage, and marriage remains women's safest route to a comfortable life, although a feckless or drunken husband can soon shatter that hope, too. But for spinsters of a certain social standing, genteel poverty and dependence on the generosity of family and neighbours are often the only route left. We see this in *Memoirs* not only in Aunt Lovisa but also memorably in the figures of the Misses Myrin, whose family once owned Herrestad. Not as wealthy as their brother and his immediate family, they are 'spare women', reliant on charity and the old-world gentility of the community, although it is never acknowledged openly. They are now confined to cramped, rented rooms where members of the community visiting them after church discreetly place items of food in the kitchen. At coffee time the two ladies bring out ancient cakes and biscuits, a gift from a visiting niece many months before. The pair live in a welter of hand-crocheted tablecloths, antimacassars and doilies which altruistic visitors buy out of pity; there is not a little of Jane Austen's Mrs and Miss Bates about them.

There is also a fine portrayal of looming poverty and conflicting motivations in the chapter 'Forty Below', when an unexpected suitor, adequate but hardly romantic, arrives in the depths of winter to ask for the hand of governess Aline Laurell. There is supreme attention to detail in the author's agonising account of how the adults of the Lagerlöf family attempt to secure a match in Aline's absence, with her best interests at heart. They eagerly display Aline's ingeniously economical home-made gifts with their decorations of fish scales, spruce cones, brown wool and scraps of leftover silk that clearly hint at the relative poverty into which fate has thrown her. She and her younger sister Emma are living in vastly reduced circumstances since the untimely death of their father the Senior Surveyor in Karlstad, and her marriage prospects have narrowed.

But all their good groundwork is undone by her own frosty, haughty attitude. She clearly allows herself higher expectations, perhaps mirroring the ambitions that Lagerlöf herself nurtured in girlhood, and the disappointed suitor takes himself off into the snow for the freezing ride back to his farm.

The Translation Process

The text used for making this translation is the complete and unabridged 1958 Albert Bonniers förlag compendium volume *Mårbacka med Ett barns memoarer och Dagbok*, although I also consulted the first edition (Bonniers, 1930), available electronically through the Lagerlöf archive of the Swedish Literature Bank at litteraturbanken.se. As I started this translation, I found it hard not to be intimidated by the challenge of tackling the deliberately dual narrative voice, the oral-storytelling style and other aspects discussed above.

As is my usual practice, I did not look at any existing translation into English or any other language, and made extensive use of the Oxford English Dictionary to avoid anachronistic language. Emulating Lagerlöf's additive technique, I kept in many of the 'ands' when commas might have seemed more correct. Lagerlöf does not eschew words that would surely have been beyond the vocabulary of a young Selma, so I did not feel obliged to limit my language choices in that way, either. A good deal of research and thought was required to get the practical details right; in a work about a self-sufficient farm and household in rural Värmland in the nineteenth century, there are a lot of those, none of which can be simply fudged over.

There were various factors behind the choice of the English title for this translation of *Ett barns memoarer*. The 1934

Afterword

translation is called *Memories of My Childhood*. 'Memoarer', however, are primarily memoirs rather than memories, and writing one's *memoirs* is quite a pretentious project for a ten-to-thirteen year old. Central to the idea of this autobiography is the idea of the retrospective account by the mature author, recalling memories as if through a child's eyes – or subtly subverting that focalisation by means of a narrator who may or may not be reliable. This ambivalence runs through the entire trilogy but reaches its most extreme form in the third part, *Dagbok för Selma Ottilia Lovisa Lagerlöf*. It also seemed important to keep the element of distancing created by 'Ett barn': *a* child, not necessarily me, the author. I experimented with various titles, among them 'A Child's Memoir(s)', 'Childhood Memoirs' and 'A Child's Eye Memoir' before the editors and I settled on *Memoirs of a Child*, which mirrors the slight strangeness and duality of the work as a whole.

Lagerlöf's fascinating autobiographical trilogy has certainly not benefited from the successive translations into English that have renewed some works of the world literary canon. It is not a *Don Quixote*, *Madame Bovary* or one of the grand old Russian classic novels. Translations inevitably age, and scholars have made the case for the desirability of new translations every thirty or at the most fifty years. The previous translation of *Memoirs* is no less than *ninety-eight* years old, although it has repeatedly been repackaged and republished in the intervening period. It was first translated by Velma Swanston Howard and published by Doubleday, Doran & Co, in Garden City, New York in 1934 as *Memories of My Childhood. Further Years at Mårbacka*.

Elin Svahn of Stockholm University has been researching the phenomenon of 'non-retranslations', that is, new translations that did not happen over the past hundred years. Admittedly her study is in the field of translation *into* Swedish, but her findings are nonetheless relevant. Is it commercial considerations that determine whether a work is enough of a classic to be retranslated, she asks. Yet here is the paradox, in my view: works like the first two volumes of the Mårbacka trilogy have been deemed of sufficient interest to merit repeated repackaging into many attractive new editions, but in almost a century, no one has ever commissioned new translations, even though the author's status has only grown in the meantime.

The fact that, as is the case with many of Lagerlöf's works that were first translated soon after their publication in Swedish, readers have had to wait almost a century for this new translation of *Ett barns memoarer*, underlines the value of Norvik Press's 'Lagerlöf in English' series. The paucity of new Lagerlöf translations applies largely to the anglosphere, however, and is not a problem afflicting Lagerlöf's work in a wider European context. As Nils Håkanson writes (p. 30), Lagerlöf's breakthrough novel *Gösta Berlings saga* (*The Saga of Gösta Berling*) has, for example, been translated multiple times into Western languages. Håkanson concludes justifiably: 'With their merits and shortcomings, Lagerlöf's translators have contributed to constructing something that we in Sweden cannot have: a *Gösta Berling* that undergoes constant transformation, that always changes with the times, a more organically living work than the original. It seems reasonable not to consider that a loss.' It is not a loss, but an asset.

For the title of his recent historical survey of the translator's art, Håkanson chose the title: *Dolda gudar. Om allt som inte går förlorat i en översättning* (Hidden Gods: On All That is Not Lost in a Translation), which was certainly a refreshing change from all those facile assumptions that the opposite must apply. I would like to end on a similarly upbeat note, putting faith in readers in the same way as Lawrence Venuti in his paper 'How to Read a Translation':

> [...] merely by choosing words from another language, the translator adds an entirely new set of resonances and allusions designed to imitate the foreign text while making it comprehensible to a culturally different reader. These additional meanings may occasionally result from an actual insertion for clarity. But they in fact inhere in every choice that the translator makes, even when the translation sticks closely to the foreign words

Afterword

and conforms to current dictionary definitions. The translator must somehow control the unavoidable release of meanings that work only in the translating language. Apart from threatening to derail the project of imitation, these meanings always risk transforming what is foreign into something too familiar or simply irrelevant. The loss in translation remains invisible to any reader who doesn't undertake a careful comparison to the foreign text – i.e., most of us. The gain is everywhere apparent, although only if the reader looks.

My thanks go to my vigilant editors Janet Garton and Deborah Bragan-Turner, to Cath Jenkins in the Norvik Press office for her close reading, enthusiasm for Lagerlöf's work and all the practical help, and to Essi Viitanen in the virtual office for cover design and layout. Thanks to John Death for many a discussion about words and for valuable early readings. Last but not least, I would as ever like to express my gratitude to Linda Schenck and Peter Graves, my fellow translators in the 'Lagerlöf in English' project, for always making themselves available to share their expertise.

All translations from Swedish are my own unless otherwise stated.

Sarah Death, August 2022

Bibliography

Bohlin, Anna, 'Mårbacka: Larders, Cow-Houses and Other Spiritual Matters', in *Re-Mapping Lagerlöf: Performance, Intermediality and European Transmissions*, ed. Helena Forsås-Scott, Lisbeth Stenberg and Bjarne Thorup Thomsen. Lund: Nordic Academic Press, 2014, pp. 60-73.

Edström, Vivi, *Selma Lagerlöf. Livets vågspel*. Stockholm: Natur och Kultur, 2002.

Forsås-Scott, Helena, 'Text och identitet: *Dagbok för Selma Ottilia Lovisa Lagerlöf*.' In *Selma Lagerlöf: Seen from Abroad/i utlandsperspektiv*, ed. Louise Vinge. Kungl. Vitterhets Historie och Antikvitets Akademien Konferenser 44, 1998, pp. 143-53.

Graves, Peter, 'The Reception of Selma Lagerlöf in Britain'. In *Selma Lagerlöf: Seen from Abroad/i utlandsperspektiv*, ed. Louise Vinge. Kungl. Vitterhets Historie och Antikvitets Akademien Konferenser 44, 1998, pp. 9-18.

Håkanson, Nils, *Dolda gudar: En bok om allt som inte går förlorat i en översättning*. Stockholm: Nirstedt/Litteratur, 2021.

Holm, Birgitta, *Selma Lagerlöf och ursprungets roman*. Stockholm: Norstedts, 1984.

Lagerlöf, Selma, *En saga om en saga och andra sagor*. Stockholm, Albert Bonniers förlag, 1908.

Lagerlöf, Selma, *Troll och människor*. Stockholm, Albert Bonniers förlag, 1915.

Lagerlöf, Selma, *Mårbacka*. Stockholm, Albert Bonniers förlag, 1922.

Lagerlöf, Selma, *Ett barns memoarer*. Stockholm, Albert Bonniers förlag, 1930.

Lagerlöf, Selma, *Dagbok*. Stockholm, Albert Bonniers förlag, 1932.

Lagerlöf, Selma, *Höst. Berättelser och tal*. Stockholm, Albert Bonniers förlag, 1933.

Lagerlöf, Selma, *The Saga of Gösta Berling*, translated by Paul Norlen. New York, Penguin Books, 2009.

Lagerlöf, Selma, *Mårbacka*, translated by Sarah Death. London, Norvik Press, 2016.

Lagerroth, Ulla-Britta, 'Selma Selmissima – en stark personlighet', *Parnass*, 1994, no. 5, pp. 6-12.

Palm, Anna-Karin, *Jag vill sätta världen i rörelse: en biografi över Selma Lagerlöf*. Stockholm: Albert Bonniers förlag, 2019.

Rådström, Niklas, 'Selma Lagerlöf gav oss berättandets viktigaste verktyg'. *Dagens nyheter*, 15 August 2021. (Acceptance speech on winning Selma Lagerlöfs litteraturpris 2021.)

Söderlund, Petra, *Selma Lagerlöf: Tal*. Stockholm: Svenska Vitterhetssamfundet, 2016.

Svahn, Elin, 'Hundra år av icke-nyöversättningar'. *Med andra ord*, no.104, Sept 2020, pp. 10-13.
https://bit.ly/3oUYNvD

Ulvenstam, Lars, introduction to *Mårbacka med Ett barns memoarer och Dagbok*. Stockholm: Albert Bonniers förlag, 1958.

Venuti, Lawrence, 'How to read a Translation', *Words without Borders*, 2004:
https://wordswithoutborders.org/read/article/2004-07/how-to-read-a-translation/

Vinge, Louise, *Selma Lagerlöf 1858-1940. Introduktion.* Litteraturbanken.se
https://bit.ly/3RT8W9K

Vinge, Louise, 'Selma Lagerlöf och högläsningens konst'. In *Selma Lagerlöfs värld. Fjorton uppsatser*, ed. Maria Karlsson and Louise Vinge, Lagerlöfstudier 2005, utgivna av Selma Lagerlöf sällskapet. Stockholm/Stehag: Brutus Östlings bokförlag Symposion, 2005.
Accessible at Litteraturbanken.se
https://bit.ly/3JbS3D0

Wrede, Johan, ed, *Finlands svenska litteraturhistoria, 1: Åren 1400-1900*. Helsingfors: Svenska Litteratursällskapet i Finland, 1999.

Wägner, Elin, *Selma Lagerlöf*. Stockholm: Albert Bonniers förlag, 1942-3 (1958 single-volume edition).

Wullschlager, Jackie, ed, *Hans Christian Andersen Fairy Tales*. Translated by Tiina Nunnally. London: Penguin Books, 2004.

SELMA LAGERLÖF

Marbacka

(translated by Sarah Death)

The property of Mårbacka in Värmland was where Selma Lagerlöf grew up, immersed in a tradition of storytelling. Financial difficulties led to the loss of the house, but Lagerlöf was later able to buy it back, rebuild and make it the centre of her world. The book *Mårbacka*, the first part of a trilogy written in 1922-32, can be read as many different things: memoir, fictionalised autobiography, even part of Lagerlöf's myth-making about her own successful career as an author. It is part social and family history, part mischievous satire in the guise of innocent, first-person child narration, part declaration of filial love.

Mårbacka
ISBN 9781909408296
UK £14.95
(Paperback, 272 pages)

SELMA LAGERLÖF

The Löwensköld Ring
Charlotte Löwensköld
Anna Svärd

(translated by Linda Schenck)

The Löwensköld Ring (1925) is the first volume of the trilogy considered to have been Selma Lagerlöf's last work of prose fiction. Set in the Swedish province of Värmland in the eighteenth century, the narrative traces the consequences of the theft of General Löwensköld's ring from his coffin, and develops into a disturbing tale of revenge from beyond the grave. It is also a tale about decisive women. The narrative twists and the foregrounding of alternative interpretations confront the reader with a pervasive sense of ambiguity. *Charlotte Löwensköld* (1925) is the story of the following generations, a tale of psychological insight and social commentary, and of the complexities of a mother-son relationship. How we make our life 'choices' and what evil forces can be at play around us is beautifully and ironically depicted and comes to a close in the third volume, *Anna Svärd* (1928).

The Löwensköld Ring
ISBN 9781870041928
UK £9.95
(Paperback, 120 pages)

Charlotte Löwensköld
ISBN 9781909408067
UK £11.95
(Paperback, 290 pages)

Anna Svärd
ISBN 9781909408289
UK £12.95
(Paperback, 330 pages)

SELMA LAGERLÖF

Nils Holgersson's Wonderful Journey through Sweden

(translated by Peter Graves)

Nils Holgersson's Wonderful Journey through Sweden (1906-07) is truly unique. Starting life as a commissioned school reader designed to present the geography of Sweden to nine-year-olds, it quickly won the international fame and popularity it still enjoys over a century later. The story of the naughty boy who climbs on the gander's back and is then carried the length of the country, learning both geography and good behaviour as he goes, has captivated adults and children alike, as well as inspiring film-makers and illustrators. The elegance of the present translation – the first full translation into English – is beautifully complemented by the illustrations specially created for the volume.

Nils Holgersson's Wonderful Journey through Sweden, Volume 1
ISBN 9781870041966
UK £12.95
(Paperback, 365 pages)

Nils Holgersson's Wonderful Journey through Sweden, Volume 2
ISBN 9781870041973
UK £12.95
(Paperback, 380 pages)

Nils Holgersson's Wonderful Journey through Sweden, The Complete Volume
ISBN 9781870041966
UK £29.95
(Hardback, 684 pages)

SELMA LAGERLÖF

The Phantom Carriage

(translated by Peter Graves)

Written in 1912, Selma Lagerlöf's *The Phantom Carriage* is a powerful combination of ghost story and social realism, partly played out among the slums and partly in the transitional sphere between life and death. The vengeful and alcoholic David Holm is led to atonement and salvation by the love of a dying Salvation Army slum sister under the guidance of the driver of the death-cart that gathers in the souls of the dying poor. Inspired by Charles Dickens's *A Christmas Carol*, *The Phantom Carriage* remained one of Lagerlöf's own favourites, and Victor Sjöström's 1920 film version of the story is one of the greatest achievements of the Swedish silent cinema.

The Phantom Carriage
ISBN 9781870041911
UK £11.95
(Paperback, 126 pages)

Ingram Content Group UK Ltd.
Milton Keynes UK
UKHW020040050423
419617UK00012B/1399